THE MISSING FLOOR

A SKYLINE MURDER MYSTERY

MARTIN HILL ORTIZ

Cover art by Dar Albert at Wicked Smart Designs

Published by Oliver-Heber Books

0 9 8 7 6 5 4 3 2 1

*In memory of my lost brothers, Paul, Michael, and Christopher.
Dream on.*

CHAPTER 1

Alan Priest

THREE A.M. and a frigid November rain had polished the roadway. My cab sped north along Lexington Avenue, wet tar lustering in the streetlamp lights. I'd describe the luminous streaks of their reflections, one coming after another, as ghosts swimming beneath the surface of a dark stream—I'd use such an overwrought description but only because I'm a lowly newshound with pretensions of being a writer.

Ensconced in the backseat, I felt that sort of shiver that comes from stepping out of a cold shower into a colder room. My skin pimpled. My teeth rattled like ice cubes in a shaken, empty whiskey glass. I wished I had a drink. I wished I had a cigarette just to inhale some warm air. I snorted like a bull, puffs of condensation blasting from my nostrils. Outside, steam crawled from curbside grates. In Manhattan, even the streets breathe, and their breath is foul.

I suppose they call these years the Roaring Twenties

because automobiles had finally won their war over horses. All the world growled, joining in the rumble of motors.

They call this the Plastic Age. Modern contraptions made with Bakelite shells: radio boxes and telephone sets. Jazz recordings with crazed dances spinning their discs at 78, composed of shellac or Amberol, all blaring a symphony of mad abandon.

The taxi's tires banged their way through potholes, water exploding like land mines. We swept past block after block of shops shuttered for the night. Streetlamps, traffic signals, the odd illumined window: their lights screamed across the backseat window. An occasional bolt of lightning flashed. Thunder rolled, unrolled, filling the concrete canyon.

They say New York never sleeps. Not true of Midtown. Here the city naps keeping one eye open, suspicious of the night. The flappers, the jazz-dives, the all-night speakeasies were far off in the fairy-tale parts of Manhattan. At this dead hour, along this avenue in the rain and the cold, even the ragged and the rummies had holed up in their flophouses and alleyways. Come three a.m. and a feller could holler "murder" down a city street, and the only response would be the echoes: "murder," "murder."

A curious dark object loomed ahead, hurtling our way. Still a couple of blocks distant, it had the form of a massive chunk of marble. The cabbie seemed unconcerned. Although the object shuddered like a live beast, it remained in the opposite lane, unswerving. As it neared and its form loomed larger, I recognized that it was a truck. No headlights. So black in form it could have been a cave; as if tunnels could prowl the world above the ground, their maws open and hungry.

When it neared, I made out that it was a paddy wagon, a Hudson Super 6. Its back end seemed sizeable enough to stash a mob of rioters. As it rumbled by, I looked out my side window and peeped at the driver, his kisser illuminated by the glow of a cigar stub. Flat-nosed, scarred brow, cauliflower ears, he looked like a boxer who led with his face. He glanced my way, grinning.

The passing took a flash of a second. *Why no lights?* I was unnerved, as though a banshee had blown by—a portent of death. I looked into the driver's rearview mirror which reflected a horizontal slice of his face. His glossy eyes met mine. We were both a bit spooked.

Up ahead and to the left, godlike in its presence: the recently finished Chanin Building, its peak illuminated by a ring of spotlights. Third tallest building in New York. The topping of its crown, coming amidst the recent skyscraping rage, had gone virtually unheralded. Nobody cares about who gets the bronze medal, especially when the race for ever-greater heights continues on at such a mad pace.

Manhattan's motto for 1928: Don't look back, just enjoy the damned ride. Hell, that was the rallying cry for the entire twentieth century. Still, I love this lousy town.

"Leave me off at the corner," I told the driver. Lexington and 41st, a block from my destination: I wanted to survey the layout of my meet-up before taking the plunge. My snitch, Lyndon Warnecki, always clung to a dash of paranoia, and it was infectious.

"S'all the same to me, bud," the hack said. "We's just a stone's throw from Grand Central. I'll swing on by and scoop me up a night tripper." Stone's throw? With the station being two blocks distant, the man must have been a champion at slinging rocks.

As I reached across my belly to dig into the right-side flap of my jacket, the cabbie shook a finger at the stump of my wrist: my missing right hand.

"The war?" he asked.

"The war." The Great War. The one to end them all. I wished I could put its misery behind me, but like a keening specter, my lopped-off hand screamed to remind me. Remind everyone. I have a good job as a reporter for the *New York World*. A fantastic wife. Still, I always feel as though I am one step away from being a street-corner cripple wearing a placard and rattling a tin cup.

He saluted, showing me he had lost a thumb. I saluted back with my missing hand.

I once had a prosthetic, a fancy one. In retrospect, it seemed dishonest. I'd gone back to being hand-free. Maybe I liked the reaction my stump caused. People had to face their discomfort. "Does my loss make you squeamish?" My veteran buddies respect it.

The change came out to be a quarter.

"Keep it," I said.

"Mike," he said.

"Mike? I'm Alan. Alan Priest."

The moment I stepped out of the cab, the downpour returned. Curtains of rain drenched me and cascaded past the streetlamps, dimming their glow.

I wore a rain jacket, oilskin, not thick enough to stave off the chill. I had buckled it so tightly that, now that I tried hurrying, my gait was stiff. My hat, a fedora, kept the torrent from my eyes.

I ducked beneath a line of scaffolding. A shudder of lightning illuminated my way forward, revealing around me a metal framework of columns and crossbeams. Alongside me, a wooden wall bordered a construction site, plywood panel squeezed against plywood panel, no slots for peeking through. With another flash I saw a series of giant heads. Plastered along the fencing, posters promoting Al Smith for President, one sheet after the other, so that if the first didn't convince a passerby to vote for him, maybe the tenth would.

Al Smith: a lower East Side kid made good. After dropping out in the eighth grade to scare up some money to feed his family, he worked his way up through local politics to become New York assemblyman, then governor, and now a presidential nominee. I kind of liked the guy. Too bad he wasn't about to win the national prize. He was Irish Catholic and the son of immigrants, bad words in the mouths of many. The cheapest trick of politicos is to blame the foreigners.

An anti-immigrant sentiment ruled America. These past few years, the Klan had taken over the South and the Midwest. They'd planted themselves in New Jersey. Hell, they were marching in Queens.

Al Smith, a two-fisted man of the people. My wife also liked him. Still, he didn't stand a chance. America prefers alliteration: Woodrow Wilson, Calvin Coolidge. Next they'd go for Herbert Hoover. Being a newsman, always grinding out a story, I've often leaned on the magical music of alliterative letters.

On the ticket for New York governor: Franklin Roosevelt. My wife was crazy about him.

After I'd passed the construction site, I leapt from the curb into the street but not far enough to avoid splashing down in the swollen gutter. Grit on the pavement kept my slick-soled shoes from slipping: gravel spilt from the day's construction trucks.

Even at this hour, the large buildings along most any other block on Lexington have some lights peeping from their windows. The ugly block up ahead, however, was pitch black and under a death sentence. The plot beneath it had been purchased for millions of dollars. What sucker paid that kind of price? One of the richest men in America: Walter P. Chrysler, wizard of motor cars.

Earlier in the evening, my informant, Lyndon Warnecki, aka, "Luckless Lindy," had buzzed me at my desk in the newsroom at the *World*.

"Alan Priest," I said.

"It's Lyndon," he whispered. I pictured him. Long, lean face, big bulbous nose, squinty eyes. He was always kind of jumpy, certain that people were listening in on him, as though anyone cared what he said. "Is it safe to talk?"

"We're on my private line."

That bought me some smirks from the nearby desks: the phone had a long cord and a dozen claimants.

"I've got the goods on the scam to bump up the land value where that Chrysler guy is building his building,"

Lyndon said. "The former owner whipped up phony blue-prints for swanky skyscrapers, huge structures no one never intended to erect. The only purpose of them drawings was to fool that clodhopper from Detroit into thinking that grand designs were planned for the spot."

"Sorry, Lyndon," I said. He probably expected a payoff for this tip. "I've already heard that chatter."

"Chatter? You think I'm just yapping? Buster, I got the goods. I've seen this room on the fifth floor of the condemned building at the site. It's got the whole thing laid out on its walls. The phony plans and the price tags, along with a photo of that Chrysler guy with a bull's eye drawn over his face. I'm telling you, what I got is worth a sawbuck."

Now he'd piqued my interest. With an eye-grabbing picture like Chrysler on a dartboard, this would make for a decent story. The kicker came when Lyndon told me the name of the landowner. "William H. Reynolds, the Coney Island scammer, sold the plot to Chrysler. You two got some history, right?"

Oh yes, we did.

"And I got me another story, something big," Lyndon said. "Only I don't know all of what it means."

"Uh-huh. We'll talk about it."

Lyndon and I arranged to meet in the dead of night, at an hour when Lyndon said that no eyes would be peeping. Always overly cautious.

I'd stowed a sleek Leica 35 camera in my inside vest pocket along with a fold-up T-bar. In my hands, the photos would be less than perfect, but Lyndon was too jittery to allow me to bring along a staff photographer. With the photograph being indoors, I could set up flash powder on the T-bar plate. I carried with me a Ronson Banjo lighter, a wonder that provides a flame with the touch of a button. I could spark a flash. Not easy for a one-handed man, but I had the practice to pull off such a stunt—and the dexterity. After all, I'd been a stage magician in my two-handed days. Before the war.

Come alone at 3 a.m.? There was only one way in which I could convince my wife, Lorraine, to let me go it alone. "It's going to be boring," I said. If I had told her the truth, that I felt a certain dread, she would have insisted on coming along. Not to back me up, but to get in on the action. She was like that.

The condemned building at 43rd and Lexington stood five floors tall. In the dark, in the rain, it reminded me of a Roman ruin, the stacked empty arches of the Coliseum. In passing by the display window of what was once United Cigars, I discerned a dim form among the shadows. For a moment, I thought it was a guard. With some scrutiny, I made out the abandoned statue of a cigar-store Indian. I pointed my flashlight its way. Its arms were folded across its chest. It smiled at me with wooden teeth. The figure was shorter than I, even when including its headdress. It seemed cruelly miniature, the American Indian as a caricature, something from the Sunday funnies' page. I've read the Apache Chief Mangas Coloradas stood six-foot-six. All else had been removed from the shop: the place abandoned and ready for the wrecking ball.

I asked myself: with so many of these wide sheets of display glass, couldn't they cut out pieces to reuse? Couldn't they carve out slabs of bricks and stand them up elsewhere as the walls of homes for some poor families? Why did everything have to be crumbled and shattered and piled on a garbage barge?

Lyndon told me the door to Bendix & Sons Jewelers would be open. In a way, it was. Although boarded over and sealed with a padlock, the hasp and its screws had been pried free of the door jamb. After this breach, the hasp had been realigned and the loose screws slotted back in place. I considered this. If Lyndon had arrived and entered, then he had a confederate hanging around outside, covering up for him, setting the lock in place. Maybe he had arranged that to keep a roaming security guard from recognizing the break-in. I also concluded that whoever pried this loose must have used a crowbar.

What if someone else was in the building? I should have brought my own iron bar for protection.

I clawed the lock free by hand and pulled open the door. It swung, creaking, revealing a hallway, the jewelry store entrance to the side.

The darkness ahead was forever deep, I might as well be looking down a mine shaft. I extracted my flashlight and switched it on. Tossing the beam around, I determined that the floor looked sturdy, the walls and ceiling, less so. I supposed that it seemed that way because I could only illuminate a small sliver of the structure, as though the narrow cone of light was all that was holding the overhead together.

As I shifted the beam around, the hall seemed to tilt: a fun house. I flashed back to my Coney Island days to when I performed my magic before a restful crowd.

The reason I arrived early was to be here before Lyndon, to be prepared for anything. I supposed if I came across a security guard, I could bargain. Still, it was best to search for some sort of weapon among the oddments and debris, in case I encountered some juiced-up squatters or feral, puma-sized rats. I might need something hefty to bash a head in.

The pieces of a broken chair littered the ground. I slipped my flashlight in my armpit and grabbed a loose leg to use as a club. I tucked it beneath the back of my belt. It stiffened my posture.

At the end of the tunnel, a stairway. Lyndon had told me to meet him on the fifth floor where he'd show me the room with the plans and the Walter P. Chrysler photo with the bull's eye. The meeting place made sense when he said it, but now, as I pounded up step by step in that doomed building, the sheer resounding emptiness pressed against me. I wished for the sound of Lyndon's yapping voice. I wished I'd brought my wife, Lorraine. Not just because she was brave, but because she saw me as brave. I could have used a bit of that secondhand courage right about now.

I kept a tally of the landings, figuring one switchback per floor. When I got to the fifth floor, I realized my count had been unnecessary. In front of me, a sign read "V," and one with an arrow pointed up the steps, saying "Roof."

I listened. I heard rain striking, water dripping. "Lyndon?" I called. I tucked the flashlight in my armpit and set my hand on the doorknob. It felt strangely cold. I twisted the knob and swung back the door. Fifth floor. Only there was no floor.

The roof above was caved in and so were two more levels down, leaving a pile of destruction well below me. This stairwell where I stood was a tower above it all. The demolition crew must have swung a wrecking ball starting at the back side. Lyndon's intel about the planning room, if it was true, must have come from days back. So much for my damning photos.

While sweeping my flashlight beam across the rubble, two stories below, I noticed an odd splash of color. Red. The sleeve of a blouse. More red. A sparkly dress. More red. Blood.

A flash of lightning illuminated the full picture. Draped over the wreckage was a woman, legs and arms askew, like those of a clipped marionette. Flat on her stomach, but with her neck twisted one-eighty so that she faced up. She wore a rictus smile. No one could survive having her head spun that far around.

I considered what to do. I'm a reporter. From my perch two floors up, I had a good angle for a dramatic picture. But … how to set up the T-bar, ignite the flash powder in the rain while aiming the camera down, one-handed?

I decided instead to wait for a lightning flash to illuminate the murder scene. Lightning bolts always run two ways, an upstroke and downstroke, a stuttering flash so quick that people think they witnessed a single event. If I pointed the camera and clicked a photo at the moment of the first flash, I might snatch a page-one photo. The lightning was coming about once a minute, so I could get in a few tries.

The Leica 35 camera was small enough to manage in

one hand. I looped its strap around my left wrist to keep it from flying. I adjusted the aperture and shutter speed and prayed. All set, I leaned over the emptiness with no hand to use to anchor me in place and pointed the lens down, peeking through the viewfinder to frame the photo. I set my left finger atop the shutter release. When the lightning flashed, I almost tipped over the edge, but managed to snag a shot. I cranked the lever to advance the film and waited for the next bursts. This second time, I made sure I had safe footing. I had some confidence in that second photo, but to be sure, I repeated the procedure again.

I considered trying to get a better angle, a closer shot, but the puzzle of navigating this wreck of a building in the dark would be perilous.

The rain coming down on me, a long wait with no more lightning coming: I gave up after three tries.

I asked myself, this dead dame, did she have something to do with Lyndon? I needed to run him down. I had the germ of a big story here.

Grand Central is located a short jaunt from the ruin where I found the body and they have plenty of pay phones at the ready. I always keep a roll of nickels in my pocket. Too many reporters still think they have to flatfoot the beat. I've learned to work the phone lines. As a bonus, if needed, that coin roll bunched in my fist can add a wallop to my left jab.

Before I called the police, before I called my editor, I first had to break the news to my wife. The operator connected me. One buzz and she picked up. "Lorraine?" I said. "You're gonna hate me."

"Oh, dandy. I'll get some of that out of my system." All purrs and sarcasm.

"I told you my little journey would be boring. It wasn't."

She mewed. "And you cheated me out of an adventure?"

"At the site for the Chrysler building. There was a dead woman. Neck broken. Expensive dress. No good reason for being in that spot short of a dump site. I'm guessing a murder."

"Did you call the police?"

"I called you first."

"Then I haven't missed a thing. I'll be right over. Where are you?"

Lorraine felt an attraction to the morbid, and it only took a hint of peril to get her charged up. It was part of what made her thrilling. And maddening.

Still, I felt I should warn her. "I don't know the cops in this precinct. They might shut me out. Or else they might haul me to the station house for an all-night grilling."

"I'll call Santarelli," she said. Lieutenant Gilberti Santarelli of the Second Precinct had worked with us on the Carolyne Fritch murder case two years back, and since then we'd kept in contact. The man was eccentric for a copper but nothing if not loyal. He treated us like he was set to be the godfather to our future kids.

Sometimes when people are generous, I just want to shove them away. Lorraine helps me counteract that instinct. She acts quickly to call in a favor, thinking it's only natural that everyone wants to be our friends.

"This hour of the morning?" I told her. "We don't need to bother him."

But she'd made up her mind and hung up. She knew if we talked any further, I'd be giving her some stiff and patronizing warnings. And I would. My trespassing and finding a body? I worried that I was headed into some unpleasantness. Maybe both of us were.

My next call was delicate. The local precinct. I could leave an anonymous tip, but if the dead dame was Lyndon's partner, I wanted to know and soon. Maybe he had never shown, and I needed to warn him someone was playing for keeps. Maybe he'd been there and set the screws back into the holes of the hasp and snuck away. Maybe he did the killing.

As for the police, some played friendly with reporters: for a price. By being the discoverer of the body, and greasing some palms, I could try to make the connections needed to shadow the investigation, to follow the story.

Or maybe they'd toss me in the clink for breaking and entering. If the cops in the precinct were lazy enough, they might even make me the prime suspect.

CHAPTER 2

Lorraine Priest

ALAN and I live in a ninth-floor studio in the Fifth Avenue Building on the southwestern corner of Madison Square. Below us, Madison Park spreads out in a spider web of cement paths strung between patches of lawn and, from our perspective, the crowns of English elms. In this mid-autumn moment, in the late-night bloom of the park lamps, the foliage burns yellow, bringing to mind that Robert Frost poem: *Nothing Gold Can Stay*. That is, if he'd been speaking about dying leaves and not the transience of spring.

On the far side of the park, the Metropolitan Life Tower hovers over us with a clock set high up, seemingly stamped over office windows. Its clock-face is bigger than Big Ben's. Its numbers and hands are lit at night. So round, floating in the sky, it's like having a full moon as a constant companion.

Mr. Moon, do you have the time?

Oh, yes. Oh, yes, I do.

Up until ten p.m., it rings the quarter hour and is a regular reminder for me to focus on my work: I've been busy trying to get Roosevelt—Frankie, not the dear departed Teddy—elected as New York governor. It's the predawn hours of the first of November—'tis no longer Halloween, 'tisn't quite All Saints—and the election loomed less than a week away. Voters had that rare choice in which the other candidate, Albert Ottinger, was also a good man. Jewish. It seems remarkable to me that, together with Al Smith, we live in an age where we have a Catholic New Yorker running for president and a Jewish New Yorker running for governor. Roosevelt's lieutenant governor is also Jewish.

Women have just gotten the vote and already we've brought about a more egalitarian world. Perhaps us gals are helping to finally put aside our country's petty hatreds.

Outside and to the right is the Flatiron Building with its distinctive snout. Our apartment is small but, with such a thrilling view, I feel like a socialite. Alan takes home a paltry paycheck from his job at the *World* but my salary as a model pays for our place.

Alan and I have been married for two short years, and he still takes my breath away. He looks a bit like that Hollywood pretty boy, John Gilbert—before the mustache. He has that photoplay star's habit of brooding. I bite my lower lip when I think of Alan coming home. When he does get home, he nibbles my lip for me.

Not many men respect beautiful women. Yes, I know I'm beautiful. Before meeting Alan, I played this town and its men like a virtuosa, and they doted over me with dopey eyes. Alan never treated me that way. Not many men appreciate the beauty of a woman's mind, and I consider myself lucky to have found one.

His missing hand, his war wound, humbles him. A ghost pain. Maybe that's what keeps him from acting out the role of a leader-of-the-pack wolf like most strong men do. He is honest, spirited, and what I like most of all, a bit dangerous.

———

"You turned," I said. "Why did you turn?"

My taxi headed up Lexington, for what should have been a straight shot to Alan and his murder. We were crossing 24th, passing the stables and Kauffman & Sons Saddlery. Each year, with fewer and fewer horses, it seemed hard to believe such a place still existed in Manhattan. Then my cab driver made a jaunt to the east and back.

"Someone be tailing us, lassie," the hack said. His brogue was as thick as skirts and kidney stew.

"Are you certain?" I asked.

"It's three and some change in the wee hours, and there be no other headlights on the street, so I padded on a needless turn to feel out the bugger, and still, sure enough, he comes nipping at our heels. There's been some late night jackers on the prowl."

"I see." The other car, not quite nipping at our heels, was hanging a half-block back and making no effort to catch us. "Can you lose them?"

"At this hour, who be there to stop me?"

I was thrown back against the seat as the cabbie floored the gas. Our taxi swayed on its chassis as it swiveled and sliced through the rain-sodden street, parting waters with the efficiency of Moses. The car behind us accelerated, matching our speed.

"Hold on to your seat, lassie," the cabbie said. "I don't hold faith that your door won't fly open."

He slammed on the brakes while twisting the wheel, and the cab skidded to the side, splashing up a wake of rainwater. Even with both hands gripping the shoulder of the front seat, I fell against it and then whipped to my side. I righted myself in time to see him pilot us into a narrow alley. The car's headlamps shuddered on their stalks. Their beams blazed along the walls of the brick canyon. The pursuing vehicle skidded to a halt at the entrance, its front left wheel bumping up the curb, not quite making a sharp enough turn.

My taxi whisked inches by lumps of humans swaddled in blankets and milling about like ragged monks. Their presence gave me an idea. I dug some change from my purse, rolled down the taxi window and flung out the coins. They ricocheted off the alleyway walls and the vagrants clambered into the middle of the alley to collect them. With the way forward cut off by a human blockade, the vehicle behind us stopped its pursuit and backed up, swerving its rear end back onto Lexington.

My driver continued down a second alleyway and onto Madison Avenue. "Just to be safe," he said. "Should they be circling over and checking for you and me at the first turn."

Wise man.

I crossed my arms and hugged warmth into my body as we continued on, the rest of the journey being uneventful. We pulled up in front of Grand Central. At street level, the place looks like ordinary storefronts. One floor up and set back is a structure rivaling the Acropolis. I gave my cabbie a one-dollar tip and he eyed me like I was Lady Rockefeller.

"Bless you, ma'am." As a further tip, I gave him one of my hundred-dollar smiles.

Alan stood leaning against the arch of one of the portal entryways, lips puckered, head slightly bowed, and delivering a soulful stare my way from beneath the brim of his fedora. Unforgivably kissable. He nodded his head to the side, and I looked that way. Several coppers in blue longcoats marched toward him.

CHAPTER 3

Alan Priest

IN THE VAST detective's room of the Tenth Precinct Station House, police gathered around Lorraine, vying for the right to light her cigarette. One proclaimed, "You ought to be a model," not realizing that she was one. "You could be on the cover of *Collier's*."

"*Collier's?*" Lorraine said with a hmmph. "That's for all-American girls. Corn-fed and cornball. I'm *Cosmopolitan*.

"*Vogue*," she added, as though relishing a dirty word.

The Vogue covers were drawings; she posed for some of their sketches. In contrast to the boyish, bob-cut, twiggy flappers in style, Lorraine had a long mane of auburn-red hair and an ample figure. No cloche hats or fringed skirts for her. For her modeling gigs, she dressed to sizzle. A beauty out of time.

I could read her mood by what outfit she wore. My phone call must have inspired the amateur sleuth in her. Tonight, she had dressed for adventure: beige polo pants and a white blouse. A thick cloth coat matching the pants, to fight back the weather.

The detective's room smelled of tobacco and hooch, the latter emitted from the officers' slack blowholes. Even with booze being illegal, this group was brazen enough to keep half-filled whiskey glasses on their desks. I'd ask for a shot, but they'd probably arrest me for violating the Volstead Act. All for the better: I've been keeping sober lately. For my gal.

Four a.m. being the most lifeless part of the dead of night, the station house had turned into an all-night boys' club. That said, I suspected the boys were on their best behavior on account of Lorraine. No cursing, and they limited their scratching to their bellies and up.

The police had parked me and Lorraine in chairs, while a squad headed out to find the corpse. They informed me they didn't want me, a civilian, to string along, not even to point out where. I suppose I described the location well enough. I didn't tell them about the photographs: my camera stashed in my inside jacket pocket to keep the film from being seized as evidence. Too late to make the morning editions, I still hoped for an evening front page story.

Being a reporter, I was used to coppers treating me like something they scraped off their shoes. The police resented how they often showed up in my paper's back pages as clod-hoppers. The comedians Keaton and Chaplin often made billy-club-twirling cops into a punchline in their flicks.

"She's my wife," I said, admonishing a patrolman who leaned over his desk a tad too goo-goo eyed. He gave me the once-over, disbelieving. I couldn't blame him. When Lorraine and I stood together framed in a mirror, I didn't believe it, either.

. . .

I heard a door flinging open and clomping on the stairs. The officers, one and all, took to their feet. I wondered whether I should also. It seemed as though holy thunder was announcing Moses's return from the mountaintop.

A bear of a man stomped into the room. It was the driver I'd seen piloting the paddy wagon. Smash-faced, cauliflower ears. He stared at me, his eyes looking like they were firing tracer bullets. He clenched his hands, and I focused on his fists. Bucket-sized, he had calluses on his knuckles. I'd seen that just once. A boxer-jailbird who kept in practice by beating the bricks of his cell wall, flattening the backs of his forefingers, turning his fists into rocks.

He gave Lorraine a momentary glance and a sneer and then surveyed his straight-spined men.

"Hello, chuckleheads," he said. "You can relax." His men exhaled. I knew his type. He was that sort of ex-soldier that transplanted his wartime authority into a new career. I wondered how far up the military command chain he'd made it. I wondered whether he screamed at kid soldiers ordering them over the walls of trenches, telling them to dodge the streams of bullets while storming machine gun nests. The kind who had screamed at me.

I stood.

He walked my way, seeming to stop when he chose to, not because his head was about to butt mine. "Sergeant Mitchell Sullivan," he said, speaking into my face. A crocodile smile. "My friends call me Mitchie, only I don't got no friends."

"Alan Priest, *New York World*." He looked at my left-handed offer of a handshake and snarled.

"You're the one who sent us on the wild goose chase to find some phantom body," he said.

"You didn't find it?" I recalled the lightning flashes and that twisted image. "You enter at the jewelry store. On the third floor, but there is no roof. She lay right in the middle of the wreckage."

"Don't tell me where I looked."

I thought of mentioning the photo and thought again. He didn't seem the kind who liked to be contradicted. He'd take my camera in his hands and snap it in two.

"You told my men that Mr. William Reynolds was running a scam out of that building. You tried to slander one of our city's upstanding citizens. Etskovitch? Write this man up for filing a false police report."

"I can show you where the body is," I said.

"My husband doesn't lie," Lorraine protested.

Mitchie turned and bared his teeth at my wife. She stood and walked over to Sergeant Sullivan, planting splayed fingers against his chest. She might as well have been trying to shove the Woolworth Building.

He looked down at her fingers. "Murphy? Cuff this lady and have her spend a night in the pokey. Assaulting an officer."

"That's—" I began to say.

Sullivan grabbed me by the lapels, pulling me to my tippy-toes. "You're nothing here, paperboy. We at the Tenth don't care what you think or what you write. We own this stretch of the city, these dead hours. When the scum of the world thinks no one can see, thinks no one is watching, we're there. We rule the night."

A short, thin man in formal dress made his arrival known by tapping his umbrella head against a desktop. I smiled in recognition. He had a drooping mustache, liquid eyes, and a bowler. With stiff posture and a genteel nod, he came across as a butler ready to announce the arrival of his lord. He doffed his hat and held it in two hands, crown-down, a beggar with a bowl. "Excuse me, gentlemen," he said. "I am Detective Lieutenant Gilberti Santarelli of the Second Precinct. Two-A, to be precise."

"And why should I care?" Sullivan asked, freeing his grip on me.

"I have come to advocate for Mr. Priest and his wife. They are ignorant of the reputation of the Tenth and have doubtlessly trod upon your goodwill. They are harmless."

"I'm not," Lorraine said.

"Captain Sullivan …" Santarelli began. I suspect Santarelli purposefully erred in promoting the man in an effort to flatter him.

"*Sergeant,*" the behemoth said in correction. "This lop-handed news hack made a false police report, a claim of murder that caused my men much alarm and wasted our valuable time. Me and my boys—"

"Tut-tut," Santarelli said, daring to interrupt the man. "I have known this pair for two years and can attest that Mr. Alan Priest had doubtlessly fallen under the spell of his writer's imagination. As a fellow officer, I humbly request that you show some sympathy to a crippled veteran and release him and his wife."

Sullivan reacted by pinching the stub of my right wrist, treating it like a piece of butchered meat. I don't let people go there. I would have punched him in the face but was afraid he'd also take out his wrath on Lorraine. Santarelli was trying to help us out of this, and she didn't deserve to spend a spell in the can.

The sergeant looked around at his men. I suspect some of them were veterans. Half the men my age had gone through the hell of the last war.

To my surprise, he relented. "Some fish you catch and throw back," Sullivan said, "on account of they smell bad." He sniffed our way. "The three of you scram, Lieutenant Dago included. Don't ever poke your ugly kissers in my end of town again."

CHAPTER 4

Lorraine Priest

Whenever I sneeze, I can never keep it down to a single blast. I don't know how single sneezers manage it. Perhaps they have larger, more efficient noses. First, the tickle appears inside my nostrils, then three quick explosions. *Gesundheit*, God bless you, and *salud*.

Six a.m. and Manhattan was waking up to nasal drip weather. I found myself leaning into my hanky. The street-lamps were still on. The shadows of dawn washed over the grimy road in front of the police station. Three more sneezes.

"*Buona salute*," Santarelli said.

I don't usually show when I am flustered, but Santarelli had the ability to see through my bravado. He recognized that I'd been shaken by the brou-ha-ha at the station house and needed Alan's arms, so the lieutenant opened the back door of his motor car and said. "Please do sit together."

Alan and I climbed into the back seat. Sitting beside me,

Alan snuck in a moment of intimacy, nuzzling my throat with his lips. Nuzzling: my second most favorite act of love.

Santarelli scooted into the driver's seat and adjusted his rearview mirror, discreetly turning it away from us.

Alan broke off, straightening himself. "Those coppers," he said. "That was humiliating. And Santarelli, your groveling didn't help."

The lieutenant shook his head. "I proffered the absolute minimum quantity of obeisance that the sergeant required, all necessary to obtain your release. You are not aware of the reputation of the night forces at the Tenth. Hours in their lock-up? They round up the rowdies and the wretched. They encourage fights among those in their cells, betting on them, even those among the ladies. You risked a brutal and perhaps disfiguring end to your evening."

"Thank you," I said. I feared just a few things, but one of those was scarring. "*Grazie.*" The detective had an Italian knight's sense of honor, and he responded to my gratitude with a satisfied sigh.

I have a keen sense of smell. The lieutenant had the odor of leather polishing oil. The only leather he wore, beyond shoes, were driving gloves. I suspect he had a particular routine for preserving their elegant calfskin. Santarelli maintained certain vanities.

He turned over the vehicle's engine, launched into gear, and swung his motor car around, joining Lexington Avenue, turning south. I barely kept my balance in the backseat. Men: always in such a hurry.

"I want to drop in on the construction site," Alan said. "I have photos of the victim, but I need to see for myself that the body is gone."

"Breaking into private property with the sun smiling upon us?" Santarelli said. "I cannot permit this. I am an officer of the law. Furthermore, I suspect they will be guarding whatever should be their nasty little secret."

"Ah! So you think they lied?" I asked Santarelli. That was my guess.

Alan answered. "I figure one of several possibilities. Number one. They screwed up and didn't look in the right place for the corpse."

"No," Santarelli responded. "They are not so incompetent and would continue to look if they did not immediately encounter the body. They would not enjoy being corrected by the demolition site workers, come morning."

"All right. Here's a second theory," Alan said. "They found the body and decided to cover it up. Reason unknown."

Santarelli said nothing, not objecting to this.

Given a moment of silence, I jumped in on the action. "Number three, someone moved the body before the police got there. Thinking like a murderer, which I fancy I can do, why bring the body to such a far-flung place to dump it? The murder occurred there. Which leads to the very good question: why would this lady in red be traipsing about a construction site? Alan, you said that you saw blood. With time and the lack of a roof, the rain would have soon washed that away. The murder must have been recent, the killer still near. The killer may well have removed the body to hide the crime."

Alan smiled. He appreciated my observations, even when they trumped his own.

"What do you intend to do with your photos?" Santarelli asked my husband.

"If I captured anything at all, I'll have them published."

"Unwise. Sergeant Sullivan will not take kindly to proof that he is incompetent or else a liar. He makes for a dangerous adversary."

"I am also a force to be reckoned with."

My husband. *Hmmph.* He had an unhealthy habit of mistaking his ego for a shield.

Santarelli's motor car came upon the block with the construction site. The destruction site. A single police officer stood posted in front of the jewelry store entrance.

"They paid attention," Alan said. "That's where I told them I'd entered."

"What sorts of national secrets could they be guarding?" I asked.

Neither of my traveling companions answered. I suppose my question was rhetorical. Santarelli turned on 42nd Street. "Let's see how many guards they have around the site."

The destruction of the building was more apparent on the far side. While the Lexington face had five floors, here the rear wall had crumbled down to two. A second police officer stood near the back of the lot.

"They appear intent on keeping the place sealed," Alan noted.

Santarelli pulled over. "There is a car behind us. It turned when we did, and now it has stopped so as to not pass us."

I looked back. "That's the same car that followed me last night."

Alan needed only a glance. "Gould the Ghoul," he said.

"Ah!" I remarked.

For Santarelli's benefit, he added, "A fellow news hack. Works at the *World* and likes to poach my stories. I've complained to my assignment editor. He says it promotes competition. Gould must have seen me gearing up with a camera and gotten word I was on to something big."

"But why did he follow me in my cab?" I asked.

"He must have missed me when I left," Alan answered, "so he staked out our building. He followed you, figuring you wouldn't be out at 3 a.m. without a good reason."

"And followed us to the precinct and now here? Persistent bastard."

"Should I lose him?" Santarelli asked.

"Nah. Take us to Park Row. My best revenge for his audacity is to get to the newsroom and file a story."

Santarelli turned onto Third, pointing south, following the overhead "L." We headed toward my preferred end of town. Some ladies favor uptown and champagne. I like the hard cider mix of immigrants, our vehicle entering a different exotic world with each passing block. Santarelli's wife is Chinese, and he and his family live in Chinatown. He enjoyed citing eastern and western thinkers, Buddha and even the Viennese eggheads.

"What would Freud say about Sergeant Sullivan?" I asked.

"A narcissistic personality trapped in the anal stage of his development."

Freud's theories never strayed far from the groin.

"The man is rigid, precise, harsh," the lieutenant continued. "Follows his own rules. Paranoiac. On an unholy mission. As for Freud, I've been leaning more toward the thoughts of Jung. More culturally global in his vision."

Alan yawned: *I suspect a comment on Santarelli's esoteric opinions.*

"Did either of you sleep at all last night?" Santarelli asked.

Late last night, we were busy at the station. As for earlier, Alan looked at me and we traded guilty smiles.

"No," I said. *But we did share some physical culture.*

"I insist on taking you to your apartment."

"Not until my story is filed," Alan countered.

I pouted. "And what am I to do while you are busily clacking away?"

"I have something in mind. Something dangerous."

Mmmm.

CHAPTER 5

Alan Priest

WHY ARE reckless and wreckless such opposites in meaning? In one case you are aiming for a head-on collision. In the other case, you are accident-free. With no sleep in over twenty-four hours, I was reckless but still wreckless. But I was heading for a crash.

First, Santarelli dropped off Lorraine at our apartment. I gave her the mission to try to track down Luckless Lindy to warn him in case he didn't know of the murder. In case he was a target. Perhaps he'd never shown up at the wrecked building. Or, perhaps he knew exactly what had happened.

I had the address to Lyndon's workplace, a penny ante crapshoot in the Bowery. A clientele composed of bus drivers and garbage men. The kind of rollers who played pick-up crap games. I figured her task would be busy-work. She would give me holy hell if she figured out my scheme of sending her off somewhere benign while I spent time getting some story writing done.

I feverishly typed away on my Remington electric, words spilling out of me, my one hand jumping between keys. My experience as a magician, the practiced discipline of sleight-of-hand, translated into fast typing.

I wrote quickly but that's not to say I didn't do my best work: a conductor only needs one hand to wield a baton. I unleashed a storm of fury directed at the real estate swindler William Reynolds for the millions he sucked out of Chrysler. Not only was he a con man, but he was also a racist braggart and lorded over slums. The two of us had history.

Once upon a time there was a nightmare called Dreamland. In 1905, Coney Island already had two entertainment parks, Steeplechase and Luna. Reynolds came along to start a third. He built Dreamland to be massive, bombastic, and outrageous. Calling it an electric city, it boasted a million light bulbs. Its attractions appealed to the lurid side of its audience. Local Negroes were hired to wander the streets decked out as imported savages. Dreamland boasted Midget City, an entire exhibition dedicated to goggling at dwarves. And if they weren't small enough, he raided hospitals for premature babies to display in glass incubators. I couldn't understand the appeal of staring at infants the size of ballet slippers.

Halfway down the Western Walkway was Hell Gate, an attraction overseen by the figure of a devil with a fifty-foot wingspan. For ten cents admission, riders boarded a boat and were sucked down a whirlpool. They continued on, floating along a river through the underworld passing a *tableau vivant* of demons.

In 1910, my mother was on her third husband and working as an actress in the Biograph Studios on Broadway, putting out fifty one-reelers a year under the direction of D.W. Griffith. At that time, as a boy of fifteen, I wanted to be in show business. I'd developed into a fairly crafty magician, smart at sleight of hand, and capable of a decent patter: rapid-fire words being as important to a routine as misdirection.

I thought I got my big break when William Reynolds, owner of Dreamland, hired me as part of a stage show. I soon discovered that he took me on because, as a child, I was cheap. Even then he never paid me, telling me I drove audiences away and cost him money.

I watched him use this same ploy against others, usually with a tinge of racism. He yelled at Persian Pete and his Belly Dancers. "You and your camel-fuckers are driving me broke. Pay you? I'm gonna replace you with some jigaboos and a cauldron for a cannibal act."

He looked like Simon Legree, the archetypal villain of melodramas. Potbellied, he sported a handlebar mustache.

Along with cheating his performers, he never paid his creditors. In 1911, all of Dreamland burned to the ground in the biggest fire New York had ever seen, still the biggest to this day. Reynolds scored a ton of money by overvaluing the land.

Since those early days, I'd followed his career. He continued on in real estate development, part P.T. Barnum, all self-righteous thief.

.   .   .

On a fresh set of pages, I wrote up the story of Sergeant Mitchie Sullivan. I described his inability to find the corpse and portrayed him as a sadist and a bumbler. I left out Lyndon's name. No reason for him to earn Sullivan's wrath. As for dragging a cop, a precinct head, through the coals, whether or not my copy editor would let me run with it depended on the quality of my photographs.

Whither went the corpse? I called my source at the Bellevue Morgue. "Bob? This is Alan. I was wondering whether you had an unclaimed woman brought in last night or this morning. Thirty, maybe forty. Broken neck. There's a five-spot in it for you to check."

"Don't need to look. No one like that."

I suspected she'd been stuffed in a weighted sack and tossed in the East River.

Just in case, I described Lyndon and asked if he'd come in. "Average height. Male. Long face. Prominent nose."

"Nope. Just a pair of very different corpses since last night. And two questions makes for ten bucks."

I promised him I'd drop by and pay up.

Earlier in the year, back in January, the *Daily News* got a great scoop. Famed murderess, Ruth Snyder was about to be electrocuted. Photographers weren't allowed at executions, so a crafty reporter snuck in with a camera strapped to his ankle. He managed a low-angle shot of the electrocution that made Snyder look like Dr. Frankenstein's monster being brought to life. It evoked the gloom of the German expressionists.

Strauss, who worked in the *World's* photography lab,

clipped three wet photo prints to his drying line. One was useless: timed badly and blacked out. But one of them … We smiled, as happy as two could be when witnessing a corpse. The black and white starkness. The rubble. The desperation on the victim's face. We had a masterpiece. Front page all the way.

The Mitchie Sullivan piece would run. Reynolds would be furious. I was about to make some powerful enemies. I'd earned a good sleep. We had two dark rooms, one dedicated to big spreads like fashion shows. Most often empty, it had a solid bench and pitch blackness for a good nap.

CHAPTER 6

Lorraine Priest

I DECIDED THAT, for my visit to Lucky Lindy's craps parlor, I'd wear something gaudy and spanking hot. I'd be the gang moll, slumming it in the mean streets and dives, untouchable under my boss's halo of protection. I even conjured up a name for my guardian: Nicky.

I squeezed into an outfit with a jade-green top and bottom, something I'd gotten for a costume party. My blouse pushed up my bosom and lowered my neckline. I tucked a hanky in my cleavage. Pink. My skirt showed a hint of my knees. The stilettos on my boots forced me to walk in mincing steps. I liked the extra three inches they added to my height.

Before I took off, I inspected myself in the mirror. I frowned, deflated. The rings under my eyes made me look like I'd just stepped out of an opium den. I needed sleep. Besides, what self-respecting gamblers would even be awake at the rooster hours of the morning? I answered my own question: Bowery crapshooters. They didn't respect them-selves. They tossed dice the way drug fiends wielded the needle.

Nevertheless, they could wait. I collapsed fully clothed on our chaise lounge and was soon out for the count as though I'd been kissed by a Jack Sharkey uppercut.

Three hours later I woke, not exactly refreshed, but the deep fog had lifted from my mind. My eyes burned, but it felt good to breathe in the fullness of the day.

The Bowery. A street and a place. It ran along a south-to-north line, said to follow a footpath of the Lenape, the orig-inal Manhattan Indians. Back in the last century, it was an upscale entertainment district. Fine theaters and hotels. Then came two sets of elevated trains, a sun-blocking pair of tracks built over both sides of the roadway and pressing up against the buildings. Trains swept by, rattling windows and jangling nerves. Their appearance began the area's descent into darkness, condemning souls to the shadows. In those first years, the engines ran on coal, soot blanketing everything. Even after switching to electricity, their cars continued to roar along, sending out tremors, buildings trembling in their wake, imbuing the area with a jittery personality.

The noontime masses spilled from the sidewalks onto the curbsides, out into the streets. Cars whisked by, inches away from pedestrians, sweeping like bulls past the capes of matadors.

My head ached, a stabbing pain made worse by the bright sun. I wished I'd brought a hat to shade my eyes.

A masher called to me, "You're a keen kitten."

"I've got me a daddy," I said. "Nicky."

"Nicky the Blade?"

As I continued down the block, other wolves responded to my claim with "You mean Nicky G.?" and "Nicky the Sheik?" Nickies get around.

On the one hand, I hate, hate, hate when men reduce me to a brainless object. On the other hand, I felt the part I was playing: the gangster's moll, and I loved the power I had over them.

The White House Hotel on Third Avenue advertised rooms with electric lights, 30 cents a night, Calvin Coolidge not included. Alan told me that Lyndon worked as a croupier for their third-floor hallway crapshoot.

"I'm here for the six-spots," I told the clerk at the front desk. "Lyndon's game."

"You a dice-blower?"

"I've come to add some decoration."

"A juju gal. Lyndon could use some good luck. He's been chinning with the trouble boys."

Trouble boys. Gangsters. Lyndon was running with a rough crowd. Just as I'd begun suspecting that Alan had sent me on this mission solely to get me out of the way, things were getting interesting. Danger provides the seasoning to the bland meal of life, and I'm always up for some added spice.

"Is Lyndon upstairs?"

"He's been legging it, in and out. Out mostly. Haven't seen him all day."

"Where might I find him?"

"He bunks at the Young Men's Christian on Third Street, just a sniff or two around the corner."

"Thanks, Buster."

He popped a kiss. "Them Christians won't see what's coming when you dance their way, Sal-O-May."

A few doors down, the Bowery's Third Avenue intersected with Third Street. Serving so many of the area's unfortunates, the YMCA on Third Street was grittier than others I'd seen and visited. It had a frowny, institutional face made of brown bricks and rising seven floors. A framed declaration in the entryway announced its mission to rehabilitate its patrons by providing encouragement and clean beds, and by promoting self-reliance and sobriety. It promised its residents new friends.

"I'm looking for Lyndon Warnecki," I told the clerk at the front desk, a man in his thirties and dressed in raggedy clothes. His eyes nearly popped out with fear. He raised a tall finger in front of his pursed lips and directed his gaze past me.

I turned. Two gangsters who must have overheard me began padding my way. One of them was miniature and wore a maestro's outfit, a black dress jacket too big for his frame. Middle-aged with pale skin and slicked-back hair, he had a spotty mustache that dotted the bottom part of his upper lip. He held a spring-blade knife in his hand. I recognized his partner, a giant, built like a train engine. He went by the unnerving name of "Icepick." Every time I'd met him, his face appeared puzzled, his brow knit, and his mouth an "O," as though the very act of breathing challenged his mental capacity.

When we last parted, he'd just been shot five times. One of those bullets left a scar creased along the line of his jaw. "Miss Loren!" he said, breaking into a goofy smile. The teeth on the side of his scar were missing. I suspect his shooter had tried to make him eat a bullet.

"Lor*raine*," I corrected him. "Hello, Icepick. And you are?" I asked the little guy.

"Dirk," he answered. Named for his knives? A *dirk* was a very different sort of blade than what he held. I supposed he could own more than one. "So girlie, you palling with Lyndon?"

It was a question, but really, an accusation. "Put away the knife," I said. "Are you really afraid of a little ole gal like me? Besides, you're spooking the clerk."

Dirk checked around. With no one else in the lobby but us, he must have concluded he wouldn't lose face by pocketing his blade. One press of a button and it retreated into its handle.

"Miss Loren … um, Lor*raine*," Icepick said. "Mr. Rothstein, you remember Mr. Rothstein, my bossman? He told me and Dirk to bag Mr. Lyndon or who else who'd he done gone chumming with, so I guess that being is being you. Sorry." Last time we'd met he apologized for being sent to kill me, saying, "I like you, but …" This time he was sorry for merely kidnaping me. I suppose our relationship was improving.

"Rothstein's word is Bible," Dirk said. "You're coming with us."

Rothstein: king of the underworld. A gentleman and a

killer. I knew him well enough to know he wouldn't hurt me —unless he had to. And he might just have answers as to why a two-bit craps slinger like Lyndon was so goddamn important to merit a visit by a couple of killers.

"Take me away," I said.

CHAPTER 7

Alan Priest

I AM NOT so modest a man that I don't delight in reading my own work. Over and over again. I had gone down to the press room in the cellar where a great monstrous machine churns out hundreds of newspapers per minute, all neatly folded and stacked, ready for the newsies. I took hold of a copy, literally hot off the presses. My story, Page One. A byline. Some of my best work. Even the photo: all mine. Carefully cropped to frame the dead woman, the rubble below her, an open door above and to her right.

Strauss, the photo developer, found me there. "I've been looking for you."

The glow of my pride burned so brightly, I would think he could have followed its beacon. "What's the deal?" I asked.

"It's right there in front of you."

I stared hard at the front page with fear, thinking that I

might have overlooked some obvious error that made it past the copy editor: my foolishness stamped into history.

"In the photograph," he said.

I stared at its dots, focusing on the dead woman, wondering what I'd missed.

"In the upper right corner."

It took me a moment to resolve the image I was looking at into anything meaningful. There, past the corpse, the rectangle of a door frame stood over the rubble. Staring in its shadow, I made out a form, a blackness taking the shape of a curtain—no, more like a cape. Above it a blank spot, the size of a head.

"I can see how someone might think that's a person. Maybe our readers will have fun with their imaginations. Besides, who the hell wears a cape these days?" A theater-going dandy? A phantom who haunts sewers beneath an opera house?

"If you look at the original print, you'll see the portrait is clear," Strauss said. "I suppose I didn't notice it immediately because I was distracted by the face of the dead woman."

It took me a moment to digest this. "What the Sam Hill?" I said. "You're saying there is clearly a person in the original photo?"

"It's not obvious on the printed page. Newspaper photos are made out of what are called halftone dots. Eighty-five lines per inch. Terrible in terms of clarity. The photo image in my lab is composed of specks of silver. Finer than the eye can resolve. On the dark room print, you can see the face of a man."

"You can make out a genuine human being?" I paused

to consider this. "That will make for a hell of a follow-up story. The Caped Killer. Who have you told?"

"Just Louie."

The chief assignment editor. The sort of boss who chops off heads if he isn't first to be notified of something important.

"Let's see the negative," I said, starting to feel giddy. "Blow up the image of the man in the cape, and we'll make him a star. The Wraith of the Rubble." I thought of how Sergeant Sullivan would crap his pants. Not only did we prove him a bungler who couldn't find a body, we'd be shoving the murderer's face straight into his kisser. This story would be a sensation. It just became must-read news. A million New Yorkers would be buying our next edition. The chiefs might even approve an extra.

The World Building has eighteen stories. When it was erected in the 1880s, it was, for a brief period, the tallest building in New York, and the tallest office building in the world: the pyramids and the Eiffel Tower lacking desks. It has a dome like St. Peter's Basilica.

As Strauss and I rode up in the elevator, I thought of continuing to the upper floors, where the Pulitzer scions kept their offices. I had a story for the ages: a killer captured in a photo, hovering over his victim. They'd award me one of their self-named prizes. After all, they'd been generous in handing those out to *World* employees, nine times in the past twelve years.

Of course, we got off on the newsroom floor. Strauss led me over to the main dark room. The door was locked. He kept it like that to keep people away from the chemicals and the delicate work and just plain because he considered it his territory.

The moment he opened the door, the moment he switched on the light, he said, "Oh, God no. Oh, crap. The prints were hanging here on the clothesline." He shuffled around some items on his workbench. "The negatives were here. Someone took them."

I immediately thought of Gould. Still, this was far beyond anything he'd tried before. Screw me, yeah, but screw *The World?* What could he do with the photos? Unless he was planning to jump to another paper. *The Sun, The Journal,* and *The Tribune* were all headquartered one next to the other along our block of Park Row. Hearst, in particular, regularly poached our newsmen.

I thought of Louie's fury. Would he hold me responsible? Not my fault and yet this story was my baby. He'd never fire Strauss. A wizard at chemistry, he could tease a chiaroscuro masterpiece out of a botched snapshot. Reporters? We were typists with pretensions, all imagining ourselves to be the next Twain or Hemingway.

I'd gone from king of the world to wondering whether I had a job. I only hoped Lorraine was having better luck.

CHAPTER 8

Lorraine Priest

I WENT SEARCHING for Luckless Lindy and wound up at Lindy's. Lindy's is a cafe just north of Times Square. They serve heavenly meals, but what makes their restaurant unique is not their menu, but their clientele. The elite of city mobsters rub shoulders with Broadway stars and cultural idols. A famous author might be penning a play while nibbling cheesecake. A sports hero might be meeting with his bookie to lay down a bet on his next performance: for or against.

Despite the presence of so many hoodlums, no gunplay takes place on the restaurant floor: The King of New York lorded over the establishment. He was the ultimate fixer, the gangster who bankrolled the city's gangs. He was Arnold Rothstein.

Rothstein held sway over both shady and sunlit businesses in Manhattan. He owned the politicians, judges, and police. He had tried to have Alan and me killed two years back, before we beat him at his own game. Afterwards, the man who set Rothstein against us, an entrepreneur by the name of Vachel Ruby, committed suicide. To Rothstein's credit, he never held a grudge. Ordering a murder and shrugging it off were just two sides of the same coin. He was into business, not vengeance.

Icepick and Dirk marched me upstairs to their boss's headquarters. The door to his office stood at the end of a long hall and was upholstered with green leather stamped in place by brass buttons, a pillow-like effect. I noted a couple of bullet holes in the fabric.

Dirk gave the door several thuds. He spit out the words, "We bagged ourselves a friend of Lyndon."

The door opened and a pair of well-dressed thugs took charge of me. They each had one hand tucked in their coats, like they were saluting the flag at a ball game, only, most assuredly, they were clutching their heaters. They considered *me* dangerous? Little old me in my brassy gangster's moll outfit? These hoods must have been on full alert. Something gave them a case of the jitters.

The parlor was furnished as a casual meeting place. Cozy chairs abutted end tables, places to place liquor glasses. I'd seen the room behind the next door: the nerve center, a round table with a never-ending poker game. I clutched the peak of a high-back chair, trying to look casual while steadying myself and my jelly-filled legs.

Mr. Arnold Rothstein entered the room, taking center stage. "This doll knows Lyndon," one of the thugs told him.

He said, "Stand down, boys. Lorraine is an old associate." The thugs lowered their arms to their sides.

In his mid-forties, Rothstein seemed to have aged ten

years since I'd last seen him a mere two years back. Thin brows, tall forehead, he had an overbite and drew back his upper lip as he smiled. He always dressed in the swellest of suits, as though set to step out to conquer the town—a kingdom he already owned. His cheeks were closely shaved, pock marks and pores wide open. I got a whiff of a spicy cologne. I noticed how his trimmed fingernails glinted with polish. His grooming included an attention to details.

"Give us two a moment alone," Rothstein said, his voice weary. The pair of thugs slipped out the front door.

His shoulders slumped. He was no longer the self-satisfied jousting knight I had once known. He'd lost his shield, and his lance was blunted and bent.

"That jade dress," he said, "it makes you look cheap." He didn't say it cruelly, just as a statement of fact—and a correct one. "Shall I get you a drink?"

As mob boss, he ran liquor from Scotland, Ireland, and the bootlegging mash-mills of Kentucky. All the best in the world. "Bourbon, please," I said.

He opened a cabinet to reveal dozens of honey-colored bottles. A peg on one door held a velvet bag lined inside with rubber and pregnant with ice cubes. He added a couple of rocks each to a pair of tumblers and filled the two glasses with liquid gold.

He handed me one. "To good times." He raised his glass.

I didn't quite trust his motives. I've heard how he'd dallied with Broadway starlets. I gave him a side eye. "To mutual respect," I said.

He brokered a smile. "Don't worry. I have a wife and a mistress and they're business enough. Besides, you're an unbroken filly. Not my kind. I shall suffice by inhaling your youth." He made a show of breathing in and then took a swallow of his drink. He winced as though the liquor had kicked him straight in the liver.

I pressed the rim of my glass to my lips. The liquor was as smooth as a lover's kiss.

"Why are you associating with a nobody like Lyndon Warnecki?" he asked.

"I've never met him. I'm tracking him down as one of Alan's assignments."

"Hmm."

"If Lyndon is a nobody, why do you care about him?" I asked.

"Hmm." The Rothstein I knew a couple of years ago was tight-lipped, not one to reveal his motives or even consider the question of a subordinate. The Rothstein in my presence was a changed man. He said, "In my job, a lug like me seldom lives to see five decades. Already, while striding the streets, I'm spying ghosts rising from the subway vents. They've come to grab me by the ankles and haul me away." He whisked his fingers with mock spookiness.

"Being Jewish, I've always had a challenge being accepted by the other races angling to control the rackets. Look at the war between the Micks and the Italians in Chicago. Here, I've kept the peace. I've kept my standing. Mostly. Until recently. The playing field is changing.

"Now, the Italian mafiosi don't like the way Mussolini operates, and Il Duce doesn't like to share power with anyone. More and more of their soldiers keep washing ashore in New York. All right, I'm okay doing business with the Italians. I've worked for a decade with Luciano and

Costello. I've got my own people behind me, guarding my back. But the newcomers, they're looking to cut me out.

"I made a bet on the election. I laid down five hundred g's saying that Hoover will win. I don't give a crap for Hoover, I just know suckers will favor Smith, the hometown hero. Hoover is going to win, but they'll kill me before paying up."

"All this is interesting," I said, "but you haven't answered my question. Why Lyndon?"

"Lyndon is a nobody, but he's got an ear and a way of figuring out what's going on behind closed doors. Who's making the power plays. He's one of the canaries I've hired to sing to me. So, why did your husband have you shadowing Mr. Warnecki?"

"Lyndon snitches for Alan," I said. "Lyndon gave him the story on the Chrysler Building, how Chrysler got swindled. You can read it this evening in the *World*." I sipped more of the liquor. My cheeks flushed. It tasted like courage.

"Chrysler? He's a piece of work. Says he wants to build the tallest building in the world so he can sit on a toilet on the top floor and crap on everyone below. Ford is a regular Jew-hater. These industrialists, they make me look like an angel."

"You're not," I said.

He nodded. "No. I'm not." He swallowed the remainder of his drink and winced again. "There's a set of hoods, they call themselves the Broadway Mob, after the street, not the theaters. I need the dope on what they are planning. Whether they are looking for war. From our previous association, I found you and Alan make for fine detectives. I'll pay you for whatever you can find out."

He took a thick wad of folded bills from his pants pocket and set it on the platform of a table lamp. "I'll let you choose what it's worth."

I'd get to choose how much of my soul I was willing to sell? I tugged back on the rubber band and riffed through the bills. At first I thought they were all one hundreds. Finally, I found a Lincoln and tugged it free, holding it up for him to see.

Rothstein squinted at me, showing me his displeasure. He didn't trust people he didn't own.

CHAPTER 9

Lorraine Priest

THE TWO HOODS who had escorted me to Lindy's Restaurant proved themselves far from gentlemen. They didn't even offer me a ride back home.

So, there I was on Broadway wearing a trollopy green dress and stiletto heels, a fine disguise to blend in along the Bowery. Standing there and looking like a street-corner floozy, I took in the judgments of passersby. I suppose I was performing a public service: allowing the masses to release their pent-up sneers. *Oh, piffle.*

I always keep mad money in my purse. Along with coins for a trolley or a cab, I held the fresh five I took from Rothstein. Fine, my stomach rumbled. I decided to hoof it several blocks over to the Algonquin Hotel, where I could hole up in a phone booth, call Alan, and wait for our rendezvous. In the meantime, I could cash in on a standing invitation to lunch with their smart set.

Midday along Broadway there roams such a herd of

humankind that it's easy to look south and imagine this boulevard and its stretch of people circling the planet. Here lies the true Prime Meridian, the New World supplanting the Old. Passing the Times Building and the shadows of the Hotel Astor and the Paramount, I turned east on 44th and headed on by the Hippodrome: the Roman Coliseum if it were a theater palace. I suppose that, considering the gladiators and lions, that old stadium had hosted a sort of show of shows.

Those who have heard of the famous Algonquin Hotel probably imagine a regal outfit. So many snobbish Manhattan hotels display a phony, gaudy, god-awful luxury, trying to evoke European monarchs with their splendor. In contrast, being a turn-of-the-century building with twelve floors of ordinary brick and limestone, the Algonquin attracted its elite patrons because of its modesty and its cheap fare, and due to the fact that so many of them were notorious pinchpennies. Its lobby spread out to its restaurant, its bar quietly hidden: after all, these were dry days. One room over, away from the bustle of ordinary visitors, was the most famous round table since the days of King Arthur.

The Rose Room. Some members of the Algonquin Circle were society brats, but most were working stiffs: if authors could be considered workers. Or, at least their *hands* were stiff—from writing. Among this crowd, even the socialites were egalitarian, composing pieces about how they cared about the common laborers. All in all, the group was comprised of playwrights, wits, some actors, and some journalists who penned poisoned columns using their spit as the venomous ink. These luminaries gathered at the Algonquin to drink and quip and insult one another and drink some more. I probably sound snide. On the contrary, I felt flattered to have been invited to join them.

I'd seen photos of their assembly. In those pictures they sat upright, conscious of the camera. At this hour they hunched over their martini glasses like horses at a trough. Or better put, they guarded their nourishment like a circle of vultures around a carcass. I recognized some of their faces.

Dorothy Parker, a beautiful wisp of a woman, famous for her books of poetry and her acid wit, sat facing my direction in a seat that allowed her to survey all comers. She wore a brutal amount of perfume. "Lorraine Priest," she said, "you've come late. We've finished drinking lunch and we're already drinking dinner."

"The gassed supper," Robert Benchley announced, raising a toast my way. He wore a dress jacket and had a broad face with a permanently pixilated expression and a sniffy air. Sobriety was for lesser mortals. Along with serving as drama critic for *Life* magazine, he'd just finished starring in the first-ever all-talkie.

Dorothy introduced the man sitting next to her, asking me, "Do you know Robert Sherwood? The 299th best playwright on Broadway. Fortunately for him, there are 300 theaters."

He was absurdly tall, even when seated. His head was so thin it seemed to have been compressed in a vise. "Pleased to meet you," we both said. He continued with, "That costume. Are you supposed to be an avocado?"

"Sit next to me," Dorothy said, tugging my wrist and

guiding me to an empty chair. "I'll protect you. From the others, at least."

"So, why is such a plum seat available?" I asked.

"I'm a tiny snake and the rest of those here know I can strike only so far. So they leave me my space."

I recognized George S. Kaufman, one of the funniest men alive. His hit, *Animal Crackers*, starring the Four Marx Brothers, was playing just down the street. He looked like an author: glum, lean-faced, and bespectacled. His hair stood up as though he were permanently frightened.

He was regaling Edna Ferber. She'd written a half-dozen novels. One of them, *Show Boat*, had been recently made into a musical.

"I've had this pain in my side," Kaufman said. "Our livers are supposed to be our servants. Why did they put 'live' in the name unless they weren't there to aid us to live, live?"

"You kick a servant around for too long and you're bound to get an uprising," Edna said.

"Why would I care about servants?" he retorted. "You have me confused with Morrie. Morrie is the Marxist brother."

"Oh, lookie!" Dorothy told me. "Alex cometh. Lorraine, darling, here's a tidbit: his name is spelled 'Wooll-C-O-T-T,' but it's pronounced 'Woolcoat.' Don't speak it any other way, it offends him."

A rather tubby man waddled our way. He wore a heavy woolen jacket, a wool coat, if you please, owl-like glasses, and a scowl. He stopped, hovering over and appraising me. Intense and humorless, he spoke with a sneer in his voice. "Pray tell, green lady, why do you occupy my seat?"

"I didn't know this was your seat, Mr. Woolcoat," I said. "Wooll*COTT?*"

Dorothy nearly spit with laughter, and I realized I'd been part of a malicious joke: the pronunciation was "cot," and the man did *not* appreciate games with his name. Looking at all the sly smiles around the table, I understood that offending the thin-skinned Woollcott was part of an ongoing prank.

I searched for someone who sympathized with my plight. It was only then that I noticed one particular patron turned away from me. She was so engaged in a private conversation with Harpo Marx, I doubted that she had even noticed my arrival. "Everyone is talking talkies," she said to him, scoffing. "And Jolson? You know what other group are excellent performers in black face? Black folk. And they do it without being painted like clowns."

I couldn't see her face, but I nearly froze when I recognized that voice: Gail Collinswood. My mother-in-law, the actress. Not that she would admit to anything with "mother" in its name. Too domestic, too ordinary, and she'd never concede she was older than Alan. Her hair, that is, her wig, had curls flowing down in golden locks from beneath a dreadful yellow hat that looked like a banana peel. It had to be high fashion to be that ugly. She normally haunted Hollywood. I didn't know that she had come visiting our city. Perhaps she hadn't told Alan.

"Gail," I called out.

She tilted her head my way. Her powdered cheeks had the sheen of a porcelain doll. She wore flame-colored lipstick. Her eyes were always wide and telling. She once explained to me that the secret to screen acting involved thinking loudly and gesturing quietly. I could see that in her. Her soul shone from her eyes as though they were a pair of film projectors. "Lorraine, my darling." She always treated me as though we were chums, equal in age.

"I didn't know you were in town," I said.

"I'm not. I mean, I just dropped in because I have business here, and did you know the Marx Brothers are going to make a film? Not their current play."

"We'll be filming *The Cocoanuts,*" Harpo said, "a talkie."

I heard the clip-clop of shoes approaching behind me. Or else devil's hooves.

The group fell silent. Cocktail glasses halted midway to peaked lips.

"Where went all the smiles?" I asked.

"Whither goest our grins?" Woollcott asked. "The Grin Reaper."

The whole group looked past me, chins up, stares steady. I peeked over my shoulder.

A gentleman stood behind me. I say a gentleman because he wore a suit and tie, dark and darker. And although so dressed, his performance as a gentleman seemed utterly fake. Even his performance as a human seemed phony. Stone-faced, he stood as stiff as a mannequin. Right away, I recognized why Woollcott called him the Reaper. He could wither a vase of flowers with a single glance.

He spoke to me, "Mrs. Alan Priest, madam, do you know who I am?" He had the boom of a stage voice and a hint of Irish accent.

"No." I didn't recognize his face.

"You should. Everybody should. Keeps 'em healthy." He

smiled as though about to eat me. "Jack Diamond. Folks call me Legs." That name carried the weight of a leaded sap. The whole town had heard of Legs Diamond, the underworld enforcer.

"I followed you from Rothstein's," he told me. "Lost hold of you for a moment there when you dunked your figure into this snooty dive." He drew open his jacket, revealing a gun that was as silver and as sleek as a whiskey flask. "Come with me."

"First of all, tell me why," I demanded.

"First of all? First is, we's beyond discussions."

"Are you abducting me?"

"In the polite sense of the word."

"And what if I say no?"

"Then, not so polite."

"We are witnesses to what you are doing," my mother-in-law said.

"So, tell it to the Marines."

CHAPTER 10

Alan Priest

RIGHT AFTER THE predictable lineup of historical muckety-mucks, such as Washington, Lincoln, and their ilk, the two men I'd nominate for being most responsible for changing the course of American history would be Joseph Pulitzer and Charlie Chaplin, both immigrants.

Pulitzer, Jewish, born in Hungary, came to the United States as a young man. Overseas recruiters brought him to fight for the Union. At age 17, he served in the Appomattox Campaign. For years a roustabout, he'd worked his way up the news business until, in 1883, he'd gotten enough money to buy the sickly *New York World*. As owner, he transformed journalism, making it about the little guy, launching campaigns against corruption. He raised money for the Statue of Liberty, and published Emma Lazarus's poem, championing the "huddled masses yearning to breathe free."

As for Chaplin, in earlier times, when theatrical entertainment was limited to playhouses, comedy often involved the powerful kicking their servants, or snobs making fun of those with broken English. With the arrival of the flickers, the great swarm of common folk had access to cheap, sometimes quality, entertainment. With a popular medium to back his vision, Chaplin recognized that having the little guy fight the bullies and win reflected the people's sentiment.

So came about the birth of the little guy as hero. Pulitzer and Chaplin: America was finally becoming "by the people and for the people."

Joseph Pulitzer died in 1911. His sons took over the *World.* In 1917, they established the Pulitzer Prize for excellence in journalism. Continuing their crusades, over the next few years, they often gave themselves the award, including in 1922, when they ran a series of articles exposing the violence, corruption, and power of the KKK. Still fighting for the little man. I felt proud to work for them.

Nowadays, Ralph Pulitzer oversees the day-to-day operations of the paper. I got a notice from his secretary summoning me to his office. I suspected that the missing photos had already upset those at the top.

Literally, the top. The dome that caps the World Building stretches upward for six stories. In the center of its rotunda, a stairway spirals around an elevator shaft.

The elevator boy drew back the door and I stepped out. On these upper floors, the hallway curved in a circle, with the entries leading to offices along the outer ring.

Ralph Pulitzer worked out of a suite on the second floor of the dome. Having been summoned, I went straight up to his door and knocked. "Alan Priest," I called out.

"Enter."

His office furnishings dated back to the Gilded Age. The walls were leather embossed. The lofted ceiling had frescoes. Giant windows overlooked the city. The Brooklyn Bridge, an enormous structure, seemed no more than a toy from this height, something made from an Erector Set. The bridge's Manhattan footing extended far over land and bordered the base of the World Building. An elevated train station blotted out our ground entrance.

Ralph Pulitzer had a studious look to him: more that of a scholar than a businessman. A formidable author, he wrote in an elegant and immediate prose. He was nearing fifty, and his hair thinned atop a prominent forehead. He sat in front of a rolltop desk the size of a player piano. His chair was turned my way—and toward the two others in the room.

Nearby sat his newly-minted wife, Margaret Leech, a graceful woman about fifteen years his junior. Also a polished writer, she had thick eyebrows with which to stare you down. Fiercely progressive, she belonged to the Lucy Stone League, a collective who fought for the right of women to keep their maiden names.

Across from her sat someone the complete opposite in character and style: the Coney Island flimflammer, William Reynolds, my old nemesis and the target of my article. I knew Reynolds to present at times two very contrasting looks. Half the time he oozed the gleeful polish of a conman, a swell good old guy. The other half, he looked puffy-faced and slack-jawed, like he'd barely struggled free after surviving being smothered by a pillow. Just past sixty years of age, he had arched brows and a balding head.

I was on edge: nervous, confused. Considering the smiles

in the room, I figured right away that this wasn't an inquisition, the agenda had to be something other than the missing photos or my job being in danger. Pulitzer was first to his feet, followed quickly by Margaret. Reynolds launched out of his chair, thrusting forward his hand. He outmaneuvered the other two greeters, insistent that he be the first to the handshake. He reached out crosswise for my right hand. He dropped his arm and wrinkled his nose when he saw it wasn't there.

Ralph knew me well enough to extend his left and we shook. Margaret gave me a peck on the cheek. Reynolds patted me on the shoulder. I was being treated like a hero?

"Nice meeting you," he said. His voice had sort of a grumble.

"We've met," I told him.

"Have we?"

"Nearly twenty years ago. I was younger then."

"We all were," Margaret said gaily.

Why was Reynolds treating me with civility? Had he not read my hatchet job? And if he had, did he not know that I was its author? This meeting represented a very strange turn of events.

Sure enough, Reynolds answered my questions. "I liked the way you showed me playing that upstart Walter Pissboy Chrysler," he said as though that was all I did in the story. "And you cursed his building by shooting a photo of that body." He stood close enough to me that I could smell him. One giant armpit.

I puffed out my chest, saying, "It wasn't all flattery."

Ralph rounded us and went to his liquor cabinet. "Brandy?" he asked.

"Something a tad more industrial," Reynolds said.

I shook my head. "I'm on the water wagon."

Pulitzer concentrated on filling four glasses. Brandy tumblers for him and his wife. Spritzed water in a soda glass for me. A clear and presumably punchy liquor for Reynolds. He ferried the drinks to us and then returned for his own. "Mr. Reynolds has asked me to assign you to write up a full story on him," he told me.

"A serum for some of the venom in today's article," the conman said. "You can polish aside my rough edges. Show readers my family glow. Exclaim to all my wiliness as an entrepreneur. I've survived in the real estate racket for more than thirty years, and that makes me part fox."

And two-thirds weasel.

I knew Pulitzer well enough. He was no dummy. He wasn't bowled over by this man and his slimy charms. He recognized Reynolds for who he was and wanted me to chum up to the man for a proper evisceration. And the man was offering himself up for the slaughter.

"So, how do we seal this deal?" Reynolds asked.

"Mr. Reynolds," Ralph said, "may I speak to my reporter in private?"

"Most assuredly," Reynolds said. He stuck out his right hand again to shake mine in a goodbye. I gave him a nod.

"Set your glass on the table outside when you finish, please," Margaret told Reynolds as he proceeded out the door. He wouldn't be invited back in?

The moment the door shut, Margaret laughed. "He is a bit of a scream," she said. "He has an excellent persona for a stage show. A snake oil salesman. I find those who have no self-awareness make for the most fascinating characters."

"You spend too much time hanging around the drama folk," her husband told her. "And 'excellent persona' is a polite way of saying 'prototypical scoundrel.'"

They always sounded like they spent their nights studying Roget's.

Margaret looked at me. "But theater is up your alley, considering your mother and all."

My mother, Gail Collinswood, had abandoned the stage for Hollywood years back. Not that I heard from her more than once in any given year.

Ralph set down his brandy glass and laced his fingers. "We have an opportunity here. Mr. Reynolds is on record as a racist and a xenophobe," he said, "besides being a thief. Alan, I want you to take him up on his invitation. Shadow him and expose him."

I was reluctant to bring this up, but I had to. "Mr. Pulitzer, you might soon be considering the situation in a different light. You'll shortly be learning that the original photos and negatives of the body at the Chrysler Building have disappeared."

"Disappeared?" Ralph's brow furrowed.

"They've been spirited away."

"That sounds most strange," Margaret said. "Is it strange?"

"Most," Ralph said. "I suppose they were evidence."

I imagined Sergeant Sullivan demanding to see the photos of the dead body and snarling with joy when we couldn't find them. I took a sip of seltzer water, reflexively as though it were whiskey, as though it were courage. "What's more, Strauss in the dark lab tells me that he could see in the originals the figure of a man hovering over the body. Crisp and clear. The face of a killer."

"With Reynolds just happening to drop by," Margaret said. "Do you suspect he is responsible for the photos having been stolen?"

I did. The man in the cape: Reynolds didn't want us to find him. I thought over his offer to have me follow him and interview him for a story. A conman, what if he was playing me? But what was his game?

Pulitzer's telephone box tinkled. An expensive set: wooden with inlaid brass. "Pardon me," Ralph said. "My gal Maisie is a brutal keeper of the gate. She doesn't disturb me lest it's vital." He raised the speaker to his ear and listened. His eyebrows rose. "Why yes, he is here." He put his hand over the receiver and told me, "Your mother, Mrs. Collinswood, is on the phone. She insists on speaking with you."

"My mother's in town?" I said. I supposed she could be calling from California, such coast-to-coast connections were becoming more common. Still, I could handle this from my desk. "Tell her to stay put and I'll ring her back."

Ralph was about to speak. Instead, his mouth remained hung open. Then he placed his hand over the receiver and said, "She tells me your wife has been kidnapped."

CHAPTER 11

Alan Priest

Legs. Legs Diamond. Underworld enforcer. My mother didn't appreciate the weight of that name, but I did. Cold. Pitiless.

"It happened here at the Algonquin," she told me over the phone. "The incident sent our klatsch into a positive dither!"

"Legs Diamond snatched Lorraine?" I repeated, still stumbling over the notion.

Ralph and Margaret looked my way, eyes watering with concern.

"And most rudely. He addressed us harshly, and I believe he showed her a gun when he opened his vest pocket. A *gat*, they call them. Did you see my film, *Trouble in Terror Town?*"

Unfortunately, yes. Her recent roles were shades of her former glory. I grunted in assent.

"This man was George Bancroft, only more sinister. More *Italian*."

Legs was Irish. "I have connections," I said. "I can handle this." I had no idea how to handle this. I was still numb, punchy from the blow.

"Oh, and I'm sorry I didn't inform you I've come to town. Ta." A click and silence.

I set the receiver in its cradle.

"Alan, tell us what we can do," Margaret said.

"I could ring up the police commissioner," Ralph offered. "The mayor."

I gathered my thoughts. "I'm going higher than the mayor. I'm calling on Rothstein. Ralph, get Swope to weigh in." Rothstein was the underworld's fixer. Herbert Swope, chief editor of the *World*, was a poker buddy of Rothstein and held some influence over him.

"Do you need our car and driver?" Ralph asked.

Through the fog of my anxiety, I took his question literally. Did I *need* his car and driver? Were they necessary? "A cab can get me there."

I stumbled over to the liquor cabinet and poured myself a shot of whiskey, which I tossed down. It merely served to remind me that one drink is never enough.

My spine and my limbs felt limp. I felt like I'd been sucker-punched. I stumbled past Reynolds in the rotunda hall. He stared at me quizzically. My hand grabbing hold of my hair, my head wagging; I must have been a sight.

I couldn't imagine waiting for an elevator. My feet tumbled down the spiral staircase steps from the building's dome, around and around, descending, sinking, my mind in a whirlpool as I tried to sort out what it all meant. Legs

Diamond was an enforcer for Rothstein. Rothstein didn't hold hard feelings against Lorraine and me. Or did he? Revenge for the time we beat him at gambling? That incident ended with the death of his rival and Rothstein scoring a lot of money on some insider trading.

Or was Legs playing some separate game? And how the hell did this even happen? All that I asked of Lorraine was to track down a nobody like Lyndon Warnecki.

I thought of what I would do to Legs if he hurt Lorraine. I'd gut him. Feint with my right, jab him with my left. And twist. I needed a knife.

Hacks are usually a gabby bunch. Perhaps mine read my attitude and that's why he maintained a sagely silence. I was still exhausted, and each moment I shut my eyes, I felt myself slipping backward through the wedge between the cab's seat cushions. Down a rabbit-hole? Manhattan doesn't have rabbits anymore. A manhole. A man-sized hole that sucked victims into a great underworld abyss.

Was I as red-eyed, as wild-eyed as I imagined myself to be? The cabbie dropped me off in front of Lindy's. I noticed he wore a silver wedding band. I thought of my fellow soldiers back in the Great War and how a lot of them on the front prized their rings, a connection to their women back home. Some kissed their rings before going into battle. I kissed my wedding band. I passed him a Liberty dollar and told him to take some time off. "Drive home and hold your wife."

CHAPTER 12

Lorraine Priest

LEGS PILOTED me across the Algonquin lobby, his fingernails stabbing my forearm. I studied him, noticing the skin on his face was so smooth, I figured that he'd just stepped free of a barber's chair. His jaw had a bluish tint. He smelled of cloves and wormwood, a pungent aftershave—or perhaps that came from his breath, a personal blend of absinthe.

I know how to read insecure men. Legs came across as that sort of hustler who layered on pretensions to impress the street crowd that had been his gang, desperate to prove he was the most clever.

I considered how to play up to his ego. First, broker a conversation. I'd read maybe three different versions of how he'd gotten his name. As he guided me across the Algonquin lobby, I asked him, "Why do they call you Legs?"

He leered. "Because I can dance on the floor and dance in the bed. I see what you's doing, but know this. You's only a package. Don't think to get on my good side."

"A girl can try."

Onto the sidewalk, and the street crowd parted for us: Legs had that effect. Even without showing his firearm, he was as threatening as a waved gun.

An automobile, a flivver, waited at the curbside. I would have supposed he had a better vehicle: the entire carriage rattled to the beat of its chugging pistons. An old man in a white suit sat at the wheel. Legs opened the back door and said, "Ladies first."

Considering the circumstances, I didn't appreciate his phony civility. I looked at the crowd who had stilled for our passage. I decided to let them know what was going on. "I am being kidnapped," I announced, and then told him, "If you want me in your motorcar, you'll have to push me." I wanted the onlookers to see. He grabbed my hair and thrust me, forcefully, inside. He ducked inside and proceeded to shove me across the seat.

I can put on a façade of bravura. I can also be stupidly brave. Right now, I fought hard to keep from shivering from fear. Folding my arms, I held myself still. I wouldn't let him see my vulnerability.

"The club," he told his chauffeur. I hoped that he meant a nightspot and not that he was asking for a bludgeon. The motorcar pulled onto the street, swinging around to reverse direction, west on 44th. The other vehicles swerved to avoid us.

"Now that we're past discussions," I said, "why are you taking me?"

"Shut yer yapper."

I jabbed him in his ribs. That brought a smile to his face.

He patted my cheek and then showed the back of his hand as a warning he could deliver a real wallop.

He wore a diamond ring, a tiny spear that could slice open my face.

I felt like one of those paddle toys, a rubber ball being slapped at the end of an elastic string. Rothstein's and now this, I was bouncing back and forth between mobsters' hideaways. We turned north on Broadway. We continued on past Lindy's.

I considered taking the Roosevelt campaign button from my purse and stabbing him. "I don't suppose I could convince you to vote for Roosevelt?" I said.

"Shaddup."

I've read that our guts eat themselves. They spill out juices that dissolve the meat we eat and after all, we are meat, our intestines look about the same as a string of sausages. Our guts survive by always replacing their inside lining. I felt that now. Right now, I felt like I was being eaten from the inside out.

The motor car pulled to a stop in front of the Hotsy Totsy Club, a few short blocks further up the street. In Manhattan all the buildings are crowded one against the other, and so are the rival gangs.

I remembered what Rothstein had told me. He worried that the Broadway mob was plotting against him. And I'd read something about the Hotsy Totsy Club, names sparking in the shadows of my memory. A place for heavy-hitting gangsters. Costello. The Mafia.

Legs opened the back door and clamped a hand around my wrist, dragging me out of the car as he exited. It was getting on past four o'clock and still too early for the night-club's marquee to be switched on. A hundred unlit plum-sized bulbs surrounded a signboard which promised "Girls! Girls!" and, if that didn't lasso men by their libidos, a third "Girls!"

A young man, I judged to not even be twenty, stood at the entrance: swanky outfit and Italian shoes. He tilted his head to the side in a way that said, "I'm considering you" and "You ain't worth considering." Lifeless eyes. So young to have such a dead expression. He opened the door for us. Legs whisked me past him.

He hustled me past the foyer, and we entered the show floor of the club. The red coffered ceiling rose two floors in height. Lightless chandeliers hung, suspended in the shad-ows. Spread out before me, a constellation of round, black tables, each crowned by the stick legs of upside-down chairs. An old black man pushed a dustmop from orbit to orbit.

At the far end of the room, a stage stood behind a barrier, tall enough to keep drunks from grabbing the show-girls. To my right-hand side, looming over us, a second-floor balcony with a series of private boxes. At their base, a carpeted stairway.

"Up them steps," Legs said. He held one hand tucked over his heart, where he kept his silver pistol.

I figured that if he had planned on killing me—right away, that is—he would have driven me to a junkyard or just marched me down an alleyway. Best to play along and see what fate awaited.

I walked up the steps. I felt Legs's eyes on my legs. I suppose I could have kicked back and planted my shoe in his face. Perhaps a stiletto heel to the eye. A pleasant fantasy, but I'd probably fail to do any real damage and would only make him mad.

Legs guided me into the first private box to our left, a dark, snug room. He flipped on a light. A ceiling-to-floor velvet curtain fronted the railing. Four plush chairs lined the front of the railing for viewing the show. Along the backside, near the door, a chaise lounge with two pillows.

"Do you need the facilities?" he asked me. "'Cause you's gonna nest here for a spell."

Concern about my comfort? I shook my head. "What is this about?" I thought he might finally tell me.

"I'm gonna bring you a phone line to make a call. You can tell your boyfriend ..."

"... My husband."

"The pip-squeak. You can tell him that he's gonna feed Rothstein what we says and only what we says, or damage will ensue to his package. Where can we find him?"

I considered what to answer. "Manhattan."

He raised the back of his hand. I flinched, saying, "I don't know. At the *World*. At our apartment."

"We'll corner him. In the meantime, I'm setting you a soldier outside your door. Don't yammer or we'll only got to gag you. Besides, a screaming dame ain't gonna scarcely draw an eyebrow in this joint."

He closed the door on me as he headed out. I tried the knob. Locked. I could hear the mumbles of a conversation in the hall, and footsteps marched my way. They stopped outside the room. The guard. I tried peeking through the keyhole and found my view blocked. The key. I thought of that timeworn gimmick of knocking out the key and catching it on a handkerchief. Just one problem: the floor was carpeted leaving too little space beneath the door.

I settled for locking my side, a flimsy hook in a hasp. It wouldn't stop a determined shoulder.

I can hold in my emotions, so much so, that sometimes I look down on those women who can't. Still, I wanted to cry. Cry out. Out of relief for being alive, out of the sheer release of pent-up vexation. To scream at the world and curse Legs and everyone in the Hotsy Totsy Club.

I pulled back a corner of the velvet curtain. The night-club floor was spread out below. A hundred tables. On the stage someone adjusted a microphone stand. The mike on top looked like a giant silver pill.

I thought of John Wilkes Booth leaping from the President's Box to the stage after shooting Lincoln. Broke a leg. Is that where theater folk got the saying "break a leg"? If so, how very strange.

I asked myself, *Am I desperate enough to try that?* Or else, I could free the curtain and tie it to a chair to use as a rope. Drop down onto a table. Maybe after the evening patrons began to fill the room. The mix of a crowd would discourage a flock of flying bullets.

CHAPTER 13

Alan Priest

ENTERING LINDY's, I felt like Moses must have when he crossed the Red Sea. *Listen up heathens: God is parting the waters for me. I'm on a holy mission.*

I trotted straight up the flowing stairs in the center of the restaurant to the second-floor landing. Only then did any thug dare stand in my way.

I thumped chests with a dump truck of a man. "Hello, Icepick," I said, backing off. Last time we met, my fast mouth helped get him shot. Not that he ever held a grudge —or could remember one.

"Hello, Mr. Alan!" he said cheerily.

A second goon moved up behind me and patted my sides. I raised my arms to help him complete the frisking. He confiscated the pocketknife I'd collected from my desk on my way out of the *World* office. Big enough to trim finger-nails. All that I had handy and now it seemed so silly.

"Your boss will want to talk to me," I said. "Tell him it's Alan Priest."

"I'll check on that," the second goon responded. He headed down the hall.

Icepick's eyes widened. "Mr. Alan, your doll-friend, Miss Lorraine, remember her?"

"She's my wife."

"Sorry. She came by visiting to see Mr. R. just a teeny bit ago."

"Visiting? She wasn't kidnapped?"

"Oh, no. I'm the one who tooked her. Me and Dirk, we did. Us. All nice and friendly. For a visit."

I couldn't square what happened. My mother had told me that it was a kidnapping, that it was Legs Diamond. How had he gotten involved?

The doorway at the end of the hall opened, and the second thug nodded my way. I'd been cleared to enter.

I strode down the dim hallway, my confidence not matching the cockiness of my walk. The door remained open before me and framed Rothstein as he stepped into the picture. He stood there, saluting me with an upraised martini glass. I felt like thrusting him against the wall, choking him, demanding that he tell me Lorraine's whereabouts. Yeah, right. If I laid hold of him, how long would I have before his goons hauled me to the floor and pummeled me senseless?

His other hand stretched forward, signaling me to stop. He presented me with a Manhattan two layers of golden liquids and a toothpick-skewered olive. I accepted the offer, taking the glass in my trembling hand. I tried to focus my furor, to pin him with a stare. About as easy as spearing a darting fly. He stepped to the side, ignoring my distress, and attended to his drink.

"Did your lovely bride send you?" Rothstein said. "So soon?"

"What sort of fool game are you playing?" I demanded.

He dipped his head to press the rim of his glass to his lips and looked up at me, frowning as he sipped. "When I play games, I am as serious as I can be. I'm not playing one now. Have you not spoken to Lorraine?"

"A witness called me and told me she was kidnapped from the Algonquin. By your stooge, Jack Diamond."

His brow wrinkled. His eyes searched the ceiling and then he downed his drink, setting the glass aside.

"Jack, you say?" He dabbed the wetness from his lips with his handkerchief. "I asked Lorraine to engage in an inquiry, with your help, of course, regarding some of my adversaries. In just this past month, Salvatore D'Aquila was gunned down on the street."

"D'Aquila?" I remembered the incident from a story the *World* ran. "He was a businessman."

"Few people know that he has been the Chief of the New York mafia for the past seventeen years. Joey Noes, the partner of Dutch Schulz, was shot. Some blame me. Dutch blames me. A major move is under way and it seems that Lorraine's recruitment provoked a rather immediate response."

"Response? Is that what you call it?"

"Perhaps I should have said, 'a regrettable reaction.'" Every bit as insulting. He shook his head. "I'm disappointed.

Not by her. By my own associates. I've always supposed Legs to be among my most loyal. By going behind my back to seize your wife, he has revealed a hostile design. I suspect he is holding her to ensure her silence. Probably to ensure your cooperation, as well." He took out his roll of bills, preparing to bribe me.

I answered him by pouring my martini on his carpet. "I want her free," I said. "I want her clear of any of your games."

"As do I," he said. He looked at the puddle of my drink as though the waste of liquor were one of the few actions he counted as a sin. "Your request might not be so simple a wish to grant. I trusted Legs. And for Legs to have struck so quickly after I recruited Lorraine, someone close at hand must have informed him of her mission. Before retrieving her, before making a move, I need to rethink whom I can trust."

"Give me a gun and I'll do the job." I quivered with anger.

Rothstein chuckled. So infuriating, how lightly he took this. "If you, Alan Priest, confront Legs waving a gun, I'd lay odds you'll get yourself killed. Or else snatched up and beaten until you sounded off about how I've become aware of the schemes of her captors, dooming Lorraine and yourself and, more importantly, being of no help to me. A gun? No, considering your rage and your recklessness, I think it's best that I keep you stowed away. Safe and secure." He called to someone in back of me. "Cesar?" I felt a huge presence hovering behind me, and the snort on my neck, that of a looming bull. "You and Spokes escort Mr. Priest to the Yellow Room. Treat him as a guest but make certain he doesn't leave."

"Are you jailing me?"

"Just for dinner. And a dessert." He stuffed his roll of bills back in his pocket and said, "Do you like cheesecake?"

CHAPTER 14

Lorraine Priest

THE PRIVATE BOX that made up my prison had a chaise
lounge and I lay down on it to catch some shut-eye, still
exhausted from last evening's all-night adventure.

I soon fell asleep. I dreamt of the day I'd met Alan, the
moment I fell in love. We were at Macy's, he was trying on a
pin-striped dress suit and looked for all the world like the
Prince of Manhattan. In my dream, his right hand was
restored. He fastened the pearl buttons on a twinkling white
silk shirt. He winked at me; his eyes were stars, his smile, a
galaxy. I woke to the sound of screaming.

It took me a moment to orient myself. My box overlooked a show floor and the rumble of voices coming from
below told me that an audience was gathering. From nearer
by, outside the room, down the hall, several shrieks arose,
and a woman cried out, "Oh, no you don't." Footfalls
tromped my way. A rattle. It sounded like someone grap-
pling unsuccessfully with a door one room down from here.

Then the footsteps came near. I heard the "crick" of a bolt sliding and the knob to my door turned. The door parted slightly, stopped by the hook-and-eye latch I'd set in place. A woman's whimper. I unlatched the door.

A sobbing woman tumbled in, falling against me. She wore a showgirl's outfit: long fishnet hose and a silvery, one-piece dress that ended in a fringe that dangled not far below her hipline. She wore a top hat which toppled to the floor.

"You'se an angel," she said, breaking from my hold and pressing a hand to her chest. "I needs me a spot to tuck away and snatch myself a breather." She listened at the door.

"There's no guard outside?" I asked.

"He's got himself parked down the hall, jawing with some Sheba."

I noticed that my visitor had a black eye, craftily covered by make-up. "Name's Lorraine," I said.

"CeeCee," she told me, "with four small 'e's' and two big 'C's.'" She sniffled and smiled. "This swank, in another booth. A genuine wolf. He bites." She showed me marks on her shoulder. "I draw the line at teeth."

"You can stay here."

She looked over my outfit. "You got yourself a sugar daddy?"

"I'm a prisoner."

"Ain't we all?"

"Your black eye?" I asked.

"Oh, that's from home. My poppy. Sometimes I try and sneak my money from him. I dream of saving up for a go at typing school. Secretaries snag the sweetest lugs for hubbies. Ones with soft hands."

I thought of how lonely this city was for so many women. I said, "You should just leave this joint. Just march out that door and go work in an office."

"Easy to say for you and yours. A tomato like you who gots a spiffy dress and who can jabber like a swell."

My ridiculous dress? Right now, I'd trade it for sackcloth and ashes, some sort of disguise to make me anonymous. That gave me an idea. "Look. I'll switch outfits with you. I can use your clothes to pass as one of the floor girls and hoof it out of here."

Her nose wrinkled. "Us chorus gals don't own these rags. They's gonna make me pay."

"I have five dollars in my purse."

"Five? That's only the deposit."

"And coins." Probably two dollars more.

CeeCee eyed my clasp bag. "And I want to keep the purse." She had good taste. Twelve dollars fifty from Tiffany's. I nodded.

She pulled down one shoulder strap and then another, maintaining eye contact and presenting a lascivious smile. Her top came down and she rubbed a breast while biting her lower lip. I don't think I was the first woman to be part of her private show.

I wrestled out of my dress. As I did, I considered what would happen to CeeCee when the folks at Hotsy Totsy's found out that we had traded outfits. I warned her, "They might be none-too-happy that you helped me to escape."

"When are they ever happy with me?" She rolled down a stocking.

"Look, I'm going to tie your hands. With my brassiere."

"Mmm-hmm." A hum remained on her lips.

I put my hand to her face and rubbed off the make-up from around her blackened eye. "Pretend that I knocked you out."

"And I was helpless," she purred.

I pulled her stockings over my shins, drawing them up to my hips, one leg and then the other. They felt sensuous.

We were close enough to the same size. Her showgirl outfit fit me perfectly. It was made to be snug, to compress itself around a body. She generally fit into my jade-colored gun moll outfit, a little empty around the bust.

"I'll got to use some tissues," she said.

Her shoes were half my size. I couldn't imagine running for my life in my stilettos, so I chose to go barefoot. Or, rather, in sheer, silk-covered feet, stockings which would undoubtedly shred.

She took a front row seat and placed her hands behind her back. I tied them to the back of the chair with my bra. She popped a kiss my way and I stuffed my pink hanky in her mouth. She practiced moaning to express her desperation. I tucked my purse next to her thigh.

I turned my back on her. I didn't want to imagine what would happen if they didn't believe her story about how I had overpowered her. On the other hand, I supposed that if anyone would get in trouble, it would be the guard.

I pressed my ear to the door and listened. Far down the hall, I heard a man muttering and the occasional coos and sighs of a woman. I took CeeCee's top hat and discreetly held it in front of my face as though I were tipping it to say hello.

I marched out into the hallway, just another chorus girl among the many who worked there, and headed straight for the stairs. I thumped my way down the steps and passed into a crowd of patrons in the foyer, conscious that someone looking would wonder why I was shoeless. But then, these were mostly men. They leered at my chest and legs and never even glanced at my feet.

The heavy at the front door grabbed my wrist and demanded to know where I was going.

"Legs says I can smoke me a pill," I told him, imitating CeeCee, aiming for a Brooklyn accent. He loosened his grasp and I slipped free. *Hmm.* As though I couldn't smoke backstage.

I rushed past him to the curb. Already night. Lights raced around the marquee. Evening traffic rumbled along Broadway, headlights sweeping along a city block that already seemed overlit. I had to cross the street. Right away. I wanted no one from the Hotsy Totsy Club to recognize me or try to stop a runaway showgirl.

I launched hurriedly between speeding motorcars, horns tooting, making a spectacle of myself and risking my life. Finally, stationed on the opposite sidewalk, I realized how everyone was looking at me, a foolhardy fugitive from a chorus line. Even the lug in front of Hotsy Totsy was glaring my way.

I collected myself and began walking south. I had no money, not even a coin. My outfit was designed for an indoor stage or the warmth of summer, but not for this November chill. With each step, I could feel the cold cement beneath my feet.

I thought of how Prohibition had reduced the amount of broken glass on the streets. Outside of skid row, the one thing forbidden among drinkers was waving around a bottle in public.

I thought of how Henry Ford had said, "People didn't want faster horses. What they wanted was less horseshit." Only a few years back, the boulevards of Manhattan were full of horse manure. In the summer, an eye-watering smell. In the rain, a yellow-brown runoff that turned the streets into above-ground sewers. Even after the droppings dried, bits of its straw-like grit worked their way onto the side-walks. Practically barefoot, I felt grateful that the walkway before me was clean. Except for the odd gob of tobacco spit. Except for the occasional lumps of chewing gum.

Without any money, I considered hocking my wedding band. I could return tomorrow and buy it right back, right? Or, I could hock my top hat. All I needed were a few coins. But there were no pawn shops nearby, not along this stretch of Broadway near Times Square. Too sniffy a neighbor-hood. And even a little further south, would any pawnbro-kers be up at this hour of the evening? What hour was it?

Would I have to walk all the way to my apartment? Blocks and blocks. I'd freeze to death. Then I realized: I'd left my keys in my purse!

No going back. On second thought, no problem. I could run down Giovanni, the building manager. He spent evenings near his radio. He'd let me in. He had the keys to my apartment.

I thought back to my kidnapping and the witnesses. Gail must have contacted Alan and told him that I'd been abducted. He would be out looking for me.

I peered down Broadway in the mad hope that I would see him racing my way. What seemed like a thousand yellow cabs poured along the street, none of them useful to a penniless woman. Each a tin wind-up toy, all of them wagging their snouts and rears, seeming to contain no one and go nowhere.

Coming upon 44th and Broadway, I thought of making a desperate return to the Algonquin. *No.* By this hour, anyone I knew would be long gone.

To my right I saw, less than a half-block away, the 44th Street Theatre. *The Marx Brothers! Animal Crackers.* I remembered that Harpo had witnessed my abduction. I knew something of the brothers from long ago. I'd followed them from back when I was a kid. For a time, they were fellow Chicagoans. Harpo was the sweet and sane one among his siblings. I could camp out by the stage door, shiver and wait. He would help me.

CHAPTER 15

Alan Priest

THEY STASHED me in a bare room: no windows and with walls painted an ugly yellow. I noted in the cracks beneath the baseboard, where it was hard to mop, dried crusts of blood. This was an interrogation room. The physical kind.

The only furnishings, two ladderback wooden chairs. Good enough for me. I turned them to face each other. Slouching back against one, I put my feet up on the seat of the other. I crossed my arms and dropped my head back, the wall behind me, my pillow. Exhausted, I fell asleep in mere moments.

A nap usually restores me. Not this time. Not with my pent-up fury and feelings of helplessness. Sleep was a steep drop down a dark shaft. I didn't dream; I merely fell. Accompanying my fall, screams rose from the depths of my fears, swirling around me like a whirlwind, clutching my chest, squeezing me until I was breathless.

I woke, panting, to find a tray of food at my feet. Carved

turkey, gravy, mashed potatoes, and peas. Spiced squash soup. Cheesecake for dessert. I felt hungry. With no table in the room, I knelt before it. They'd left me a spoon. They didn't even trust me with a butterknife, much less a fork. I grabbed the utensil and dug up gobs of mashed potatoes, shoveling them in my mouth. I felt primitive, like a howling beast in a cage. Not that eating furiously accomplished anything other than having mashed potatoes drop onto my shirt. I wiped it clean and sunk my hand into my pocket to massage a handkerchief, strangling it, scraping the mush from my fingers.

Feeling the glory of having a bit of food crash down into my empty belly, I took several deep breaths, collecting myself. I crossed my legs, stiffened my back, and spoon in hand, scooped up the soup unhurriedly and savored it, returning to being human, even if it was only an act.

I thought of Lorraine. Rothstein had a hundred times more power than I had to find and rescue her. But was that his goal? She was a pawn in a game where the players would just as soon flip over the chessboard.

I tried to imagine Lorraine's abduction and how it took place with my mother there. It seemed to be fiction, like one of my mother's photoplay dramas.

My mother's films played in the motion picture palaces and, over the years, in the absence of other contact, I'd come to think of her as being as unreal. I suppose her moviegoing audience felt a closer connection to her than I did.

I recalled her giant head floating up on the screen, her face artfully painted to reveal her thoughts and to hide her age. Make-up which seemed so fake when seen in real life.

There in the theater, the accompanist pounding out melodramatic organ music. The vast emotions on display on the silent screen, and how she conveyed both innocence and passion. I pictured her that way as I recalled her words over the telephone line. The histrionic way she conveyed her alarm over Lorraine's safety. Her cheerful *ta!* to say goodbye as though every plot twist was guaranteed to have a movie ending.

I felt angry at her, as though she were behind this. As though she could have stopped Legs. *Legs.* I pictured the hook-footed limbs of a bloodsucking louse. A hundred-legged centipede skimming along the floor.

My thoughts returned to Lorraine. How she would often laze one calf over mine when we were lying naked in bed, atop the sheets, looking at the ceiling, talking small talk in the afterglow of love. How the mere touch of her skin could make my body hum.

A knock on the door. A strange bit of politeness: did the thugs care whether I was decent? "Come in," I croaked. Nothing happened. I took a seat in a chair and then with a little more effort and clarity, repeated, "Come in."

The door parted and Herbert Swope, the long-time executive editor of the *World,* stood before me.

Swope possessed an extraordinary gift: wherever he went, he belonged there. Legend has it that, when he was a European correspondent, he strode through palaces, entering whatever chamber he chose without being questioned by guards. He had that sort of confidence. Among the other, varied worlds in which he traveled, he was also poker buddies with Arnold Rothstein and political scammers like Harry Sinclair. As he described it, "I seek out the company of men who, like me, have a soul-connection to the sporting life."

And now this man, who consorted with kaisers and kings, high rollers and criminals, took a seat across from me.

In his late forties, his hair was drawn back, as though washing over his crown. He wore pince-nez and examined me with paternal concern. I begged him with my eyes. I suppose I appeared less like a prisoner and more like a found puppy. He pocketed his spectacles and glanced amusedly about the room. "Yellow," he said.

"Yellow, indeed," I echoed. "They have Lorraine."

"Not anymore."

I caught my breath, mid-gasp.

Swope pressed his hands together, peaked as though in prayer. "A source from the Hotsy Totsy Club has informed us that she escaped."

Of course, she did. Lorraine was crafty. The poor saps holding her hadn't stood a chance.

"Where is she?"

"We don't know. She snuck away."

I wiped my hand across my face, rubbing life back into it. I felt like slapping myself. I was coming fully awake for the first time in hours.

"I need to find her."

"Arnold tells me you are free to leave."

I thought about the tall shimmering island of Manhattan and how it was a labyrinth with a million cul-de-sacs. I thought of home and how she'd probably head there. Was that safe? Perhaps Legs had learned where we live.

"Mr. Swope?"

"Herb."

"Talk to Rothstein, he listens to you. Tell him I don't appreciate his schemes or making us a part of them. Tell him I blame him for putting Lorraine in danger."

He rubbed his jaw and said, "There are worse forces than Rothstein out there. He is a bulwark against them."

"I don't believe that," I said. "Rothstein corrupts everyone and he's as cold blooded as any killer. Tell him if Lorraine is hurt, I will come after him."

CHAPTER 16

Lorraine Priest

BACK IN MY CHICAGO DAYS, back in the 1910s, when I was a budding young woman, I told my ever-so-ambitious mother that I wanted to perform on stage. Too often giving in to my whims, she enrolled me in Minnie Palmer's Chicken Farm. The name sounded hick or, perhaps, suggestive, but it referred to how we were as untutored as freshly-hatched chicks, fledglings ready to be molded and trained in song, dance, and comportment.

And yet it did turn out to be quite indecent. Minnie Palmer was both the mother *to* and the manipulative manager *of* the Five Marx Brothers during their vaudevillian days. My teacher turned out to be none other than her son, Leo Marx, soon to be famous as Chick-o (later, Chico), named for his pursuit of the ladies. Part of my fellow class-mates' daily exercises included being chased around the stage by the king of leers. At twelve, I was too young for his philandering—barely—however already I was not so naively starry-eyed to fail to recognize that I needed to ditch this sort of "training."

I didn't meet the other Marx brothers during my brief period of showbiz lessons, but still I remained intrigued by them, enough so as to follow their careers from afar.

The great showman Eddie Cantor once said, "It takes twenty years to make an overnight success." Quickly pared down to four, the Marx brothers separately and then collectively, struggled for nearly two decades on the vaudeville circuit before making it to Broadway. These past couple of years they'd stormed Manhattan and reigned as conquerors of the Great White Way, the masters of musical mayhem. Alan and I had caught their previous show. They were brilliant: their energy, creativity, and timing miles ahead of other comedic stage acts with their rubber chickens and punchless puns. They presented a Marxism more anarchic than the Bolsheviks, and certainly more crowd-pleasing.

Standing below the marquee of the 44th Street Theatre, contemplating the caricature of Chico on a poster, I realized that he no longer held a menacing sway over me. He was just another skirt chaser. I'd survived a few in my life. I had come a long way.

So had they. I smiled at the cartoon heads of Groucho, Harpo, and Zeppo.

Music by Kalmar and Ruby. Top-notch songsmiths, their tunes were helping to sell a million radios. *I Wanna Be Loved by You.*

Margaret Dumont starred as Mrs. Rittenhouse. A matronly foil under a constant barrage of insults from Groucho. The woman had the patience of a saint.

I was shivering. Although only a half mile, considering

that I had walked on a cold night wearing silk stockings and a one-piece that might get me arrested if I wore it at the beach, it had been a long, frozen journey from the Hotsy Totsy Club. One block back, the soles of my hose had sprung and drawn up to my ankles. Every subsequent step prickled the skin beneath my feet. I felt like some sort of showgirl-bum.

Manhattan can be cruel and indifferent. In spite of my bedraggled appearance, no one among the crowds I passed offered me help. They all marched by, imprisoned in their portable private worlds, certain their own troubles were all that mattered. I vowed to never be like that, to be so unfeeling and oblivious.

I concluded that I had no chance of busting through the front entrance of the theater in my disheveled state, so I decided to head over to the alleyway to the stage door. Maybe I'd be mistaken for a chorus girl who got trapped outside.

I imagined my face in a mirror. Frightening. Placing my fingers on my cheekbones, I felt the smudges and the speckled grit of eyeliner. My former purse had my make-up kit. I couldn't even fix my face.

The walls of the alleyway at the side of the theater acted as a megaphone. I heard a distinctive voice before I caught a glimpse of the speaker.

She said, "In Hollywood these days, there are only two roles for women: plums and prunes. I'm not ready for the pickling jar."

My mother-in-law, Gail Collinswood. She wore a knee-length red coat with a fur fringe that rounded her neck like a boa. She was talking to a man. He had that sort of beaming smile and snazzy grooming that made me believe he was an actor. Hair perfectly sculpted, gelled into place, and with a razor-sharp part.

She saw me coming. "Lorraine, darling!" she called out, gasping, pressing her hand to her chest as though about to succumb to the vapors. "Was all of that a bit of sport? My dear, your exit sent our gathering into a tizzy. I gave a shout to Alan …"

I came up to her and kissed her on the cheek. "It was real," I said, "I managed to slip free."

"Did you? Thank God that's behind us." She took a moment to look me over, head to foot. "That tawdry outfit of yours. What were you thinking? And your face! Oh, darling, where are your shoes?" I had a feeling that her greatest concern at this moment was that my appearance was embarrassing her in front of her friend.

Her companion's expression was an indecipherable squiggle, head dipping, waiting for introductions.

"Ah, my dear! This is Monta Bell," she said. "A producer. He works with Paramount, their Astoria studio. Monta, this is my sister-in-law, Lorraine Marquette." I understood why she called me her sister-in-law, not wanting to admit to her age, but not why she used my maiden name. "Monta and I had to step into this alley. We're conspiring."

"I haven't agreed to conspire," he said.

"We're conspiring to conspire."

"Can we head inside?" I said. "I'm freezing." I shivered to demonstrate.

"The brothers are going through their big first act finale," Monta said. "I doubt the stagehands will be attending the doors."

Monta passed over his dress jacket. I said, "Thank you," and set it over my shoulders, closing it around me, hugging it.

"I, at least, dressed sensibly," my mother-in-law said. Then she leaned my way as though to speak in confidence, even though she had a theatrical bray to her voice. "The brothers are making a talking picture out of their musical, *The Cocoanuts.* I would be magnificent for a part. Since they are changing from stage to film, where I have oodles of familiarity, I'd fit in perfectly to take over the role played by Margaret Dumont."

I'd seen *The Cocoanuts.* "Why would you want to play the part of Mrs. Potter? They're so mean to her."

"I know how to take abuse. I've had three husbands."

"Four," I pointed out.

"I still *have* Joseph. And he doesn't count as a husband. He's normal."

"I haven't agreed to drop Mrs. Dumont," Monta said. "She has quite a royal presence and a Broadway voice. She can handle talkies."

Gail heaved a sigh and spoke with affected grace. "And so am I a maestra at elocution. Wouldn't you prefer someone in her thirties?"

I considered blackmailing my mother-in-law. Give me money to get home or else I'd reveal her birth year.

A boom of applause arose from within the theater, a sustained ovation that told me the act had ended.

The stage door parted, and a head peeked out, a man scouting the alley. When he was finished, and before the door could close, I rushed up to its breach and inserted my hand, opening the door and entering. I needed a little warmth. I tossed Monta his jacket.

Piano playing rang out from the stage, mad in style. The work of Chico banging out an encore. Something extra for the audience.

Chorus girls poured around me. The stagehand who had attended the door, considered me standing there with a bit of puzzlement. "That's not one of our costumes," he said.

Men are not observant, or he would have concluded that, in my disarray, I looked more like I'd been mauled by a lion than that I was a wrongly dressed chorus girl.

I ignored his assessment, merely smiling. Backing up next to a radiator, I let it feed me its warmth. I took off my top hat.

Having just heard the scheming going on behind her back, I felt uncomfortable when I laid eyes on Margaret Dumont passing among the cast members. She sat, filling a chair. I imagined she had her own dressing room. Perhaps she was taking the moment to collect herself.

Dumont. A stocky woman, she sat with perfect posture. I knew something of her personal story. After a brief career on stage, she married a sugar baron and hobnobbed with the gentry. A few years later, he died during the great flu epidemic. She discovered he had left her no money, so she reluctantly returned to the stage where she played a character close to her former life: a widowed society matron. As part of their routines, the Marx Brothers mocked her, savagely, repeatedly.

Perhaps my unique costume made me stand out among the other chorus girls. Perhaps it was my Junoesque figure. I drew the attention of Groucho. He loped my way. Up close, his painted-on mustache and eyebrows looked ridiculous, but he'd probably take the word "ridiculous" as a compliment.

"I'm the man your mother warned you about," he told me.

Chico followed closely behind. "I'm the one she should have warned you about," he said.

Both spread their arms for a hug, together forming a wide arc that left me little room for escape.

"We've met before," I told Chico. I cupped my hands in front of my belly as though it had once been heavy with child. He backed away, and then spun, ready to skip town.

"I'd like to apologize for my brother," Groucho said, "but first I'll need all the disgusting details." I stepped off to the side, bumping into Harpo, squeeze-horn bulb first.

"Lorraine?" he said. He looked like he'd seen a ghost. He wore his full stage outfit here, disheveled trench coat, a blond, frizzy wig, and a rumpled stove hat.

Harpo's use of my name served as a declaration of familiarity and Groucho abandoned flirting with me. I supposed the reason was the fact that Harpo was the only brother who was not married, and they kept their hands off the women he knew.

"That was Legs Diamond who took you, right?" Harpo said. "Actually Legs Diamond?" He looked me over, noticing my distress. "Are you …? What happened to you?"

"I escaped. From nearby. I came here because I thought …" And then I realized that Gail would forward me the funds to make it home. No need to bother this man. "To hide out."

"You look shaken," Harpo said. "Do you need my dressing room? Some real clothes? Something to eat?"

I found myself sniffling. Not from the recent cold. My eyes were watering. Out of gratefulness. Having found someone who could see beyond my façade of bravery.

"Yes, please," I said. "Yes, to all that. Especially some clothes."

With a wide grin, he passed me his rumpled top hat, placing it on my head. I laughed and handed him my hat. I later learned that he finished the second half of the show wearing it.

CHAPTER 17

Alan Priest

I'D ONCE SEEN an article in *National Geographic* with photos of a vast necropolis called Wadi-us-Salaam in the Arab land of Iraq. Black and white images. Stark. A cemetery built above ground with millions upon millions of burial chambers of so many sizes.

Stepping outdoors and onto a sidewalk of Broadway, Manhattan felt like an immense cemetery. Its buildings looming around and above me, all massive crypts. The people in the streets, the wandering dead.

I hailed a cab. The moment one stopped, I told the cabbie that I'd made a mistake and to head on. I needed to try a more immediate connection. I plodded over to a phone booth.

I peeled off a nickel from the roll in my pocket and listened to the coin's heavy bong as it dropped. The operator said, "Number, please." I gave her my exchange and four digits.

I let it ring a dozen times, imagining the hollow echo of its chime in our small flat. I thought of the empty rooms and the view out the window to the Metropolitan Clock Tower, imagining its *dong.* My watch read ten. Still early in the night.

I needed to hire out a message-taking service for our home line. Not only for times like these, but practical for my line of work.

I asked the operator to connect me to the building's manager. He picked up on the first ring.

"Hullo, this is Mr. Marco." I'd seen him speak into a phone. He always addressed the device by leaning in, as though confiding to a person inside a box.

"This is Alan Priest."

"Mr. Priest, signore! Yessir, I recognize your speaking voice. Hullo! You are there? You are fine?"

"Yes, Giovanni. This is extremely urgent. Have you seen or heard from Lorraine this evening?"

"No, sir. Not this night. Not at all. A big man came looking for her. A big man like a gorilla."

No one would call Legs a gorilla.

"Did you get a name?"

"*Polizia.* Sergente Sullivan. He had fists like cement blocks. He showed me them high up at his chest like a boxer. He had a little man with him. He demanded for your key."

Dropping by to serve a little revenge for my article? He had learned where Lorraine and I live. Not difficult for the police. *I own the night,* he'd told me. That was a warning: just you wait.

"You let him into my apartment?"

"He is *poliziotto.* I bring him to your place. Him and me

and the little man with a box. He made me wait outside. He sees I am not lying. You are not there. And not Mrs. Lorraine."

A man with a box? What game was he playing? "You did all right. You had to do what they said. Mr. Marco?"

"*Sì?*"

"I'll be there soon. If you see Lorraine before I come, could she stay for a while in your apartment?"

"It would be my honor to be of service."

"*Grazie,*" I said and ended the call.

Marco made me think of Santarelli. I thought also of Luciano and Costello and the mob forces Rothstein described coming here from Italy. Why is it that I lump people together based on nationality and not simply as to whether they are good or bad?

I rang the *World,* hoping that Lorraine had left word there. I got the night desk and asked whether anyone passed along a message. Nothing—but they would check my desk.

I asked to speak with Ralph Pulitzer.

"Herbert's here."

"Swope?" I'd just left him at Lindy's.

"Pulitzer."

Herbert, the youngest of the Pulitzer brothers and a carefree playboy. Tragically, his father left him most of the estate in his will. Herbert seemed determined to use his financial influence to bankrupt the *World.* Did I want to talk to him? Never.

"Just take a message. For Ralph and Margaret Pulitzer. Tell them that Lorraine is free and thanks for their help."

I asked to speak to the night desk manager. Haines was filling in. He described a note left on my desk: a sketch with what looked like a croquet ball passing through a wicket. The words: Up for a match after you sort things out? *Wm. Reynolds.*

I imagined that image and an irrational surge of anger swelled in me. That drawing, probably no more than a swirl, trivialized the hysteria I'd felt. I placed my hand over my mouth and breathed steadily, calmly. What was wrong with me? I felt I was going mad.

CHAPTER 18

Lorraine Priest

WHILE I FIXED my make-up in his dressing room mirror, Harpo left to collect some clothing from the costume department. Before stepping out, he loaned me his woolie slippers. Soft and warm. My toes rejoiced. If they could have sung, they would have—the five-piggy serenade. Two feet, a full choir.

He returned with a bundle of clothes under his arms, giving me my pick. I chose one of the outfits. Before my stepping behind a screen, being a gentleman, Harpo shielded his eyes as I dressed.

I stepped out for him to see. Ta-da! In fake fur and twinkling gown, I felt like a star.

"Ma-jestic," he pronounced, and then, as a whisper, "what happened with Legs?"

I narrated the story of my escape, and he listened, round-eyed.

Harpo said, "I know these guys. Some gangsters, they

hang around us actors figuring that our fame is like magic sparkles that will brush off on them. They all want to be big shots and they claim they're our friends."

Knuckles rapped on his dressing room door. "Three minutes."

"Act Two," Harpo said, apologetically.

"I have to go home to let my husband know I'm okay."

"I understand."

"I'll get these clothes back to you," I promised.

He shook his head and frowned, his eyes like big buttons. I gave him a peck on his cheek and when I did, he dropped back in his chair, mouth wide open as though slugged. He clasped his hands together and blushed on cue. My heart fluttered.

Only after he left did I discover a ten-dollar bill in my coat pocket. Did he think I needed a week of groceries? I made one last inspection in the mirror. Presentable. Ready to meet the world.

On my way out, I came across my mother-in-law standing just inside the stage door. She seemed forlorn, alone, and for the moment, not trying to absorb the worship of the world.

"When I was a younger actress," she said, "I could sneak an extra bow, slip upstage, or just plain steal a role from unsuspecting actors. I perfected stealing men's parts, convincing the director I could do them. Now, I'm losing my nerve. I saw Mrs. Dumont sitting there. She could be me in … ten years. I'm not going to take the movie role from her." Her forehead wrinkled. "I must be growing … *senti-mental.*" She said it as though it were a worse word than "old."

"You'll always be my mother," I told her, and she shuddered. I can be mean.

I took a subway home rather than a cab, a direct run from Times Square to Madison Square. Maybe I wanted that crowd of people around me to feel safe. Besides, my recent trips in backseats had been traumatic.

While walking to the front of my building, I looked over at the Metropolitan Life clock. Its ornate trimmings lost in the dark. Its long arrow-like hands glowed. Slanted just a little to the side, one next to the other as though the two were leaning on one another for support. Minutes before eleven. A single yellow light beamed from one of the building's upper windows, just to the side of the "9." It framed a silhouette: an observer looking out over the world. Or, who knows? A living, breathing gargoyle. I don't ever remember having seen that figure before. The clockkeeper? So high above the world. The image seemed phantasmagoric. It unnerved me.

I stepped up to my building's door. Home. I felt rejuvenated. I wanted to wake up my neighbors, to hug and kiss all of them. First, I needed to get inside. This was past our doorman's hours, and the building's front door was locked. I first rang my place hoping for Alan. No answer.

I felt a bit guilty for having to disturb the building manager; nevertheless, I pressed the ringer to his apartment.

A friendly, familiar, "Hullo?" He didn't sound groggy.

"It's Lorraine ..." and before I could apologize for the hour he said, "*La mia regina di bellezza.*" A buzzer sounded and the front door unlocked.

CHAPTER 19

Alan Priest

PEOPLE WHO KNOW me know that I am an aficionado of skyscrapers. I've written special interest features detailing their histories for the *Sunday World*. The Pulitzers and Swope always appreciate "This is your city" type of stories. Behind every building is a fascinating tale.

The three-hundred-foot bell tower of St. Mark's Cathedral in Venice collapsed in 1902, having stood for over seven hundred years. The Metropolitan Life Tower, a block away from where I lived, was constructed to look like St. Mark's, a homage to the lost campanile. Completed in 1909, it briefly reigned as the tallest building in the world. Massive clocks were set in place spanning its twenty-fifth to twenty-seventh floors, one on each of its four sides. Their faces are made of glass tiles revealing the white face beneath. Their minute hands are 17 feet in length and each weigh half-a-ton. The Metropolitan Life company advertises the beacon on the roof of the building as "the light that never fails."

The original designs planned for a multiplex of skyscrapers. In 1920, they tore down a gorgeous church fashioned by the architect Stanford White to build a north tower. Less than ten years had passed, and now they were ready to tear down that tower to put up an even taller one, one-hundred stories in height, the tallest in the world. Taller than Chrysler's soon-to-be tower and higher up than his plans for a toilet from which to crap on the world.

The clock read eleven-thirty. Some of my neighbors complained about its familiar *bong*. I found comfort in its voice, and wished it rang all through the night. Its bells stay silent for these dead hours. I felt the coldness. The quiet. The aloneness. Not being certain where Lorraine was. She had time, so much time since she'd escaped. She had either made it home or else had been recaptured. These hours. I wondered whether it was possible that Sergeant Sullivan had returned for another visit. Perhaps he was waiting for me.

I unlocked the front door to my building and then hurried down the hall to Marco's apartment, having asked him to protect Lorraine. I didn't trust her being alone in the apartment with Sergeant Sullivan calling on us.

I knocked with trepidation. My heart leaped as I heard footsteps racing to the door. I recognized the cadence of those steps. Perhaps she'd recognized my knock.

The door swung back and Lorraine fell against me. She wrapped her arms around me and I felt for a moment as though I couldn't inhale. I kissed her hair, my entire body shivering, and whispered, "Thank you," not certain what I meant. *For being here. For being you: the bravest woman in the world.* As a couple, we're the pluckiest lady and luckiest guy.

I breathed her in, taking a moment to compose myself. I

kissed her on the lips, lingering in their warmth, drinking their suppleness. A soft landing after a long fall.

I found myself crying. Marco teared up. Only Lorraine remained dry-eyed, her wellsprings of composure running deeper than mine.

"The police, including that sergeant, have been to our place," Lorraine said.

"When I called Marco, he told me." My mind whirred. "He said Sullivan brought along a partner—a guy carrying a box. I believe they placed a wiretap on our phone." Wiretaps had been around since the first days of telephony. A recent Supreme Court decision declared that police could plant them without a warrant.

"I don't feel safe in our room," Lorraine said. "I left behind my purse at the Hotsy Totsy Club. Legs has our front door and apartment keys."

"There's an empty apartment on your floor," Marco said. "You can camp out there."

"Camping? Thanks." Perhaps I sounded dismissive, but I meant it sincerely.

I thought of what I'd need to extract from our place. My shaving kit. A couple of suits. My journals and my lists of contacts: I'd best move them, lock them up in my desk at the *World*.

Bed sheets, some covers, and a pair of pillows. I thought of Lorraine and me lying on the floor among a swirl of blankets. I looked at her, a sensual smile on her lips. We were thinking of the very same thing.

CHAPTER 20

Lorraine Priest

ALAN HAS ALWAYS HAD an acute sense of duty. I suppose some army instructor drilled it into his head. Or it could have been discipline from his days as a magician on the stage or from his mother's counsel: he told me that he fed her lines for practicing her dramatic roles since he'd first learned to read. He adopted the credo that, no matter what, the show must go on.

After we made love, with the musky mix of our body odors still fresh in the air, he busied himself scribbling in a journal in the nude. Two a.m. and then some. Regardless of yesterday's disasters, he was determined to get right back on track. "I'm composing a war plan," as he described it. I took a peek at his work. He had numbered the things he intended to do, the kind of list you spirit gum to the swing door on a cabinet.

I let him work. I knew what it would say. I knew what he would say to me. Of course, he would admonish me before heading out come morning, telling me to stay safe and stay holed up, not involving myself in such dangerous matters. I'd burn for a moment, reacting to such patronizing instructions, but I'd forgive him for his concern. He'd later forgive me when he learned that I had ignored his advice. He knew damned well that I'd be heading back into the fray.

I woke up before dawn. He lay there sleeping on the floor, bed sheets scribbled over him in the shape of a question mark, not quite covering his naked figure. I got up to look out the window. A giant crown of light hung over Manhattan, a fiery brilliance rising into the night sky and shutting out the twinkle of the stars. Entering stage east, the beginning of daybreak. The sun: a star with an attitude.

Alan had laid out his clothes atop the kitchen counter. I found a copy of the *World* folded up in his inside jacket pocket. He always kept a lot of things there: a notepad and a couple of sharpened pencils, no erasers—he's the kind who just crosses out his mistakes. A single glove.

I spread the newspaper out across the counter and read his front page article: the discovery of the corpse amongst the ruins. He certainly knows how to tell a story.

I yawned, stretched, and laid down next to him, wrapping an arm around his body, leaning against him, his form supporting mine.

I can be a bit macabre. I imagined us lying there, never moving through Judgment Day and for millennia beyond until we became nothing more than commingled bones and dust. Together forever. The thought made me happy.

We woke at nine a.m., late for us. Alan's movements stirred mine. He was the first to the shower. I stood in front of the radiator, my fingers splayed, soaking in its warmth.

Ice needles clung to the outside of the windows as though the very panes were transforming into snowflakes.

Steam in the bathroom. I shivered at the thought of it against my skin. The thought of Alan's soap-slicked hands.

I studied his journal. His list of things to do today.

1. Report to the assignment editor at the *World*.
2. Make an appointment to follow up on the task of tagging Reynolds.
3. In the meantime, track down the missing photos.
4. Track down Lyndon.
5. Sneak in to visit the murder scene in case there're still clues among the wreckage.
6. Keep Lorraine busy elsewhere. And safe. And distracted.

I decided to poach number five. Too far down his list for him to pop in and interfere.

As Alan headed out the door, I told him that I would be checking in with my agent to see if he had a lead on a modeling gig. It's not lying when he should know me better. My kiss goodbye wasn't false.

Having read through Alan's front-page story, with its photo of the rubble and the corpse, and having listened to his account at the police station of how he had gotten there, I figured that piecing together the exact spot where he'd been and where the body lay would be simple. Getting there could be a bigger problem. This time I'd be fighting police or private guards and sunlight while workers actively tore down the building.

I had to consider that another day had passed. Between

the police covering things up and a wrecking crew taking another swing at the walls, would there be anything to find? Alan had taken his photo looking down on the body to where it lay on the third floor. Did the third floor even continue to exist?

I thought of myself as an archaeologist, like that British lady, Gertrude Bell. After all, I was preparing to visit a ruin. A pith helmet might save me from a falling brick or a Sphinx dropping its nose. If only I owned a hard hat. I did have a beige canvas jacket, good for explorers. A long woolen dress for the cold. Sensible loafers for treading over rough terrain. On the other hand, they were not thick-soled enough to stop a rusty nail. I winced at the thought. I tucked yesterday's *World* under my arm and headed out.

I enjoy days that are chilly but sunny. The sunshine seems like an apology from God, one spoken with a shrug, Him saying, "I have to make some days cold. Here, let me brush your face with a tickle of warmth." Thank you, God. I smiled His way.

I jumped aboard a trolley car along the Third Avenue Railway and tottered my way down its aisle to the rear end, my favorite set of seats. From that perspective, it looked like those sitting in all the rows before me were my personal chauffeurs and chauffeuses—I don't get to use that latter word often. Okay, all the passengers at my service is a silly notion, but with yesterday and its trauma behind me, and having launched on a fresh adventure, pardon my flight of fancy.

With so much motor car traffic and the reckless pedestrians in Manhattan playing "dodge me," it's not unusual for a trolley to pull to a sudden stop. *Hmm.* I remembered when the Brooklyn baseball team was called the Trolley Dodgers. Timing my departure with the sudden screech of brakes, I didn't risk twisting my ankle when I disembarked on the corner of 3rd and 42nd. There, standing before me, was the back end of the building being torn down to make space for the new Chrysler monstrosity.

Being midmorning and what must have been break time, a demolition crew gathered 'round a pair of food carts. Bad news but good news. So many workers to steal past. But, it was best to go exploring without being menaced by a wrecking ball. With the workers idle, it seemed as though I could sneak in some quick snooping, get in and out.

Or not quite sneak. A blue-coated guard stood at the one opening. He had a police star pinned to his chest and a toothpick between his teeth. I asked myself, were the police guarding the building? Or had this officer been hired out, and was picking up extra money during his off hours? He nailed me with a stare. I was certain he'd guessed my intentions. I decided to meet him head-on.

"You're guarding this building?" I asked.

"Tenth Precinct," he said, as though that answered the question.

I recalled the unpleasantness at his stationhouse; however I couldn't place his face with that confrontation. He must not be part of the night watch.

"I recognize you," he said. I thought he meant from my magazine covers, but he continued with, "Your type. I see you got yourself a copy of that news story. Made fun of our department, it did." He took out his toothpick and cracked it between his fingers before dropping it. "Us police got us a name for you dames. Fame fatales. Like the ones who writes them love letters to execution row killers."

I thought my way in was irretrievably blocked but then he presented a wild smile, like some Sunday comics goofus.

"Come along. I'm no judge. I'll give you a tour for a buck. You'll find what we found: there was no body."

No body. I thought of that Marion Harris song, "*I Ain't Got Nobody.*" I handed him a dollar. The bluecoat passed through the doorway and shook a hand for me to follow. I felt the eyes of the demolition crew judging me as I passed them and stepped into the building.

We walked down a shadowy hallway, our transit getting darker with each step. Of course, the lights and electricity were gone from this shell of a building. I heard the hollow thud of his feet on the stairs, and boards creaking above me before I saw the stairway. Up ahead, at the top of the stairs, he swung open a door and daylight flooded in, the second floor open to the sky.

He stayed there holding the door and, when I arrived, I saw why. There was virtually nowhere to go. A few feet of board lay ahead covered by crumbled bricks. Good for walking the plank or else a casual slip to the side before falling into a pit.

He said, "Now, I got word that the reporter claimed the body was on the third floor. That ain't there no more. But that photo would've looked down on the spot of where we are, only one floor up."

I realized that this was a fool's errand. Did I expect to see blood? A spare leg left behind? An IOU note from whoever snatched the body? And yet something among the rubble did catch my eye.

A small cloth pillow shaped like the inside of a coffee cup and about the same size. A little point on the tip. I recognized what it was. A brassiere insert.

After the dawn of the twenties provided women with the vote, we threw off our shackles and trashed our corsets. Many gals reacted to their liberation by going with the "flapper" style: clothes that made them look flat-chested. They bobbed their hair short and took on manly habits like puffing on cigarettes and partying like frat boys. Encountering a brassiere insert anywhere was rare enough these days: few women these days bothered to plump out their chests. But to find a bra stuffer at a demolition site? One with a prominent nipple? Evidence.

The police officer was looking over his shoulder in the direction of the exit, probably counting down the moments before this venture ended. Since he was properly distracted, I picked up the object. Damp, it was still spongy from the rain a night and a half ago. I trembled with a sudden insight. I had a notion of what this discovery meant.

A work whistle sounded. The bluecoat tugged my jacket sleeve. "Ma'am, it's time. We gotta go."

I knew my next move.

CHAPTER 21

Alan Priest

FRANKLY, I spent the morning obsessing over William Reynolds, the real estate developer who ripped off Walter Chrysler. His appearance at the *World* headquarters coincided with the disappearance of the photos that would have revealed the face of the killer who stood in the building's ruins. Perhaps Reynolds had a motive for getting rid of the body and the photographic evidence. Was he still financially entangled with the building he had sold? I remembered back to a different sort of ruin he presided over: the smoldering ashes of Coney Island's Dreamland.

Years ago, much more so than today, fire held a gruesome fascination among the public. In 1904, Manhattan watched in horror as a fire aboard the General Slocum steamboat killed over a thousand, just offshore. The Triangle Shirtwaist Factory fire in Greenwich Village killed nearly 150 in 1911. Also, in living memory the Great Fire of

Chicago. In our fears, we all lived one cow-kick away from a city-leveling inferno.

Over the past decades, New York strove to become flame-proofed. Terracotta bricks covered the steel skeletons of its new towers. No one wanted the horrific vision of five-hundred-foot-tall torches.

Fire was a major theme of Reynolds's amusement park, Dreamland. His "Fall of Pompeii" spectacle had fake lava and real flames. With the "Fighting Flames" exhibit, spectators paid a quarter to watch firemen battle a blazing hotel.

So many of Dreamland's structures were nothing more than papier-mâché and scrap wood. Kindling. Reynolds had built a tower for his Coney Island theme park, 375 feet in height, the second tallest structure in New York City at the time. The tower looked something like the Metropolitan Life building. From its observation deck, it provided tourists with a glorious view of inglorious south Brooklyn. Flimsy, flammable, it might as well have been made of guncotton.

1911. Just two months after the Shirtwaist Factory fire. One week after Coney Island's summer opening. I was a teenage magician, staying after hours, practicing my act. I saw Reynolds standing in the mouth of the Hell Gate ride, talking to workmen. I particularly remember Abelardo, a hunchbacked laborer who seemed to dote on Reynold's every word. I thought little of the meeting at the time.

Sometime in the early hours, in a subterranean chamber of Hell Gate, a tin worker spilled hot pitch over a lantern. The laborers scrambled to escape as flames quickly rose through the ceiling. The fire literally came from hell.

The park was well supplied with fire hydrants. They failed as the attractions from the nearby rides diverted the water to soak their structures to prevent the flames from spreading. The non-play-acting firefighters whose firehouse was less than a block away arrived to find they were left without water pressure. Nothing could be done to stop the raging blaze.

The wildfire spread. Heroes rescued the incubator babies. Hip, a circus elephant, terrified, refused to leave its pen and burned to death. Black Prince, one of the lions, escaped its cage and rampaged through the streets, its mane on fire. Another lion climbed the roller coaster to escape. No humans, but sixty circus animals, lost their lives. Dreamland, along with five city blocks, became a smoldering ruin.

Through a combination of stiffing his partners, overvaluing the property, and backdating deeds, Reynolds emerged from the devastation as a rich man.

I awoke from the ashes of Dreamland, no longer a child. Dreams were as phony as the cheap wooden façades and bombastic barkers of an amusement park.

From the very first, I was certain that Reynolds had planned the blaze. Afterwards, he made a career out of bilking the public.

———

Ralph Pulitzer had spoken to my supervisors about yesterday's crisis with Lorraine being kidnapped, and so they were surprised when I showed up, back on the beat. Maybe I was cold, maybe I was overly zealous, maybe both. Yes, I cared about Lorraine, and only a night had passed since she'd been held captive, but I had a mission. She had been abducted while trying to track down Lyndon. I felt convinced that the dead dame among the ruins was tied to Reynolds. Lyndon and his disappearance was the key to understanding this whole mess. What's more, he could be in danger.

I sat at my desk, figuring that I needed to pound out some sort of teaser article, something that would follow up yesterday's story but would dance around the fact that I had virtually nothing new to say. Reynolds had asked me to do a story on him. I typed out, "The *World* will soon have an exclusive profile of William Reynolds, the real estate operator who flimflammed the industry giant, Walter Chrysler, the new owner of the ruins where the body was found."

No more words came to me. I postponed writing my follow-up.

I checked the city directories for Reynolds' business number. Down in Long Beach, an hour by train. I called and left a message with his secretary responding to Reynolds' squiggle of a note. *Croquet?*

And now for the unpleasant part. Tracking down what had happened to the photographs and negatives and, if possible, recovering them. The thing is, their disappearance had to be an inside job or at least partly. Besides myself, only Strauss in the photography lab would have known the exact number of relevant photos and where to find them.

Strauss, had to be in on the disappearance. All right, or else, maybe he told someone. Someone said, "Great photo," and he returned with, "Yep, I've got two more like them," and then left them on top of his work counter.

. . .

The warning light was off in front of the dark room. I tried opening the door. Locked. Now, he decides to play safe. Why wasn't he this careful before the photos went missing?

Jim, the guard, is a friend of mine. In his seventies, he'd been working at the *World* going back to Joseph Pulitzer's first days. He considered retiring as the same as death. Not having family to support him, and too old to find a job elsewhere, it probably was.

He unlocked the door for me and asked, "Anything else, Mr. Priest?"

"No. But thank you." After he left, I thought, I should have given him a tip. Doormen get gratuities.

Just as I began turning the doorknob, the warning light changed to red. I read that as "Leave me alone." I opened the door.

Strauss sat slumped in his chair. He wore his chemical bib and mottled jeans, their color blanched in spots from occasional splashes of his processing fluids. "I locked the door because I wanted peace."

"I have to track down what happened to the photos," I countered.

"I knew this would be coming."

I noticed a tumbler of what was not a developing agent on the table beside him. Too golden.

"Care for some?"

I shook my head. He'd known me in my drunkard days.

He said, "I told one of our runners to bundle up a package with the negatives and the photos, figuring I'd show them to the nabobs in the tower. I thought of asking them for a raise."

"Who? Who did you ask to make the bundle?"

"Jeffrey."

Jeffrey. I liked the boy. Trusted him. He had gotten his start as a snot-nosed newsie, looking like something a cat had dragged in. Frankly, a lot of the streetcorner paper sellers bumped up their trade through sympathy. Smudged faces and threadbare clothes: hey, mister, support an enterprising kid. Over the years, Jeffrey had grown too long in the legs to play the street waif, so he'd switched over to errand boy. He told me he wanted to be a reporter. Saw us as heroes.

I asked around and hunted down Jeffrey in the printing room. With a job that involved pouring molten lead, sometimes the boys on the linotype machines asked for off-the-book favors like running down a whiskey bottle or two. The linotypists were a wild bunch.

When he saw me, Jeffrey tensed as though about to run. He didn't. I guess he knew avoiding this encounter would mean his job. So, instead, we hiked to the stairwell. I shut the door. It was private and not so private. With the towering echo, it was easy to imagine someone twenty stories above could listen in.

"This man, a fancy swell," Jeffrey blurted out. "He passed me a twenty. I hardly see me a twenty in a whole week. And I live with my mum, and she needs help."

I happened to know that he got his start in the Sisters of Charity orphanage and now lived with seven other former newsboys in a single room on the East Side. Still, I had some sympathy. His life had been a lot rougher than it would have been if he had had a mother.

"And you know, you had already published the picture. So what were they? Like trophies? The guy musta been thinking, 'look what I got.'"

"He was wearing a suit and a tie," I said, describing Reynolds. "In his fifties, and he had a kind of a big belly and a mustache."

Jeffrey nodded. "You know him? Is he a friend?"

I shook my head. "Jeffrey. What you did hurt the *World*. A lot. And you hurt me. I've always trusted you. But I'm not going to snitch on you to the bosses."

"Thank you."

I heard the echoes of footsteps and murmuring of voices somewhere far above. Maybe angels were hovering over us listening in judgment.

"But you've got to learn from this."

"I learned my lesson." His hands were shaking. "Mr. Priest? I looked at them photos. There was this man, in a cape, he looked to be leaning over the body, excepting he wasn't. He only seemed that way 'cause he had a hump on his back, like that guy, that ugly guy in that flicker from some years past. The one with the church."

An actor? "A hump on his back? The hunchback of Notre Dame."

"That one."

The killer was a hunchback? I thought of Humpty Jackson, East Side's famous humpbacked gangster. He now owned a pet shop in Harlem, being one of the few to get out of the life and retire. Or did he? I thought of the hunchback Abelardo, a great beast of a man. I knew only his first name. Reynold's onetime flunkie. In Dreamland.

CHAPTER 22

Lorraine Priest

THE BELLEVUE MORGUE FILLS A LONG, ugly building at the end of 26th Street, on the shore of the East River. The main room spreads out as big as a gymnasium with enough dissection tables to support those occasions when Manhattan is hit by a mass disaster. This time of year, in early November, they keep their windows open, and the cool autumn air makes it a much more welcoming place. In the summer, the place reeks of rotting flesh. I can tolerate disgusting sights much better than disgusting smells.

Alan, through his reporting, maintains contacts there. Among those, Bob works the weekday afternoon shift. He rules over the massive room with its dozens of dissection tables, a warehouse for the dead. Tagging along with Alan, I'd met him on a prior visit. He knew me and he would help me—but with Bob, it was always for a price.

Bob was a little over fifty. He had that sort of bleached,

bloated face that made him look like a corpse fished out of a chlorinated pool.

He stared at me dull-eyed, the pilot light in the furnace of his brain unlit. It took a sawbuck to ignite his flame.

"Miss Marquette," he said. He knew me from my maiden days.

"It's Mrs. Priest, now." I gave him my most gracious smile.

"Of course. Your hubby called me a day back. He asked me a couple of questions, and I answered him with two things. First, I said, no, we didn't get an unknown lady corpse in the last two days. And then he asked about someone who might fit the description of an informant of his. Also no."

"What sorts of bodies don't come your way?" I asked.

"Lots of them. We get the unclaimed. Cases and victims that got to be autopsied. Those who die on the Bellevue wards. Poor folk on their way to burial in the pauper's trenches. But a good number of folks, they go straight to the funeral homes. And with murders, like how he was asking, some of them get junked in the rivers."

"I suspect that you didn't tell him about a man who dresses like a woman?"

I first got the inkling that Lyndon might be part of that world when I learned he lived at the Bowery YMCA. The Bowery had a reputation for its diverse entertainments, and the men at the YMCA for their varied habits. Also, Lindy was a snitch, and entertainers were often in the middle of a world of gossip. Alan was meant to meet him and instead encountered a dead woman. Then, when I found the brassiere insert, the pieces came together.

Now more than a hunch, it was an idea worth hunting down.

"You mean a boy-girl," he answered. "We got one, but no, Alan didn't ask. My mind works kinda literal, I mean, when someone don't say exactly what they're saying."

"Show me the body."

"Come with me." He led me between a pair of tables with covered corpses. "I'd a doubted a swell like you would soil herself by knowing a thing about the pansy craze, but they've set up their own speakeasies. They got their own shows where they dress like girls. Their goings-on. They'd bring some scarlet to your cheeks."

Men dressing as women. With the prohibition of alcohol promoting the underground world of speakeasies, a number of other concealed cultures had begun to flourish. The twenties were a time of wild partying. Some folks hid it, others flaunted it. High society had its drag balls. Some of the most successful of all nightspot entertainers were men and women who dressed opposite to their sexes.

Me? Naive? Blushing? I'd dated English lords who had bred into them generations of peculiarities. As a fashion model, I was well-acquainted with men who liked men and women who liked women.

My friend, Mae West, a Broadway star, continued to shock New Yorkers with her plays "The Drag" and "The Pleasure Man." Rumor had it that she had created her ultra-feminine persona by copying male performers.

Most of the cadavers in the room were covered up to their necks, although often their toes and toe-tags poked through the bottom. The corpse on the table that Bob led me to had a sheet drawn over its head. Feet exposed, the toenails were painted red.

I drew back the sheet to the belly. Not nearly the first dead person I'd encountered, the revelation merely made a dull thud against my chest. The head was at an impossible angle. That alone would have been fatal. An ugly welt covered one side of the corpse's longish face. The bra cup over the right breast had a stuffer. The bra over the left breast was torn back and was missing any filler.

I noted a fine red, sparkly dress, long sleeves. Expensive. He was a class act. I noted earrings in the form of the letters LW.

I pointed these out to Bob. "The initials of Alan's informant. The one he was supposed to meet." I showed him the brassiere insert. "I found this at the crime scene. Have you performed an autopsy?"

"Do you see a cut?" He took out a cigarette and coughed before inserting it between his lips. His breath reeked of tobacco and Juicy Fruit. "This place is better on the tongue and the nose if you smoke. Want one?"

I shook my head, asking myself whether formaldehyde was flammable.

"He could a died from a fall," Bob said. "That would explain the bash to the head and the spin of his neck. Or someone could've twisted his head before tossing him."

"Alan wrote a story ..."

"I seen it. I get a lot of bodies here, and they all swim in my mind, and so I only figgered how this was another one. And even when Alan gave me that call and asked for a woman, I didn't put two and two together. I'm never good at that. I'm good at cutting, though."

"The body disappeared from the building wreckage. Do you know where they found it?"

"A church turned it in. They found him on their steps. St. Agnes."

Catholic. "Across the street from the wreckage site where they're building the Chrysler Building."

"I didn't know that."

"Do you have a telephone?"

"Uh-huh."

I had the operator connect me with the *New York World,* the evening edition floor. "Alan Priest. The pressman's floor."

A couple of rings and then, "Hello. This is Alan Priest."

I recognized that voice, but it took a moment to place the name. Gould the Ghoul. Calling himself Alan and poaching my husband's calls. "This is Lorraine Priest, and you're not my husband. I'd like to talk to Alan."

"Lorraine? He's stepped out. You can talk to me. We can work together. If only you'd clue me in."

"Do you know where he went?"

"A note here says he got a call to meet up with one Lyndon Warnecki."

My breath caught in my throat. Whoever had summoned him, it wasn't Lyndon.

CHAPTER 23

Alan Priest

WHEN I RETURNED to my desk I found that Lyndon had left me a message to meet him in the Gas House District at the corner of 20th and First Avenue. Little Italy.

With Lyndon being so jumpy, I was surprised he had chosen such a rough part of town. I guessed that he had something to show me. Another Reynolds scheme? I packed the camera. A daytime shot, no worries about lighting.

Lindy calling me? I'd lucked out. Lorraine would be impressed. Finally, I'd get some answers.

Going back a hundred years, in an area verging on the East River, Manhattan built coal gas plants to supply the street-lamps and home stoves, abandoning the use of whale oil. Although a technological marvel of its time, the manufac-turing process exhaled a brew of toxic fumes, layering the Gas House District with sulfur, ammonia, and coal dust. It became the worst place in the city to live, relegated to the poorest of the poor and to those newly arriving immigrants with nowhere else to go.

For decades, giant tanks called gasometers, ten stories tall, dominated the area's landscape. At the end of the 19th century, with lamps and stoves converting to electricity, the plants had shrunk in size. Only a few of the giant tanks remained, including those at my destination.

I grabbed a Checker Cab, the kind with lots of legroom in the back. I kicked out my feet and bent my neck back, announcing, "20th and First," a shady destination. The driver turned to give me the eye, assessing me. He didn't refuse me service. I must have fooled him into thinking I was respectable; he shifted into gear.

"There?" he said. "You know what you are heading for, mistuh?" A white man, he had a British Caribbean accent, one I associated with Jamaica.

The Gas House District had a storied reputation. At the turn of the century, it was the dominant breeding ground for mobsters, the "Gas House Gang." The was before the War, when gangs still grew up from the streets. Before the big money of rum-running and the rise of Rothstein.

"Just a quick jog, in and out," I said. "I promise. Just picking someone up." After whatever business he had that had taken him there, I'd convince Lyndon to join me in the cab, and we'd skedaddle to somewhere safe for a full interview.

"Okay, mistuh."

"Call me Alan."

"Max."

Max had rosary beads looped around the base of his shift lever and a St. Christopher prayer card dangling from a string below his heating vent. The patron saint of safe journeys. I could use the good luck.

It was nearing noon. The weather had warmed, and even with its meager autumnal angle the sun gave me a break from the chill. Or else: I pressed my fingertips to the window. It still felt cold. I must have been feeling the cab's heater.

Max took Lafayette to Fourth Avenue and then Fourth all the way up to 20th. Turning right on 20th, the cab made one of Manhattan's breakneck transitions from the polish of Broadway to the soot belched out by its rivershore industries.

The dirty brick apartment buildings to either side were squat by Manhattan standards, usually three floors. Some rule said that, being in a residential neighborhood, they couldn't be built more than one-and-a-half times taller than the width of the street. Nearby smokestacks towered over them, their height guaranteeing that their fumes would disperse as widely as possible.

Truant kids played in front of Public School Number 40. Across the street, junk cars without wheels sat in front of an auto repair business.

We approached our destination. Along this stretch, the Second Avenue L lorded over First Avenue, and a train rumbled overhead, northbound.

I scanned ahead for Lyndon. On the northwest corner stood a pair of overdressed men: black suits, thin ties. Lean and young, they squinted, surveying the approaching vehicles, including mine. They maintained one hand tucked into their business jackets. Hoodlums. Armed. Waiting on someone.

They would have scared Lindy away. Or was this reception for me? Before I could warn him, Max glided his vehicle to a stop at the corner. My destination.

I barely got out the words, "Keep going," when another thug stepped in front of the taxi, gun drawn and pointed forward.

Smartly, the killer aimed at the driver. With him dead, I'd be easy pickings. Max slammed his foot on the gas pedal and the vehicle lurched straight at the hoodlum. He fired, drilling a hole through the window missing both Max and me. The slug punched a hole in the seat to my side.

Like a leaping spider, the killer bounded atop the taxi's hood. For an instant, I thought it was a controlled jump. Rather, the taxi's forward motion had provoked his maneuver and he tumbled to his side. His shoulder and half his face smashed against the windshield. The glass exploded and pellets and splinters flew. I ducked their flight. Shards sailed over me. The man tumbled in, plowing headfirst into the front passenger's seat. Blood spurted onto the front seat; the man had a nasty cut from chin to ear. His legs stuck out behind him through the broken windshield, feet flailing, kicking against the hood.

I rocked against the back door as Max swung the cab around the corner, shooting south on First. The traffic ahead was sparse, and he accelerated. Gunfire. I looked back. A pair of street hoodlums stood in the middle of First Avenue, spraying bullets our way.

The killer in the front seat continued to squirm. "*Merda!*"

he cried. I agreed with his sentiment. I knew some Italian having fought alongside their forces; they had been our Allies in the Great War.

He groped about the front seat, presumably for his gun. He latched onto it, but before the goon could get his finger over the trigger, I leaned forward and yanked on his trench coat, drawing it over his head, constraining the movement of his arms.

"Are you all right, mun?" Max asked.

The killer grunted as though the question had been directed at him.

"I don't know," I said. Grains of glass on my jacket and in my lap. I ran the back of my right wrist across my forehead and checked it for blood. None.

"Were you hit?" the cabbie asked.

I thumped around my chest, searching. I didn't know. Could I have been? I'd seen those in war, wounded and unaware. "Were you?"

"No."

"Pull over and let's heave this man out." I wasn't sure how much longer I could pin his movements.

"No, can do. We got us some Furies on our trail."

I looked out back. A black motorcar, the kind with a long nose to hold an engine built for speed, sailed after us.

I thought it lucky that we were on First Avenue. No trolley line. Light crowds, no people on the street, nothing to block our mad dash. All along the sidewalks, pedestrians gawked at the racing cab with two legs thrashing out the front window.

"*Vi ucciderò entrambi,*" the gunman said, vowing to kill me and my heroic driver. He clutched the gun, but with his trench coat pulled up and his arms forced over his head, he couldn't aim. He wasted one bullet shattering the back window.

I had a crazy idea. "Max, I'm going to lean over your seat and take the wheel for a moment. You have two hands. Grab the man's gun."

Letting go of the killer's trench coat, I leaned back and then sprang up on Max's left side, setting a third hand on the wheel. Max let go and bent to his side, engaging the killer, who refused to relinquish his weapon.

The street ahead seemed to be flying straight at us, as though we were plunging from a great height, driving down the face of a skyscraper, gathering speed, moments from a crash landing. The pavement was mostly smooth, but with every occasional bump, the wheel lurched and the cab swerved. The remains of the back window shattered as well-aimed bullets from our pursuers flew through.

"I got the gun," Max said. He didn't bother spending time brandishing his trophy. Instead, he seized the wheel and passed the pistol to me.

I used it to smack the killer over the head. In the motion pictures, that move knocks a man out. It did nothing but make him angrier. He struggled free from the confines of his jacket. Finally, he pulled his full body into the cab and sat upright. He pressed one hand against the cut on his face and neck. Blood seeped between his fingers. He fired bullets with his eyes. I nodded my pistol with its very real ammo. More gunfire pinged off the frame of the cab: our pursuers gaining on us. I thought of the war. I thought of the trenches. I kept my head low and muttered a prayer.

We raced at sixty miles per hour, a death-defying act on

a Manhattan street. Max hit the brakes, slowing down to avoid a pedestrian.

"*Vai avanti e sparami, codardo.*" He invited me to shoot him. When I didn't, our uninvited guest responded by opening the passenger-side door and leaping out.

I looked back. He rolled like a loose tire coming to rest on the sidewalk. We must have been doing forty. To my surprise—and relief—the motorcar behind us pulled over. Hoodlums poured out to collect their comrade. The distance between us and our hunters grew to one block, then two. I set down the gun. "We're free."

"I'll drive to the police," Max said.

"To Park Row," I countered. "The World Building. It's across from Town Hall and they wouldn't dare follow us there." From recent encounters I didn't feel safe with the police, and Santarelli's precinct was across town.

The elevated train line over First Avenue twisted and turned and accompanied us along our journey even as we switched streets. I kept looking back for any sign we were being followed. None. The L ended at the station at the foot of the Brooklyn Bridge.

"Park here in front of the World building," I told Max. "Straight up on the sidewalk like you had no choice. With all the bullet holes in your cab, people will see that you barely escaped with your life. I'm going to arrange to get the paper to buy your story and help pay for repairs."

He nosed the cab onto the sidewalk, near the building's front steps. A crowd immediately began making a ring around the vehicle. I handed him all the cash I had and shucked myself from the back seat, promising him, "If you get stuck with the repair bill, I'll make it right. Alan Priest." I left him with my name to seal my promise.

To my surprise, Lorraine stood there near the door to the building, arms folded. She looked over the bullet-pocked cab and said, "How is it that you have all the fun?"

CHAPTER 24

Lorraine Priest

ALAN SLUNG an arm around my waist and leaned against me. We inhaled each other for a moment. I told him about my encounter at the morgue.

"Lyndon was dressed in women's clothing?" he said. "I didn't even think of that. You're a genius."

"Clearly, I am," I said, kissing him, "that goes without saying." I was glad he said it.

A smile trembled on his lips.

Once we'd parked ourselves on a bench in the entryway lobby, he spelled out the story about his meet-up, the gangsters in wait, and the car chase. With his journalistic skills, Alan is a master storyteller. He finished by saying, "Only now you tell me, they'd already taken out Lyndon. The trap must have been all about me."

"But, why?"

"The killer who planted his head in the cab's front seat spoke Italian. Rothstein told you of mafiosi arriving from

Italy. They're planning a power play. They must think we know more than we do."

"Still, that makes no sense," I said. "Or at least, not enough sense. Kill everyone who might know something? And do we know anything at all? For certain?" My brow furrowed. All this mess was going to give me premature wrinkles. "How did Lyndon fit in?"

"I don't know. I think Reynolds might be the key. Lyndon died in the wreckage of Reynold's demolition site. Reynolds stole those photos. That was quite a risk."

"And Rothstein picked me up when I went looking for Lyndon. As an informant, he must have been on to something important, something bigger than the Chrysler story."

Alan escorted me to the journalist's floor, that is, to the one for the evening edition. I'd visited before but always felt surprised by how it was so very much a man's domain: like a construction site and with just as many leers. When thinking of the *World*, I recall Nellie Bly, the trooper who set a new record racing around the globe, or Marie Wright and her legendary trips across the Andes. I suppose that was an earlier age.

A message on Alan's desk carried an invitation to Reynolds' estate. It read, "Did you get my note? A game of roque?" Alan considered this. "Roque? What's roque?" he asked.

"I've played it. Like croquet only more hard-nosed."

Alan nodded somberly. "I should go meet him. Find out what he's up to."

"Why do I feel the need to go along to protect you?" I noticed my question drew smirks from his co-workers.

"Because you're my good luck charm."

I bridled. Alan knows me. He knew that was not the right answer. He reduced me to a trinket to save face with his colleagues.

While a game of roque at someone's manse certainly didn't sound dangerous, Alan nevertheless did have a habit of getting into trouble. And, what's worse, he did so without me. And, what's both worse and more, this Reynolds guy possessed a sinister side. I would join Alan on the trip. I wasn't about to let him go blundering around alone.

He called up the operator and connected to Reynolds' office, getting the man's secretary. "My wife and I will be there at four, if that hour is good for him."

Alan jotted down the words, *Long Beach Terminus.*

An electric train connects Grand Central to Long Beach, a small city built on a slip of sand on the southwestern corner of Long Island.

Seated alongside me on a train car bench, Alan pressed the stump of his wrist in his jacket pocket to avoid stares from his fellow passengers. From my point of view, he had forced his right arm down so deeply that it only made the missing hand more obvious. He carried a lot of shame in that missing hand. He still hadn't forgiven himself for the circumstances leading to his war wound, what he considered cowardice. Men can be so pig-headed.

Alan is a handsome man. When we are alone, our love makes us equals. When he is beside me in public, where people judge others by skin and defects, he becomes defensive. He acts as though he has to apologize for his amputation, as if it is a personal failure. He felt ill at ease sitting next to a fashion model. In my view, the public obsession with idolizing beauty is a peculiar sort of malignancy.

"You mentioned you've played roque," he said.

"Like croquet, but it's played on a packed clay court, so the balls move quickly. Instead of an out-of-bounds, it has walls, a border that the balls rebound off of."

"Like in a game of pool?"

"More like billiards since there are no pockets. The playing field is about half-the-size of a basketball court. Other than that, you have mallets and balls and posts and arches, and you are expected to act all sniffy like you're playing croquet."

"Will my one hand be a problem?"

"The mallets are shorter than croquet clubs but a bit larger than lobster hammers." When this comparison didn't register in his eyes—a man who has never cracked a lobster! —I held my hands about two feet apart. "You don't need two hands to swing them."

He nodded. His lips were pursed with deep concentration and he inhaled stiffly. I had the feeling that the terrors of his morning motorcar chase were just now catching up with him. I decided not to disturb him, that is, beyond gently massaging his forearm.

After a time, he spoke. "Reynolds essentially built the whole of the city of Long Beach, a huge project. As a publicity stunt, he borrowed elephants from his entertainment park, Dreamland, to carry lumber to make the boardwalk. He announced that he would sell homes exclusively to white Protestants and did that for as long as he could. He's been convicted twice for embezzling city funds. The man has always been a menace. A privileged bastard."

Although Alan's mother had gone on to be a photoplay star, when he had lived with her, she'd toured the vaudeville circuit, filling in that strange spot that sandwiched dramatic recitations between dancing acts and cornball comedians. Alan grew up poor and punchy, always suspicious of the rich.

My parents, before they went to prison, were well-off. A sizable home. My sisters and I had private tutors. Mom and Pop indulged us in our aspirations and fantasies. I still fight the notion that I am a princess in exile. Alan's experiences seemed much healthier. He didn't think so. I suppose living with his mother could be a bit challenging.

Long Beach has a charming station house with a Spanish tile roof and white stucco walls: a taste of the Riviera. I'd been to this burgh before, back in the days when I played the social butterfly. Its hotels serve as resorts for the wealthy; some of those gentlemen included my former lovers.

Reynolds sent a personal limousine to meet us. The chauffeur was a black man. White gloves, flaring collar—he dressed like a Pullman porter.

"No baggage?" he asked.

"We'll only be visiting for a couple of hours," Alan said.

I had been to Miami Beach once, before the Big Blow of '26, and this island reminded me of that resort. A thin sliver of land, lots of swank buildings: all-in-all, the sense that the whole of the island was a yacht tied to the mainland.

From the outside, the Reynolds' mansion didn't appear particularly ostentatious: broad-shouldered and similar in features to so many Mediterranean style homes we had passed along the way. Being a real estate baron perhaps he intended to announce to his neighbors: come buy into my development. You, too, can live as richly as I do.

Inside, however, the house possessed a nouveau riche insecurity. A broad reception room was populated by plaster statues of Greek and Roman gods and goddesses, each mounted atop a waist-high pedestal, the main theme being nudity. Not-terribly good landscape watercolors hung on the walls of the entrance hallway. A wide grand staircase boasted a light blue carpet flowing down its steps like a cascading waterfall.

There, by a marble stand and its gaudy urn, stood a recent acquaintance: Legs Diamond. He wore an innocuous outfit: a white jacket and polo pants. However, with that thick brow, creased smile, and tightly coiled posture, he reeked of menace. I'm good at hiding my agitation. I locked eyes with his and could have won a stare-down.

Unlike myself, Alan had never met Legs, knowing him only through his public images, the occasional front-page mugshots. Frankly, although Legs had the intensity of a mob boss, his tough-guy features could be swapped for those of any of a dozen angry hoods. Alan merely gave the man a puzzled look, unable to place him. Perhaps it was the unexpected context. If my husband had immediately realized that this had been my kidnapper …

"Alan?" I whispered. "I'm going to tell you something. Can you promise me you'll not do anything impulsive or crazy?"

"Of course," he said. Still, I didn't quite trust him.

"That tough guy is Jack Diamond." I tossed my chin in the direction of the man.

Alan's entire body stiffened as though shot from a cannon.

Mr. Reynolds took that moment to come trotting down the grand staircase, two mallets tucked under each arm. "Ah, Mr. Priest and your beautiful wife—Lorraine, I believe. Who needs a mallet?"

Not taking his eyes off of Legs, Alan raised his hand and said, "Me." I wasn't sure whether he should be entrusted with a blunt instrument at that moment.

Legs walked over to Alan. "They call me Gentleman Jack," he said. As with most of those who first meet Alan, he extended a right hand to shake. Alan jabbed the stump of his wrist into that hand. I'd never seen him do that. For an instant, Legs seemed unnerved. Then he presented a barracuda smile and they shook.

Reynolds thrust a mallet into my hand and passed one to Alan. Alan pressed the blunt head of the mallet against Legs' chest and shoved him back.

"Mr. Reynolds ..." Alan began with a nod.

"Call me Bill."

"Call me Mr. Priest, *Bill.* As a businessman, why do you associate with a petty hoodlum like Mr. Diamond?"

Legs remained unperturbed. Sticks and knives can end some lives but words ...

Reynolds brayed with a laugh. "Petty hoodlum? Not hardly. Mr. Diamond possesses the swagger I need to get certain things done. Keeping business rivals in line. Real estate is a cut-throat enterprise. Besides, we share an interest in making our country pure again."

"Pure?" I asked.

"You are thinking 'But Mr. Diamond is Irish,'" Reynolds said. "While I'm no fan of foreigners, I appreciate how his people came to New York early and built up their political muscle. Only, nowadays we're flooded by the Italians and the Jews and Eastern and Southern Europeans, and their presence stains the whiteness of our nation."

"Mr. Reynolds," I said. "Mr. Diamond snatched me up from the Algonquin yesterday. At gunpoint."

Reynolds seemed to react with more confusion than concern.

In contrast, Legs lazed his head to the side as though studying me. "Oh, I had me a gun," he said, "but never had I *pointed* it." He swung his mallet so it rested against his shoulder. "And what is more, my friend Lorraine, here, flung one of my club's dolls a handsome shiner." He blew me a kiss.

I tapped my mallet head against my palm. At least it sounded like CeeCee got away with playing the victim and not my helper.

"Sounds like you two are even," Reynolds exclaimed. "Let's all have a friendly round of roque. Did you know it was named after croquet? They lopped off the first and last letters. Maybe you can promote the sport in your article. And Mr. Priest, keep Legs out of it. For your report, ask me about me." He pointed the handle of his mallet toward his patio door. "Shall we?"

Alan had described Reynolds as having the face of a melodrama villain. I couldn't see it. I saw a sixty-year-old puffy-eyed, balding man with sad bits of a mustache, hairs that seemed to have been snorted out of his nostrils. A circus showman who had fallen on hard times.

He led us along a short path to a roque court, an area surrounded on three sides by tall, well-manicured hedges.

"I figured you'd want an anecdote-filled interview, and what better way to pass a couple of genteel hours than with a gentlemen's game of roque? Plenty of time for questions. I let my guests choose ball color."

"Black," I said. That meant white would go to Alan.

"Red," Legs said.

Reynolds tucked his mallet in his armpit and rubbed his hands to fight back the chill. "I'll have Joseph stir up some Bronx cocktails. Made with the juice of fresh Florida oranges. I have them delivered straight from the boats."

"Just the orange juice for me," Alan said.

Reynolds tossed me a black ball.

Unlike croquet, the game of roque uses solid rubber balls made for distance and speed. Drives can rebound off the ankle-high curbs like a three-rail billiard shot. When playing in teams, black and white take alternating turns against red and blue. There are ten wickets, called arches, to pass through and two stakes to knock against to score.

The main strategy is to keep in mind the "danger" ball. The danger ball is the one about to go next. Because team players alternate, the danger ball always belongs to the opponent. Defense demands that its progress should be blocked at all costs.

The balls are set up with the partners at diagonally

opposite ends of the court. I was first up, and because I was wearing a long dress, I lined up to the side of my black ball. At the left-hand corner, directly across from me, Legs had the danger ball, the red one. Reynolds owned the court, so I suspected he was the real nemesis. Legs was bound to be as much a beginner as was Alan. I chose to go after Legs because he wouldn't know how to stop me.

I leaned over and whacked my ball. It came to rest a shoe-length distant from the front of Legs's red ball, at an angle that blocked his progress to the first arch. A good player knows how to make their ball jump over a block. A good player takes advantage of the extra shot that comes after hitting an opponent's ball. I doubted Legs was a good player.

I was right. He took personal offense and aimed at my ball, driving it halfway back to where it came from and sending his ball to the side of an arch, a useless position. Ambitious, he used his bonus shot making a ricochet off the back wall and toward the first arch. He struck it too hard and at a bad angle, winding up once again next to the arch, on its other side.

"After I attacked you in my article, why did you invite me to write more?" Alan asked Reynolds.

Reynolds snarled at the question. "Because there's no such thing as bad publicity."

"I'd like to change that equation," Alan said.

His turn. I called over to him. "Stay on your end," I told my husband. "Move in front of the arch." He stroked his ball, rolling it only a little, positioning it in the center. A safe place. At least according to my plan.

That left Reynolds alone on his end. With no play on us,

he chose offense, dinging the inside corner of the nearby arch, set for some quick scoring. I'd hoped for this. That meant Alan and I would both be scoring against the hapless Legs.

"When you first began the development in Long Beach, a fire broke out in the town's largest hotel," Alan said. "Your hotel."

"That's right," Reynolds said, clenching his mallet. "Burnt to the ground. Made all the papers at the time. Eleven hundred guests made it to safety."

"One died," Alan said. "Five years later, Dreamland burned down. Fires follow you."

The businessman nodded. "Tragedies. I rebuilt the hotel from its ashes."

"But not Dreamland. You cashed in."

"I have the Midas touch. And I've made a tidy sum on the new hotel."

I knocked aside Legs's ball, it lolled to the corner while mine stopped near Alan's in front of the arch, setting me up for an easy point.

I used my first bonus shot to score, and my second to thread the following arch. Rather than position for another arch, I chose to block Legs, again rolling my ball in front of his.

He quickly responded with fury, not caring about his own position, knocking my ball as hard as he could, nearly to the center of the court. Unwisely, he aimed his bonus shot at my ball again, this time missing and scurrying far down the court.

Alan managed to thread his white ball through the first arch. With his bonus turn, he bumped against the inside edge of the second arch, leaving his ball halfway through. Reynolds played for position to begin going after the second pair of rungs. I suppose he intended to gather all his points before mucking with his opponents.

"Ah, Joseph," Reynolds said, raising a hailing hand.

Joseph, a dark-skinned man, brought out a tray holding a dozen orange-colored drinks, placing them on a counter to the side of center court. Three cocktails for each of us? That many would knock me cold.

Considering this servant together with his black chauffer, I concluded that Reynolds had set out to assemble his own private plantation.

"Roosevelt or Ottinger?" I asked him.

"Ottinger is a Semite. Do you want a governor under the influence of the global cabal of the children of Shem?"

Children of Shem? I'd heard of that. Since, according to some, Noah's family were the only ones who survived the great flood, racists divided up the world into the descendants of his several children. How desperately strange.

Alan gave several of the drinks a sniff. Having sworn off booze, he'd be trying to locate the ones without alcohol. He downed a selection in one swig and set his empty glass on the tray. He said, "Mr. Bill, what do you have to say about the body found among the ruins of the building you sold to Chrysler?"

Reynolds grabbed a glass and immediately gulped down half of it. He licked orange pulp from his mustache. "The police looked into the matter and found nothing. The *World* should apologize for running a photo that could have been staged anywhere. Ask me about my grand plans for the future. My hopes for this election. Ask me about the fucking stock market."

I took a drink from the tray and took a sip. Heavy on the booze. I discreetly used the remainder to water the hedge. After a baby burp, I returned to the game. Figuring that Legs would come after me again, I nudged my ball to a spot, aligning it to score through the second set of wickets while standing guard by the loop of an arch. Legs didn't have a direct shot at me.

Alan asked, "Bill, what do you tell the Great War veterans who are immigrants from the countries you don't prefer when you refuse to rent to them?"

"They have their own neighborhoods." He drank a gulp and continued. "The Great War serves as a lesson. The eastern nations of Europe have never flourished, they've never known democracy. Their immigrant class lowers the intelligent quotient of our country. We need to maintain the genetic purity of our blood. That's science."

He finished his second cocktail. I imagined his eyes being a glass gauge which was filling with orange, rising to a marker labeled "Danger." The purity of *his* blood was 200 proof.

Reynolds continued to opine. "The Balkan people carry primitive genes. See how Serbia turned the noble countries of the world against one another."

"It seems to me the war was more of a fault of the noble countries," I said.

Reynolds' face twitched. "Your woman is doing the interview?" he said. And then to me, "You don't exist." He proceeded to do a very odd thing: he took his mallet by its head and swung its handle back and forth as though it were the point of a fencing sword, fencing in my direction.

Legs took a full gulp of a drink and then slammed his ball directly at mine, missing it, caroming off to the side of the protecting arch.

Alan slid his ball through the second arch and then positioned himself for the third. Reynolds made a pair of deft offensive plays, scoring through the third and fourth arches and then laid up for the center arches.

I took a second drink, again sipping some and pouring the rest into the hedge. Legs must have seen my maneuver. He took a swallow of a fresh drink and emptied the rest of his. That hedge was going to wind up very drunk.

"I don't like my hooch to taste like fruit," he told me.

"Mr. Reynolds, do you know Lyndon Warnecki?" Alan asked.

"Never met the man," the real estate magnate replied. He pressed his mallet to his side as though guarding his liver. I found his answer curious. How can anyone be certain of never meeting someone? And why not just say, "I don't know anyone by that name?"

"We've identified his corpse at your destruction site. Warnecki was supposed to meet me to give me the lowdown on how you scammed Chrysler."

Reynolds made no response to this revelation. Considering what had been printed in the paper, describing the victim as a man should have surprised him. Instead, he answered by tottering over to the drink table and exchanging his empty glass for a full one. "I played Mr. Chryst, Mr. Chrysler. I played him for the chump." He pinched his nose. "Good business. Played him fucking good. Goodly."

In two shots I sent my ball through the third and fourth arches. I used my second bonus turn to whack Legs's red ball as hard as I could. I suppose I could have played him for position, but really, making him mad was most important.

Legs immediately whacked his ball back at mine, missing, and caroming off the wall with a spinning hop.

"You thimble-headed Mick," Reynolds screamed. "Stop reacting. Start thinking! Block the reporter's shots."

"Mick?" Legs called back. "Mick? You want me to block his shot? You want me to block his shot?" Legs walked over to the arch nearest to Alan's ball and swung down his mallet, again and again, pounding the metal until it was no more than a crumpled piece of wire, smashed flat against the court.

"What the living fuck?" Reynolds said. He closed his eyes as though about to drift off, then toddled over to the counter and grabbed another drink.

And that was the end of the game.

CHAPTER 25

Alan Priest

Legs and Reynolds are working together.

Reynolds knew Lyndon Warnecki but avoided admitting it.

Reynolds hates Italians and Italians are in the middle of a gang war.

Seated on the train next to Lorraine while jotting down notes, I looked up on occasion to eye my fellow commuters, realizing how many were lost in a newspaper world, evening editions held in front of their faces. Others were closed-eyed, sipping in a tranquil darkness, knowing they would be awakened when the train came to a stop at the end of the line. Like us, most were probably headed to Grand Central, with its connections to anywhere in Manhattan. Hell, iron rails stretched out from there in an unbroken web across the whole of the continent, from the Atlantic to the Pacific shore and off to the Arctic and the Mayan jungles.

Those passengers who sat in pairs seemed unaware of their partners. I considered how moonstruck kids were the only people I ever saw kissing in public. Well, I thought, why not give these folks a show?

I leaned into Lorraine and pressed my lips against hers and licked around those lips as though cleaning a smidgeon of whipped cream. They tasted sweet, a lingering hint of Florida oranges. She gave one of her tiny gasps. Then she kissed back, pressing me so hard I felt her head and her mind inside of mine. Physically. Spiritually.

We got some stares. Envy. Disapproval. Wistfulness.

Grand Central. The train pulled to a stop and dimmed its lights. If it hadn't been the end of the line, we would have sailed on by, distracted by bliss.

We changed to the train that connected us to Madison Square and home. The subway station's stairs opened up at the foot of the Fuller Building, named for George Fuller, the father of the steel skyscraper—not for the Brush King. Okay, nearly everybody these days calls it the Flatiron Building.

Twilight ruled: the weak shadow of the not-quite night. The departing sun abandoned those of us outdoors to a sharp autumn chill. A giant swath of low-hanging storm clouds hid the stars, a gray dome illuminated from below by the glow of thousands of city lights. The Metropolitan Life clock rang the half-hour. Seven-thirty.

Lorraine and I walked arm in arm.

I'd asked Marco to signal us by placing a triangle of paper in his window if the police had returned.

I took a nervous peek. Nothing. But then, this was still only the leading edge of night, not yet the hours Sullivan claimed as his dominion. The respite felt good. I looked forward to a few minutes in our apartment to change and refresh before setting up camp in the next-door flat for the night.

I stuck my key into the lock at the front of the building. Fancier buildings have twenty-four-hour doormen, a beefeater guard at the door or, at least, a barely sentient senior, even if the protection provided by the latter was minimal. As for our abode, at this hour, any killer with a crowbar could muscle his way in.

Lorraine and I traipsed down the first-floor hallway. Our elevator is semi-automated. Although there was no operator at this hour of the evening, the controls were straightforward enough. All right, sometimes older residents, intimidated by modern devices, conscripted Marco into service when they arrived home late. Still, the press of a call button was enough to bring the elevator to meet us.

We stepped in and, after securing both doors, I drew the crank up. As we ascended, Lorraine said, "The police will be listening in on our telephone."

"That's how it figures."

"I need to make a call. I have a lead I want to follow."

Lorraine was a slick detective. She regularly puts my skills to shame. "And that would be?" I pulled down on the lever scooting the elevator to a halt, leaving a short step up to the twelfth.

Lorraine released one of her *pffts*, telling me she could have done better. "Mae is acquainted with the world of female impersonators," she said. "And Lyndon was dressed up when he was killed. Someone among their set might have been close to him, close enough to know what he was last up to."

"Hmm." Mae. We first met Mae West, the Broadway

diva, when she helped us with the Fritch murder case. She and Lorraine had kept in touch since then, conspirators in late night chit-chats, Lorraine breathlessly whispering into the telephone set. Mae did indeed have connections to entertainers in a broad range of venues.

Her first big New York hit, the play, *Sex*, ran for eleven months before the police decided that it had to be shut down because of degeneracy, and that she had to be thrown in prison. Always a provocateur, she was just getting started. Broadway had an unspoken decree: even though many a comedy milked laughs out of actors playing "fairies," men known to be homosexual could not perform on stage in any role with speaking parts. Mae's next show smashed that rule to pieces. Earlier this year, she produced *The Drag, A Homosexual Comedy in Three Acts*, featuring men in women's clothes and love between men. What's more, shameless for publicity, she held the casting call in a drag bar.

Her play was shut down in a heartbeat. Never dispirited, she followed that up with her biggest hit yet, and was currently starring as Diamond Lil, a saloon singer with a heart of gold and necklaces full of hard-earned jewels.

"Mae can show us the hot spots for drag entertainers," Lorraine said. "She might even have known Lyndon."

"It's Friday with an evening show on tap," I said. "I doubt she'll have the energy to show us around."

"Mae? Not having stamina?" Lorraine said, scoffingly. "You ought to hear the stories she tells. They would straighten your curlies."

Mae was famed for her sexual prowess and endurance, but no, I didn't know how much of that legend was true. Whenever we met, she was always purring, always sizzling like an ice cube on a hot skillet, but that could be an act. When I once asked her whether she maintained the same extravagant personality when she was alone, she answered, "Only I know. When I'm alone, there's no one else to see."

I couldn't argue with that.

Lorraine knew Mae much better than I did. And I do confess, I judged the woman. Maybe I had an old-fashioned streak. To me, being adored by many is poorer than being loved by one. I sensed that, short of worship, on stage or in bed, Mae had little human interaction.

"When she isn't performing," Lorraine said, "she often hangs out in her dressing room in the backstage of the theater. She considers herself a writer, even more than an actress, and she is obsessive about making notes and constructing scenes. She keeps a private telephone there and sometimes calls me about her latest piece. I'll wager she's planning to stay after the show until midnight or later. Those are the hours for the drag shows."

"Let's scrub up and change clothes," I said. "It's going to be a long evening." Arriving at our apartment, I unlocked the door. Looking in, and thinking of the telephone tap, I could only imagine the grubby ears of the police. The place felt dirty.

Lorraine and I showered and changed. I stuffed my jacket pockets with the basics: a couple of pencils, a notepad, some Scotch masking tape, good for when I had to tape a page to my right arm sleeve, for when a firm surface wasn't available for jotting down quick notes. Lorraine packed her industrial purse, the one big enough to carry some of everything. One wallop to stop a charging rhino.

Before leaving I used my home phone to make a call to the message service at the *World*, leaving some info behind knowing that the police would be listening.

"I got a dispatch from the Turk," I said. "Says he has some keen info on the Tenth Precinct. When he calls, tell him we'll meet him at the fight."

When I hung up, Lorraine asked. "Fight? What fight?"

"That's what Sergeant Sullivan will be asking," I said. "Friday night, the city? There's always a fight card some- where. And I don't know anyone called the Turk. Tracking all this down will keep our busybodies busy."

CHAPTER 26

Lorraine Priest

I HAD Mae's dressing room phone number, but with our telephone being monitored, we couldn't call her from our apartment. Nevertheless, I hoped to reach her before the curtain went up on her show—not to talk, she would be busy preparing—but to arrange a time to talk. By the time Alan and I got to the street and encountered a phone booth and made the connection, I was too late, the show had started. Instead of Mae, her younger sister, Beverly, answered. She was also an actress, also in the production. We had some time to confer before her scenes: time enough for me to explain the whole of the situation.

Beverly was a bit of a lush. She spoke loudly, a slur slathering her Brooklyn accent. "Mae told me about you and how you and Alan chased down the murderer of Carolyne Fritch." That's not exactly what happened, but I was not about to correct her. She went on, "My sister's a regular booster of yours. She'll be keen on joining you."

Alan overheard her braying voice. "Join us?" he whispered, shaking his head, no. "Mae can just point us where to go. We don't have any use for a prima donna."

I put my hand over the receiver and told him. "We need Mae to get us an in at the drag bars. To get them to talk. They can be quite cliquish."

Alan squeezed his eyes shut, frowning in surrender.

"We'll be happy to have her along," I cooed into the receiver.

"I gobbled up that story Alan wrote about the victim found in the ruins," she said. "Do you really think we can help find her killer?"

"We?" Alan said, this time loudly enough to be overheard.

"Don't think of shutting me out," Beverly said. "Mae's got a swell-sized limo. You'll find there's plenty enough shoulder room for all of us."

"Nothing doing," Alan whispered.

Beverly couldn't hear that. "We'll come collect you after the show," she said sternly.

I gave her a local address, a diner. She followed this by mangling a British accent, asking, "The game is afoot?"

"I promise you," I said, "the game is afoot."

"Oooh."

That line from Sherlock Holmes also gives me the shivers.

Alan and I waited for Mae's limousine while dining at a nearby cafeteria with the droll name of Consolidated Lunch. The food was little better than that of an automat, but Alan said he liked the place because it sat on a corner which provided it with two wide windows overlooking 22nd and 5th. He claimed its view helped him to people watch—and we do that sometimes as sport—but I suspected he was feeling antsy and wanted to catch sight of all comers. The night served as Sergeant Sullivan's domain, and we were just a block from our building—and he knew where we lived. Scanning the streets explained why Alan looked past me as though I wasn't there.

I had a sensible egg salad sandwich, while he chose a plateful of a pungent corned-beef-garlic-hash-brown-potato concoction. A better meal for breakfast and one which showed no regard for future kissing.

"Mae and Beverly and you," he said. "I'm going to be outnumbered by women, three to one."

"Three formidable dames. Be on good behavior."

One of the many things that I loved about Alan: he never felt that strong women menaced his manhood. All right, sometimes he did. However, he was about to encounter the world of drag. Included among their artists are the most overtly feminine creatures on the planet. I knew a little of their world from my days out and about as a society siren. Quite a few of them act as outrageous vamps and flirts. Alan was about to experience a very different sort of female attention, one that would challenge his masculinity. I asked myself how well he would handle that. Would he be flustered? Would I be jealous? I chuckled at the thoughts.

We had plenty of time before the end of Mae's show and Alan decided to use it for taking notes. He extracted a sheet of paper from his coat pocket. Using his one hand, he folded it into fourths, creasing it flat. This allowed him to write out notes like they were on the pages of a tiny book. When he was done covering four sides, he unfolded the paper like it was a blooming flower and wrote on the back, a sort of second draft. A peculiar habit, but it worked for him.

As he became quite lost in his labors, I recalled how Mae spoke of herself as an author, and how she bemoaned the "onliness" of writing.

While waiting, I reviewed the case in my mind. Lindy to Rothstein to Legs to the Italians to Reynolds. How did it all connect? Or did it? Was the sadistic Sergeant Sullivan part of the same mix or was he a parallel threat? And how did the hunchback fit in?

A tootle from a horn announced the arrival of our ride. Mae had a spanking new Rolls Royce Phantom, this year's model, silver. Her current chauffeur, James Timony, was also her lover and her lawyer. He was crazy about her. Although Mae professed to live in a perpetual thrall to dozens of men, considering the devotion she and James shared, they were closer than most married couples.

James opened the back door for us, revealing Mae sitting in the back seat. She is short, barely five feet when standing. That fact gave her the head space to wear a tilted picture hat with an ocean of black ruffles. She wore a knee-length sequined dress, one that emphasized her curves. Skin-tight. No, that's not correct: her costume was her true skin. A fox fur rested on her shoulders, completing her ensemble. Its head drooped over her chest. It had beady, black eyes and a mouth agape, probably marveling at her bosom.

Although Mae is physically compact, there is nothing small about her. She once told me, "Life can be overwhelming until you learn to live larger than life."

She percolated with sex. With unnerving violet eyes, her gaze felt more intimate than most men's kisses. Was Mae playing a character she invented? No. She didn't invent a character. She invented herself.

In contrast, her sister sat beside her in a modest beige evening dress and plain cloth coat. Beverly was broader in features with wide-set eyes. Her lips were not so pursed. While Mae was blissfully seductive, Beverly came across as a stern matron, her peepers dull, her overall aspect currently blunted by liquor. Mae seldom drank. The two held hands with woven fingers.

"Lorraine, Alan," Mae said. "Come scooch in beside me. Make yourself friendly, if you know what I mean."

I moved in next to Mae, providing one degree of separation between her and my husband. All right, I was a bit jealous. Alan pressed beside me and shut the door.

I inhaled the tang of Mae's *L'Heure Bleue* perfume. I looked about. This Rolls Royce had a coachman and elbowroom for four of us in the back. It was a royal carriage.

"Where are we headed?" Alan asked.

James pulled out onto Fifth Avenue. "There's a drag joint on West 70th," he called back over his shoulder. "Mae has some chums up there. If not there, we'll try the Village."

"Did you know Lyndon Warnecki?" Alan asked Mae.

She shook her head. "The name doesn't ring a bell. But you know, these performers, they seldom advertise their true selves, know what I'm saying? And, as for you, Alan, nothing goes in the papers without their strict say so."

Alan crossed his heart and gave the Boy Scout salute.

"A few rules about the drag world," James called back to us. "Unless you are in, you're not in."

"There are no rules," Beverly said with a *hmmph*, her brow furrowed. "You know, my sister took writing her play about drag performers very seriously. She studied what the European head doctors have written and quoted them and all the latest science about those people."

Those people? I personally had a more strained opinion of the psychoanalysts than that of "those people." And the scientists? God bless them, they tried hard. They attempted to see what was plain in front of them by using telescopes or microscopes. And even then, they were looking through the wrong end.

"Mae is sort of a queen to them," James said. "She's the epitome of womanhood."

"I have a pair of 45s and the guns to protect them," Mae said, patting her hair.

"By guns she means nipples," Beverly said. I had guessed that.

Mae pressed her chest and inhaled. "Do you know of the drag star Bert Savoy? She taught me to be who I am. How to be a siren with a bullhorn. Not some starving flapper."

A hush came over those in the vehicle. We knew the name. Bert Savoy. The legend. The tragedy. "She was such a gentle soul," Mae said. "She taught me to be a Woman with a big 'Woo.' My Diamond Lil outfit came from her dress." Mae's voice, so husky, so well-fashioned for the stage, cracked. "I remember the day she died, reading about what happened. The story goes that she and her friends were walking along Long Beach. A lightning bolt struck nearby. She said, 'Well, ain't Miss God cuttin' up somethin' fierce?' The next bolt hit her."

When our vehicle came up to Central Park, James turned left. "Talk about their clothes, their dresses," he said. "Flattery will get you everywhere."

From my limited experience, that was too simplified.

"How do I address them?" Alan asked. "Sir? Ma'am?"

"Follow their lead," James said. "They call themselves by a dozen names, some you might think of as insults. This one might use the term pansy, that one a daisy. Some are proud to be fairies."

"The men about town who come with their group, they like to be called bachelors," Mae said.

So much advice. You would think we had to choose the proper fork when dining with royalty.

"Just be yourself," Beverly said, amending her statement to add, "but don't be an asshole."

CHAPTER 27

Alan Priest

LORRAINE SOMETIMES TREATS me as being less worldly than she is. True, I can't claim, the way she can, to have witnessed the secret sins of so many snooty folks, but when I was a tyke, I did crisscross the country getting lugged around by my mother, a stage actress. We stayed in flophouses. Their mattresses provided a home for whatever bloodsuckers lay in waiting.

What went on backstage among theater folk was eye-popping. Scamps, tramps, and thieves. Bawdy songs and saucy music. Half of my fellow sojourners were the most open-minded people on earth. Half of them were insecure monomaniacs. All of us lived as though we were one freefall away from slumming it on the dreaded burlesque circuit.

I also knew something of the hidden side of Manhattan. Reporting on scandals, making the rounds of the courts and the prisons. And my colleagues? Newshounds comprise a salty and diverse crew. In their time off, some of my guy friends haunted the fringes of conventional society.

The Rolls turned onto a block of West 70th. Both sides of the street were bracketed by tall brownstone row houses. For most of the residences, amber window shades were pulled down and lit from behind, forming a honeycomb of radiant cells.

Midway down the street and to our right, the sounds of a raucous party emanated from a basement, half sunken, with a door at the bottom of several steps. Cars crowded the curb in front, so we had to park far away at the corner.

"The Horticulture Club," James said.

I'd heard some members of the homosexual class refer to themselves as horticulturists, a self-mocking designation, chosen because of how some called themselves by flowery names, pansies and daisies.

James opened the back doors for us. We poured out. He remained behind, guarding the Rolls.

From somewhere within the depths of a building, a wailer with the voice of Bessie Smith belted the blues. Mae, Beverly, Lorraine and I walked toward the music. The first-floor steps were roped off, making a basement door to serve as the entryway. Lights blazing from all the building's windows announced that the party filled every floor.

A pair of bewigged female impersonators stood in the basement well. One wore platinum hair as tall as that of Marie Antoinette and the other wore a bob with a tiara, a princess version of the "It Girl" style. Both sported knee-high skirts, black stockings, and white evening gloves. Both flaunted footlong cigarette holders. They wore lipstick the color of Broadway neon. Their upper arms bulged as much as those of a bouncer.

"Mae, it's Mae the original," Marie Antoinette said, calling out and cooing. The way she started huffing, I thought she'd need a fainting couch.

"There are very few women who are goddesses," the bob-haired lady said, greeting Mae as we arrived, "but you, my dear, are a goddess."

Mae patted her hair below the brim of her hat and rolled her eyes. "Goddess has nothing to do with it."

Beverly swept right by the pair and into the basement, doubtlessly seeking a drink.

"Mae, you're the woman I want to be when I grow up," the It Girl purred.

"Never grow up, child," Mae said.

The music hit a crescendo. Cheers rose from the basement. A host spoke into a booming mike amid more cheers.

"Don't the neighbors mind all this noise?" I asked.

"Honey, we are the neighbors," Marie Antoinette said. "My name is Dinah Mite."

"I'm Destini with an 'i-n-i,'" the other said, winking. "Welcome to the Horticulture Club."

"You know my name," Mae said to fawning smiles.

"I'm Lorraine."

Destini oohed. "Girl, you are a darling."

"I'm Alan Priest."

"A veteran?" Dinah asked, pointing at my missing hand.

I nodded.

"We lo-ove veterans," she said. She acknowledged my war wound by kissing the back of her wrist. Something about the gesture moved me. I supposed she was telling me that it was okay to be different.

"We're looking for some info on a Lyndon Warnecki," I said. "He dresses like you."

"No one dresses like me," Dinah said, fist to her hip. Destini tapped her cigarette holder against a stone, shucking the butt. Seeming to have lost interest in us, she turned a cold shoulder. I supposed it was because I was prying into the life of a fellow performer.

"I wrote the story about the woman found in the wreckage at the Chrysler Building site," I said. I was delighted when Dinah displayed wide-eyed approval: she'd read my work.

"And I discovered the corpse was Lyndon Warnecki, dressed in drag," Lorraine added.

Dinah cupped her hand over her mouth. "They torment us," she said. "No surprise that they're out to kill us."

Destini squinched her eyes, coming alive, returning to the conversation. "Lyndon? You don't mean Lynn Dawn?"

She and Dinah Mite exchanged a quick back and forth. "Lynn Dawn?" Dinah said. "We know her. I haven't seen that child for a night and a day." With sudden realization, she whimpered. "Oh! The poor girl."

"We're looking for whatever you can tell us about her," Mae said.

"Who she hung out with," I added. "If she was afraid of someone."

"Is she really dead?" Destini asked. Lorraine nodded and squeezed her hand.

Beverly rejoined us, sashaying out the basement door, drink in hand and a pair of gentlemen in tow. Both were dressed in crisp tuxedos as though fresh off a male chorus line. They had slicked hair and carved smiles. One had a line of mustache dotted across his upper lip; otherwise, the two were interchangeable.

"Meet Melvin and Louie," she said. "They knew Lynn Dawn."

"Melvin," the mustache said. He presented his hand to Lorraine, palm down, as though it were there for kissing. She gave it a squeeze.

"Darling, you look just like Mae West," Louie told Mae. "Only prettier." He winked.

"No one is prettier than Mae West," Mae said, purring.

Melvin and Louie spoke quickly, an intimate back and forth, completing each other's sentences.

"We were on East 53rd …"

"… the dark reflection of here."

"Turtle Bay. Louie and I share a walk up. And we were just strolling along the street, Lynn Dawn at our side, minding our business."

"When the prude patrol pulled up in their wagon."

"Their paddy-whack wagon."

"Lynn Dawn was the only one of us three in a dress. Melvin and me, we were the same as now, just two bachelors."

"And the police hustled the lot of us into the back of their van."

"Where it smelled from pee and spew."

"Pee-yew. And they had a vanload of these small fry, kids for sale, painted up to be bargain boys, rounding them up, running them in for being victims. All them tykes had wide eyes like those church icons we saw at the Met."

"Byzantine."

"And it was just sickening."

Both paused for a moment, made bilious by the memory.

"And the wagon was driving along," Melvin said, "and Lynn Dawn started acting loony."

"Loonie-tic," Louie said.

"She banged on the panel to the cab and screamed, 'I gotta get out of here! I gotta get out.' The girl had some priors for dressing as a woman, and another offense might send her away for a year or more."

"And she called out, 'I got some primo dope. I can help you.'"

"She used the word 'primo.'"

"And 'dope' means inside information," Louie said.

I knew the word from writing about corruption at the races. It came from the horse track from gamblers who learned which horse was being medicated, charged up.

"And the van stopped. And they took Lynn Dawn out of the back."

"And that's the last we seen of her."

"You didn't learn what sort of news she had?" Mae asked.

Both gentlemen shook their heads.

"They went on to carry the rest of us to the police station in Turtle Bay," Melvin said.

"That place is a genuine nightmare," Louie added.

Turtle Bay. The Tenth precinct. Sullivan's domain. *Brrr.*

CHAPTER 28

Lorraine Priest

IT NEARED ONE A.M., and I felt the fingers of sleep crawl over my body, tips digging into my muscles, reminding me of my exhaustion. Beverly and Mae had night jobs, performing in *Diamond Lil*. After midnight meant nothing to them. The pair still ran on the adrenaline from their performances—and for Mae, the adulation of the drag performers —and, for Beverly, booze. They declared their desire to stay at the party and promised to continue to ask around about Lynn Dawn. I'd already been going for a full day and night, and implored Alan to join me, returning home to collapse. Over the last few days, we'd had a series of nightlong adventures. I might have blamed my exhaustion on sidling up to thirty, but then Mae and Beverly had years on me, and they were still full of life.

Before the law shut them down, my mother and father had sold patent medicine. I thought of the special "pick-me-up" ingredients in their concoctions. My mind drifted to that Kansas doctor who promised the invigorating miracle of goat glands. Be a kid again. I could use some of that.

James gave us a ride home. Most of the vehicles still left on the road were taxis, yellow or checkered, carrying commuters out too late to hook up with the tram and rail lines. The other motor cars? As Ford said, his customers could have any color they wanted, "as long as it's black."

"Lorraine?" James asked me. "You share such a rapport with Mae. But you two are so different."

"Everyone is different from Mae," I said. "I bring her something else."

"What?"

I felt tired, my guard was down. Honesty spilled from me. "We share a similar pain."

I had told Alan about that, but when he pressed me on what I meant, I said there were no words. There was a word. Before we'd met, I'd considered suicide.

"I want to be a beautiful corpse," I'd once told Alan. Strange, because half the time I think of my beauty as a curse. Men treat my shell as though I'm hollow. And yet I play the glamour girl for magazines. Press me flat on a page and I'm perfect.

Alan accepts me in all my dimensions. He even worships me. But does he truly know me?

When I told James that Mae and I shared a similar pain, he said, "I think I understand." If that was true, I was jealous. He understood me even though I didn't.

James left us in front of our building. I felt so cold. A damp night chill crept up my arms, as if my coat were sleeveless.

Alan halted in his tracks. "There's a paper triangle in the

window," he said. That was our building manager's signal to warn us the police had come to visit. "You stay here. I'm going to speak with Marco."

Alan seemed surprised by my lack of protest at being left behind. The reason was quite simple. I walked over to Marco's apartment and tossed up a penny at his window. A moment later, it opened with a jolt.

"Mrs. Lorraine," he said. "You must come inside. You look cold."

"Giovanni, darling. Have the police dropped by?"

"Ah, yes. A fine gentleman. An Italian. Signor Santarelli. He insisted on waiting outside your door."

Santarelli.

I thanked him and let him go. He had to answer Alan's knock on his door.

I joined Alan in the hallway. He wore a sheepish look on his face. Big lamb eyes.

"I figured it was safer and quicker to simply rap on Marco's window for attention," I said.

"I suppose."

Our elevator has a pair of accordion mesh doors that allow the riders to see each hall and the industrial in-between space. As we rose, we viewed the inside guts of the building, an alien point of view. We arrived at our destination, the floor sinking to the level of our feet.

Down the hallway, Detective Gilberti Santarelli stood leaning against the wall across from the door to our apartment, scribbling in a notebook. He became animated as our elevator opened.

Santarelli stands an inch or two shorter than I do. He is well-groomed and well-dressed, more in line with a waiter in a prissy rooftop restaurant than a police detective. His mustache is large and arches down, a style better suited to the days of muttonchops. He spread a toothy grin when we joined up with him in front of our apartment door.

"Miss Lorraine," he said. He clasped my extended hand.

"*Mrs.*" I responded. He'd known us going back to before our marriage.

"Yes. And Mr. Alan."

My husband nodded, saying, "Gilberti."

Santarelli tipped his head. "After some private investigations, I attempted to contact you via telephone without success. I decided to venture here to pass along a note. Some words of warning are best carried in personal communication."

"What have you found?" Alan asked.

Santarelli studied his note, holding it at arm's length. He read it aloud. "Dear friends. With substantial concern I pored over Alan's newspaper account of the dead lady encountered among the building ruins and considered its sensational photograph taken in the lightning and the storm. With greater unease I pondered our shared experience with those at the station house of the Tenth Precinct. *Urm-mm.*" He cleared a knot in his throat. "I've concluded that Sergeant Mitchell Sullivan is not someone to be trifled with. You have waved a red cape in front of a pawing bull."

Santarelli lowered his notepad. "I had not the opportunity to complete my composition. Perhaps for the best. Speaking allows me to elaborate to a greater degree. I have researched your adversary.

"A young Mitchell Sullivan entered the Foreign Legion before the Great War and fought alongside France for all its four years. During this period, he traveled the military circuits as a featured pugilist. It was said he could crack a skull with a single strike of his fist. After a head injury of his own, he briefly served as a drill instructor.

"Since joining the New York police, he has rented out himself and his men as enforcers. In the service of crime bosses. To union-busters and in rounding up immigrants. His corruption and methods go unpunished due to powerful supporters in the underworld and sympathizers among officials who approve of his anti-immigrant crusades. He has ensconced himself in the graveyard shift to avoid scrutiny. To quote the immortal Milton, 'It is better to rule in hell than to serve in heaven.'"

Santarelli paused in his recitation. He sniffed. "Mrs. Lorraine. Mr. Alan. From what I have been told, your status as honorable citizens will afford you no protection. Sergeant Sullivan will think nothing of killing the two of you if he sees you as a threat."

"No matter who protects him, he can't just go around killing people," Alan said.

"He will perform his murders in a way to hide his responsibility."

In the back of my mind, I heard the elevator being called and starting to descend. It didn't mean much, merely a late-night tenant requesting its service. The telephone began to ring inside our apartment.

"Thank you for the report," Alan said. He responded to the sound of the phone, taking out his key and inserting it into our apartment door lock. "And for coming here in person to deliver it."

"It is wise to steer clear of Sullivan and his men," Santarelli said. "He has forcible associates. You have not the power to defeat them. Nor do I."

"They have been monitoring our phone," Alan said, pressing back the door. The phone continued to ring. "Still, I'd like to know who felt the urgency to call at this hour." He went in to answer it. In the corner of my eye, I saw the floor indicator above the elevator pointing to the lobby.

"Alan and I appreciate your concern," I told Santarelli. "But you know we are not the kind who back down from a fight." The elevator again began to hum.

"Mrs. Lorraine, now that we are alone for a moment, allow me to speak intimately. You are aware that I follow the great thinkers of our times. And of history. Deciphering the human soul aids me in capturing those who perform crimes."

As a detective, Santarelli was strangely highbrow in his approach. He often quoted philosophers, alienists, and even Buddha.

"Freud," he told me, "declared that all dreams represent unexpressed wishes. When some of his patients spoke of dying in their dreams, rather than admit he was wrong, he contrived the notion of a 'death wish.' And yet is his conclusion a fallacy? I am worried that you undertake unnecessary risks. And you enjoy doing so."

Since meeting Alan, I've redirected my self-destructive impulses. Did I want to die? No. I wanted to stomp on death. That explained why I had a reckless attraction to danger. A mania that I would soon learn, was about to again be tested.

I heard Alan slam down the handset of our telephone. He rushed to the door saying, "Lorraine, Gilberti. That was Marco, our landlord. Sergeant Sullivan is in the building, heading our way."

I thought of the police listening in on our line, a hook-up down at the phone exchange. They would learn that Marco had warned us.

I looked to the end of the hall, where I could see through the mesh of the closed elevator doors. Inside the shaft the cable twitched as though it were a strand of spider web stuck to a struggling fly. Fear welled in my throat as I saw the dial on the floor indicator climb.

"The type of corruption he represents," Santarelli said, "does not listen to reason or the authority of a fellow officer. Prudency compels us to seek refuge in the opposite stairway, leaving no trace that we had been here."

"There's no time," Alan said.

He was right, for the elevator cabin now climbed into view. As it ascended, I saw, bit by bit, the rising figures of Sergeant Sullivan and a second officer: heads and shoulders, chests, and soon full bodies. The elevator jolted to a stop and the accordion doors drew back.

Sergeant Sullivan was the first to step out. "Lookie here!" he said. "The unholy three." His lips puckered as though preparing to spit. The man was huge. His barrel chest strained against his black jacket. As a prizefighter, he must have intimidated even his heavyweight opponents. His reach was that of a gorilla, his fists as huge as anvils.

By his side, about as tall as Alan but dwarfed by the Sergeant, was a wiry officer in police blues. A billy club extended from his arm. He wagged it as he approached.

"Lucky me finding you," Sullivan said, a smile cracking his face. "The wop downstairs told me you was out. Having you here saves us some time poking around. So, Mr. and Missy Newsfuckers, cough over your notes and names on the Chrysler Building body, or Bergen and me will needs to lay waste your furnishments while scaring up your secrets."

"You said there was no Chrysler Building body," Alan said.

Sullivan snarled.

I tried a different tack. "You'll require probable cause to enter our apartment," I said. Or maybe I should have said "a warrant." Those terms confuse me.

"Probable cause? It's prob'ly 'cause I want to. So you all, put me wise: where you keep your stash of notes?"

"We reserve our right to silence," Alan said. I nodded.

"You can't push us around," I said, "Detective Santarelli is a police lieutenant, and he outranks you."

Santarelli shook his head. He was right: confronting this thug was risky and probably futile. But so was giving in.

"Or we can settle this matter at Midtown," the heavy-built sergeant said. "Mr. Alan Priest, you are under arrest."

"On what charge?" my husband asked.

"Trying to steal my service .45." Sullivan drew his revolver so smoothly it seemed as though the bulky gun was lighter than air. He pointed its barrel at Alan's chest.

Alan stiffened his arms against his sides. His hand became a fist.

"Bergen, frisk the man."

The wiry thin officer looped his billy club over his wrist and began patting down Alan.

"My gun is not so shiny," Santarelli said, drawing a sleek, black pistol and directing it at Sullivan. "Sergeant, perhaps you are a capable shootist. However, I am reasonably certain that if you should chance redirecting your aim my way, I would first be able to deliver a gut shot."

A gut shot. Alan had told me that soldiers feared those more than straight-out dying. A hole in the innards, and no medicine could stop the infections from eating you from the inside out.

"If you did get off a first shot, I could still target you with the same favor," Sullivan said. Bergen set his hand against the side of his holster. I suspect he knew that drawing it would initiate a gunfight.

I stayed frozen. Not that anyone would suspect me of hiding a pistol in my outfit.

"Alan? Lorraine? Come, let us make our way to the elevator," Santarelli said. The three of us slowly backed off while keeping eyes on Sullivan and Bergen.

Sullivan's smile widened. As we entered the elevator cab and closed the door, he called out, "When we meet again, Lieutenant, you can reckon on a bullet for a hello."

CHAPTER 29

Alan Priest

ONCE WE WERE SHUT inside the elevator, Santarelli took hold of the control lever. He drew it up.

"Where are you taking us?" I whispered. There were only a few floors before the roof.

Lorraine matched the questioning look on my face but added a smile and a shrug saying she trusted Santarelli to have some sort of mad scheme.

"We are going to play a game," Santarelli said. "The sergeant and his man will see our elevator cabin rising and question why. The indicator dial will show us stopping three floors up. We will be suspended above him, like a lure on a fishline. If he tries calling the elevator, I will make certain the elevator remains in place. At least, that is, until they commit to following us." The detective pulled the elevator to a halt and began opening the screens.

"I will listen at the door to the stairway," Santarelli continued. "When I hear them begin to climb up, I will return to the elevator, and we will descend all the way to the first. A ploy merely intended to irritate."

I had to laugh. After all, Santarelli had been the one to warn us about waving a red cape in front of an angry bull. And his description was right. I imagined Sullivan pawing the dirt with his hooves, ready to charge, only to discover that the matador had left the stadium.

Santarelli parted the door to the stairs and cocked an ear. After a few moments, he softly shut the door and returned to us. "They're coming up."

"Gilberti, you are the devil," Lorraine said. She kissed him on the cheek.

Santarelli's maneuver provided us the opportunity to gain some distance in case Sullivan and Company decided to follow. When we got to the street, we found that even though well past midnight, there were some lingering, huffing cabs, this being Madison Square.

"If Sullivan can find our place," I told Santarelli, "he can find yours."

"My wife and my children are my strength," he said, "I prefer to be with them, staying safe together." A cabbie stepped out to open the back door for him. "Besides, we live in Chinatown. People there look after one another. They'll point a crooked finger when strangers or police ask directions."

I thanked him as his cab headed off.

23 skiddoo. It means to fly away and escape. They say the phrase came from the winds that swirl around the Flatiron

Building at 23rd and Fifth and how they make a hat fly or a dress flutter.

As for Lorraine and me, we skiddooed down a couple of blocks along 23rd over to the Hotel Chelsea. I'd always wanted an excuse to stay there. It had a reputation for being a haven to writers. My heroes, Twain, O. Henry, and William Dean Howells had all holed up in the place, along with some of the best painters of our times. I've fancied that one day, after I'd stuffed my head with worldly wisdom and mustered up something worthwhile to say, I'd try my hand at hacking out a novel.

The Hotel Chelsea building went back to the early 1880s. Although only eleven stories, it was one of the tallest habitable buildings in the world at the time it was built, elevators having just become practical.

The building had a European façade with an American muscularity. Stretching across each story and fronting the rooms, balconies provided outdoor walkways. Their grill-work possessed elaborate flourishes, vigorous but graceful, giving the sense that eccentric blacksmiths were the crafts-men. Black grills and rust-red bricks alternated in bands, the floors layered like icing and cake.

The place began as a commune with artist studios in its lofts. It maintained a Bohemian attitude—including a Bohemian snobbishness. When we checked in, the clerk studied us up and down to determine whether we had the proper degree of artistic attitude or uncultured culture to stay there. It probably didn't help that I asked for a room with a private toilet and shower. Still, he gave us the nod. I suppose everyone appears rather like a vagabond at two a.m.

The elevator ride was interminably slow. We arrived at our room with the clothes on our backs, my wallet, and Lorraine's fat purse. It took us only moments to skin down to our underthings and crawl beneath the covers. Showers could wait for the morning.

While Lorraine acted kissy, I felt sad and serious, still shaken by our encounter with Sullivan and his drawn gun and the certainty that our apartment was about to be wrecked. I deflected her advances. It surprises me how any pair of individuals can align their passions. I suppose the frenzied fervor of our early marriage usually overwhelmed any countervailing desires to be alone. Now, already two-years married, not every moment could be like the first days.

I lay in bed on my side with my back to her. She salved my distress by kissing my shoulders for a time before surrendering and lying peacefully on her back. When she sleeps, she has a mesmeric, gentle rhythm to her breathing. When I heard that, I turned to watch her. Her placid figure lying there, vulnerable and yet so strong. I knew that I would love her forever. I only hoped she would continue to tolerate my moods.

I woke at eight a.m., the Puritan in me chiding me for being lazy. All other diurnal creatures begin their days at sunrise. I include Lorraine in that group, already out of the shower, and currently powdering her underarms. The depths of her purse contained all sorts of soaps, talcs, and cremes. I decided to borrow her eau de toilette, something to mask my skunkiness.

"I have to head into work," I told her.

"It's Saturday," she said.

"Oh." I don't often write a feature for the *Sunday World,* so Saturday was my sometimes day off. Still, I was a victim of my own success. My bosses at the *World* had blessed the Chrysler Building murder story with front page copy and would demand that I continue to milk it. I'd yet to write up the Reynolds interview or to release the bombshell that the victim was a man in drag. I supposed I could beg off from my obligations by saying I'd serve up a sensational story come Sunday night. The bosses liked to start Mondays with a splash, a teaser that would string readers along for the week.

Lorraine drew out of her bag a Maidenform brassiere, an undergarment she swore by—an endorsement lost on my comprehension. "I'm going to call Mae," she said, tucking her breasts in, "to see if she learned something more at the party."

"Ask her if I can use her name in my story," I said.

We didn't have a phone in the room and so, once fully dressed, Lorraine headed down to the lobby, leaving me to my morning grooming and ablutions.

I thought about the coming day and the few leads I had to follow to solve this mystery. Legs knew something, but he wouldn't sing. I couldn't randomly insert myself into the world of Italian gangsters. I couldn't fool Reynolds into speaking up again. Maybe the toughest nut to crack would be determining how Sullivan and the Tenth Precinct were involved. That is, without getting my head blown off.

However, I had an idea of how to look into the story of the hunchback who was photographed looking over

Lyndon's body. Which left me with the eternal riddle of how to keep Lorraine involved while keeping her safe. I concluded it'd be best if we investigated together.

I stared at the end of my right wrist, thinking about getting a new prosthesis. I had no excuse for continuing without, that is, beyond general pig-headedness. That missing hand held on to my anger, motivating me, I told myself. A sworn vengeance against the world and its injustices. *Raise your right hand* … isn't that what you were asked to do when making an oath? And yet that conceit: the idea that my missing hand as a depository for pent-up fury. That was just me as a hack writer, contriving a cheap metaphor to avoid living my life. A prosthetic wouldn't end my rage.

Lorraine meanwhile, had returned from her foray to the lobby with a cat's smile on her face. "Mae had a great idea," she said. "She knows someone in the Chanin Building. The building has the perfect view of the Chrysler lot."

"Someone in the Chanin Building?" That didn't sound particularly promising. Some random employee witnessing something meaningful?

"Irwin Chanin."

I whistled. "She knows Mr. Chanin?" One of the most prominent builders in the city and one of the few successful men who truly impressed me. I'm not a socialist, but in my opinion, there are few ethical millionaires.

"He owns the Royale Theatre, where Mae is playing. He helped finance her show. She says he's quite the benefactor."

I supposed that Chanin could pass the word along to all his employees. Some late night worker could have seen something significant. An out-of-place vehicle. A swarm of thugs. Maybe the police carrying out a body.

"Mae has arranged a meeting for you and Chanin, come eight tonight."

"Thanks," I said. "I've been thinking about our next step." She smiled at the word "our." "I know a gangster, one who's accommodating. He's a hunchback. Thomas Jackson. Goes by the name Humpty."

"A hunchback? You think he's the one in the photo?"

"No. But he may give me a lead on a character I worked with at Dreamland. A hunchback by the name of Abelardo. I suspect him because he worked with Reynolds."

Lorraine rolled me a stare, a pair of snake eyes. "You're saying all hunchbacks know each other?"

"Give me more credit than that. Humpty knew Abelardo from his street days. He may help me trace him. Or at least give me a last name."

"This Humpty. He's a gangster?"

"Retired. He once ran his own pack of thugs. Back before Prohibition turned mobs into big business."

"Is he dangerous?"

Not really. But I knew that wasn't what Lorraine would want to hear, so I told her, "Fairly."

CHAPTER 30

Lorraine Priest

"JACKSON'S STORY IS LEGENDARY ... UNUSUAL," Alan said as we boarded the Broadway line. "A street gangster but he's literate, well-read. He quotes the classics. He walked away from the game. He's become a peaceable guy. But that wasn't always the case.

"Twenty years back, he ran his gang while squatting on top of what he called his throne, a tombstone in the 11th Street Cemetery. He passed out a menu to prospective clients. Two black eyes went for four dollars. Scooping an eyeball cost ten. 'The Big One'"—Alan slit a finger across his throat—"started at a hundred and went up, depending on whether the victim was a mug or someone with authority. He finally got caught after shooting a copper four times. He pleaded down, sentenced to a mere two-and-a-half years. He had in his possession too much blackmail material on too many of his clients to receive a harsher sentence. After a stint in the joint, he just decided to give up being a hoodlum and opened a pet store."

We got out at 125th, up by Harlem, just a block from Grant's Tomb. Who's buried in Grant's Tomb? Why, Julia Dent Grant and that husband of hers.

We strolled down the quiet lane of LaSalle Street to where Humpty Jackson kept his pet store, a little hole in the wall. A small brass bell on a side mount hung in front of the entrance, a leather shoelace dangling down from its clapper as a bell cord. A hand-painted sign instructed us to "Ring First." So I jingled.

"Open the door slowly," a woman's voice said from inside. "Just enough to squeeze your body in. Just the one of you first. Just the lady."

I went in. The interior was wall-to-wall cages crowding the floor and those strung from the ceiling, head-high. The place smelled of poop and ammonia; my nose was tickled by floating feathers. A tough looking woman eyed me, aiming a revolver my way.

"Don't fret yourself," she said. "I won't smoke ya. Just keepin' heedful."

A man sat on a stool. "We've had some threats," he said. "Old enemies promising to drop by. My Bella keeps me safe." He nodded her way.

I could see how he got the name Humpty. He was remarkably egg-shaped, with a squat body and a roundish head. He had a broad flaring nose, and I thought he looked a lot like that slugger Babe Ruth, almost a twin. Except for his hunch which made him appear as though he was constantly shrugging. His grin was as wide as a xylophone, toothy, and a little manic. His eyes seemed to hold whirlpools, a stare that could suck you under.

"You is fine," Bella said. I had no place on my outfit to hide a weapon. "Tell your man to enter. A quick squeeze in. Don't want our birdies to go flyin' the coop."

Birdcage doors hung open and canaries flitted about. Loose cats, mothers and kittens pawing at Humpty's pant legs, seemed uninterested in an avian meal.

"Your turn, Alan," I said. He tucked himself through the doorway and shut the door just as a yellow bird tried darting for the great outdoors. He waved the bird away from his face.

"We've met for a couple of stories," he told Humpty.

"You're that reporter with that *World* paper," Humpty said.

"Name's Alan Priest."

"You trust him, Tommy?" Bella asked.

"Sure," Humpty said. "A free smudge of news ink always does the business good."

"Do you point your gun at all your visitors?" I asked.

"I keep only two bullets," Bella said. "One for a warnin' shot and one in case the folks don't listen right." She placed the gun in a table drawer.

"My lady watches over me," Humpty said.

Bella gazed at her man with obvious love. "Saturday is playtime here," she said. "We let our critters run free to join the fun. Come evening we set a shellac on the phonograph and play our pets some opry music."

"Do you like opera?" Humpty asked.

I started to answer, but Alan spoke over my words. "No,

I love it," he said. A bit more passionate a response than I would have guessed, knowing and not knowing him for two years. He loves opera? We'd never been to the Met, and we didn't even own a gramophone. I supposed he lied to sweeten up to Humpty.

"I have all the recordings of John McCormack," Humpty said. He closed his eyes. "More than Solomon's riches, I wish I could sing." His eyes popped open, and his smile fell flat revealing a vertical scar that traced along the crease of his cheek. "What brings you here, Alan?"

"I believe a particular murder may have been performed by a hunchback."

Bella looked as though she could have spat. "And you suspect my Tommy?"

"No. There's this other hunchback …"

"Harry Riccobene?" Humpty asked. "Making a name for himself, but he mostly sticks to Philly."

I was beginning to suspect there was an entire cosmos of humpbacked mobsters.

"No," Alan said again. "Someone you knew from your Gas House days. Abelardo."

"Lardo," Humpty said, eyes closed, smiling. "Ran with Spanish Louie, my best lieutenant. A crack shot. You know, after Louie got drilled from a passing auto we found seven C-notes in his boots? We discovered he was a rich kid from Brooklyn. Playing at being a thug like it was some Sunday sport."

Humpty's old gang seemed surreal and intense.

"Abelardo Visconte," the hunchback continued, "and, yeah, he had a hump. The two of us being mistakes of God, hmm, we shared our sorrows. He loved machines, kept our one auto chugging. Back when us kids ruled the gangs. Today's mobsters, they're monsters. They'd squash a puppy just to see the juice …" He reached over and scratched a baby bulldog behind its ear.

"Lardo went on to work at Dreamland," Alan said, "at Coney Island, servicing the mechanical parts to the rides. He worked for Bill Reynolds."

"Reynolds," Humpty said, sneering. "There's a real piece of work. My team ran jobs for him. Breaking up picket lines, busting bones. Not that you'll get me to snitch on him. Not to any particulars. I'm no canary."

Canaries: snitches who sing to the authorities. An ironic phrasing considering all the canaries flitting around us.

"Do you know what happened to Lardo?"

"Yeah, I do," Humpty said, a wistful smile growing on his face. "Got out of the business, same as me. Worked down at Coney Island. You said that. Always good with gears and things. Went on to get himself a job working the clock at the Met Building."

The Met Tower? I shuddered That moon-faced clock that watched over our apartment from across Madison Square. Was it the sometime-home to a killer who had been gazing down on me all this time? Spooky.

CHAPTER 31

Alan Priest

LORRAINE and I planned to continue our stay at the Chelsea. We'd made a few enemies in recent days, and our apartment had become a target. However, having become jealous of the volume of my wife's purse and all its contents, I wanted to visit home to collect my own set of accessories and a change of clothes or two. I figured our place was safe to return to in the daylight hours. Mostly. Lately, it seemed that our place on the ninth floor was getting as busy as Penn Station.

So, when checking in with Marco, I wasn't that surprised when he told us we had a caller upstairs. "A rude man from your newspaper," Marco said. His lips were pursed, his face flushed. "Bumptious." These visits annoyed him, too. "He had a high hand and this card that said 'Press' in a hat band like one of them reporters in the moving picture shows."

That described a few people I worked with, although not my bosses. A hat with a press pass could get you special entry to crime scenes and events. Had the powers above me placed a second player on my story? I was lagging behind in filing my reports.

"And those *polizia* in the dark night," Marco said. "Late, after you and Lorraine left, they came back downstairs and treated me with disrespect. I saw how they treated your room with disrespect. Like those dominatores in the old country."

"I'm sorry," Lorraine said, reaching out and squeezing both his hands. She had the power to soothe with a touch.

"It's fine," Marco said, breathing more calmly. "But, Mr. Alan, I wish you had a more quiet job. Like a baker. Or like Signora Lorraine."

Yeah. Me, modeling for Cosmopolitan.

Riding up in the elevator, I told Lorraine, "I'm thinking about my appointment to meet Chanin tonight. It'll probably be routine, but you can tag along."

"I'll be busy. I hope to run down Abelardo, that hunchback," Lorraine said. "Or I'll at least run down what hours he works in the clock tower."

I didn't like the sound of that. Maybe, like Humpty said, Abelardo had stepped away from the world of crime. Or, maybe, he was the man in the photo hovering over Lyndon's body. What I did know was that he was a goliath. During his Dreamland days, I once saw him tip over a Tin Lizzie for the fun of it. I'd prefer to be there with Lorraine when she met up with him. I'd prefer to have an armed brigade tagging along. Or else ... I chided myself: I was overly concerned. By the time of his Dreamland days, Abelardo had become a gentle giant.

Lately, coming home to our apartment had been a chancy undertaking. After last night, even the empty hallway held an air of menace. It was the long and hungry throat of a beast. I studied Lorraine to determine whether she felt the same uneasiness. She didn't show it, but she was like that, inscrutable at times. Coming up to the door to our apartment, I found someone had splintered the wood around the lock.

Before we could enter, a man spoke from within. "I can hear you thinking," he said. I recognized that raspy voice. He added, "Pal."

No, he wasn't my pal or anyone else's. I pushed open the door, and Lorraine and I passed into the front room.

The speaker was Jessie Gould. Gould the Ghoul. The reporter at the *World* who regularly went out of his way to poach my stories. He was thin, slick. A heavy mass of jet-black hair atop his head added two inches to his already tall height. He wore another pile of hair under his nose. Whenever we'd stood face to face, I had to look up into his furry nostrils.

He sat with his feet up, stretched out between two chairs. The second chair had its back broken off and served as a stool. All around the room, furniture lay overturned and smashed to pieces. Papers strewn everywhere. The closet stood open, and clothes were torn and cast about. I guessed Sullivan, last night before he left. The police wouldn't have found anything important. I'd moved my notes to my office —except for those I kept on my person.

"I was gonna wait outside," my rival said, yawning, "but with your door being all busted and inviting, it told me 'Be my guest.'" He waved a hand about at the mess, chuckling. "Your gal, Lorraine's not much of a housekeeper."

His impudence. I bunched my fists. Lorraine seethed. She didn't often show that anyone had gotten under her skin, but Gould had a special talent for burrowing. Not that he noticed. He was sincerely oblivious to his crudeness.

"Mr. Gould? Kindly leave," Lorraine said, setting down her purse. She began slamming closed kitchen cabinet doors.

"In good time." He crossed his legs. I kicked his footstool out from under him.

He refused to be flustered, taking to his feet. "Alan, you're one of the Pulitzer pets. Ralph, him being a war correspondent, he's got a mushy heart for you cripples. And you know how to play that kissy game." He sucked a knuckle, a schoolyard insult.

"What brings you here?" I asked. My bosses knew all too well how I felt about Gould. They wouldn't assign him to work with me.

"I've tried sneaking behind your back, but now I kind of figgered with you, you having snagged a tiger by the tail, we could buddy up and share in the glory of that dead dame's demise." He had a natural inclination for alliteration. His writing was as subtle as a Harding speech.

"We don't need your help," I said wearily. I had been fighting so many hoodlums and scofflaws that I didn't have the energy to grab him by the collar and heave him out the door. The busted door. I looked about at all the litter on our apartment floor. I wondered whether this place would ever feel like home again. If we would ever feel safe. The telephone was intact, still ready to catch our calls.

"Ah, but you do need my help," my nemesis said.

"What can you bring to the story that my Alan can't?" Lorraine asked. More pragmatic than I expected her to be —and calmer.

"Mrs. Priest, I heard how you were out snooping and got snatched by some bad agents. Now, wouldn't it be better to have a man chumming at your side? To keep you safe?"

Lorraine gave that sort of smile that was oh, so sweet, and which I knew meant utter contempt. The irony was, I wished someone were there to watch over her, but I was wise enough to not suggest it. "You'd protect little old me?" she asked.

"It would be my honor as a gentleman," Gould said. "I got me a lead, um, I have a lead on finding that Lyndon Warnecki."

"Lorraine met up with him," I countered.

Gould seemed startled. "What did he say?"

"Not much," Lorraine answered. He was dead.

Gould tried again. "Okay, then. I got an idea on the identity of the dame in the ruins."

"Lorraine met up with her," I said—leaving out that it was, again, Lyndon, and that he was in the morgue. "My wife gets around."

"You found her alive?" Gould said. "Or she was dead, right? She had to be dead."

"She didn't say," Lorraine said.

Gould wrinkled his brow and nose. "You're playing with me."

"In other words, you haven't a thing to offer us," I said. "We're gonna pass. It's time for you to up and ankle far from here."

Lorraine folded her arms. Gould read how little he'd impressed us. "How's this?" he said. "I got an inside man at the Tenth Precinct. They got some sort of scheme going, all hush-hush. And I could give you a heads up on when they're coming for you."

This proposal intrigued me. I had no source at the Tenth. "The Tenth is certainly in the center of this," I said. "And I don't know their angle."

"I'm figuring they're stooges for Reynolds," Gould said.

"Something more," I remarked.

Lorraine glared at Gould. I had the feeling she preferred Sullivan to Gould. Still …

"Let's say, I could double agent them," Gould said, "make them think I'm selling you down the creek, all the while getting prime info."

I considered this. That could be helpful. And he'd be taking on quite a risk.

Then he added a threat to his offer, "If I'm not chumming around with you, I'll have to return to sneaking behind your back."

Why do they say "behind your back?" I asked myself. Isn't that in front of you? I shook off my distraction and answered him, "If you can get me something more on Sullivan and his gang, if you can find out what sort of game they're running, I'll share a byline."

"Deal." He grabbed my hand, not so much shaking it as

to pull himself forward and lean into me. He leered and whispered in my ear, "If you die, I get first dibs on Lorraine." He thought it a fine joke and laughed. His nose was near enough to bite. I restrained myself.

"Let me discuss our partnership with my wife," I said.

Gould nodded. "I'll duck into the hall to give you some whisper room." And to listen through the keyhole.

I followed Lorraine to the bedroom corner of our studio apartment. The police had knifed our mattress and shaped the loose stuffing into a heart, leaving us a valentine.

"My vote is to go on without him," Lorraine said, taking a seat among the lumps of cotton. "He's found out very little on his own."

The truth was, I wanted him to shadow Lorraine, to keep her safe. My wife is a remarkable woman, but I can't help but worry. Sullivan or Legs or whoever the Italians represented might show up at any time. Could I always be there for her?

"I could use him to get the goods on Sullivan," I said. "This is what I figure. I'll meet with Chanin tonight. Huffy rich guy, probably boring." I emphasized the monotony so Lorraine wouldn't think I was cheating her out of an adventure. "You keep Gould busy while looking into Abelardo. Find out when Abelardo works and such. When you have that info, we'll confront him together. And I promise to babysit Gould for his next outing."

She spat on her hand and we shook.

That decided, we announced our plans to Gould and arranged for Lorraine to meet up with him later. "This

Abelardo Visconte," I said, "we think he might have been there at the time of the murder of the woman in the ruins." That was intriguing enough to get him out of our hair, for the moment at least. In theory, we could always change our minds and stand him up and be no worse off.

With Gould having departed, I made my way to our closet. My blocky suitcase lay cracked open, courtesy of Sullivan. I tested its latch, and found it still worked. Lorraine and I packed up some items. For me: a change of clothes, a sweater and a glove, and a variety of cleansers and tonics, including Listerine and soapy toothpaste. I was becoming that sort of consumer that Madison Avenue craves: one who always frets over hygiene.

I prepared my jacket for the evening ahead, stuffing the special pockets I'd had sewn inside of the right flap with a set of needful items. Stubby pencils and notebooks for writing. Masking tape for when I need to secure something to my right-side shirt sleeve for easy access. My Banjo cigarette lighter. A Wenger Swiss Army Knife.

I thought about visiting a pawn shop and getting a gun. I haven't even fired one since my service days. But, given what had happened in the last few days, I'd earned the right to be paranoid.

CHAPTER 32

Lorraine Priest

ALAN and I spent the afternoon in our hotel bed holding and kissing and talking sweetly and softly about violent things. What lay behind us. What lay ahead.

Come sundown, Alan would go to the Chanin Building and meet up with Irwin Chanin. Either Mr. Chanin was one of those compulsive achievers that worked all hours into a Saturday night, or else, being Jewish, he'd scheduled the meeting for the end of Shabbat.

I was to join up with Gould and together we'd visit the Met Tower to track down the hunchback, Abelardo Visconte. Maybe learn his home address. *Visconte,* an Italian name meaning viscount. I'd dated a viscount once. British. He warned me in advance, "I am a peculiar chap." He didn't lie.

I agreed to go along with the plan to work with Gould to soothe Alan's caveman instincts to protect me. Had it been solely up to me, I would have declined. Although investigating a murder meant blood and corpses and visits to morgues, Gould represented an entirely different species of disgust.

While Alan headed off for his appointment, I spent some time with my friend Giovanni, the manager of our building. He had a way of distilling Italian espresso into a sharp, savory brew. As soothing as a kiss and as bracing as a slap. Too bracing: a demitasse was all that I could handle.

I finished up the coffee and looked out his window across Madison Square. High above and beyond the park trees, the hands of the Metropolitan Life clock pointed straight up and down. Six p.m. Its bell began gonging, a dulcet tone, B flat, summoning me to the hour of my rendezvous.

"Fare thee well," I told Giovanni.

"*Arrivederci*," he said, adding, "stay safe."

I walked along the puzzle of paths that crossed Madison Square Park. No great hurry. I could be a little late. Gould could wait.

Being November, with autumn beginning its decline, the sun had set an hour ago. I shivered from the cold. I shivered at the thought of passing another night knowing Sullivan would be out there, prowling the streets. What was he really up to? Why did he obsess over Alan and me?

A blocky building, a sort of "hunch," was attached to the Metropolitan Life Tower. The tower itself was insanely tall and ended in a spire. Or perhaps, it seemed to soar so high because of its narrowness.

A beacon shone from its peak. The insurance company used a drawing of it as their logo. The lit tower and its mind-boggling height made me think of the multicolored spotlights that illuminated the crown of the Chanin Building. Alan had probably told the truth, his interview would be routine and boring. Still, I worried about him being alone, off by himself. He had a habit of finding danger.

The entrance to the Metropolitan Life Tower passes beneath a square arch: if arches can be square. I heard my footfalls transform from outdoor background noise into echoing clacks. The foyer spanned the breadth of the building: a mostly empty court with a bank of three elevators in front of me.

I could feel Gould eyeballs crawling over me even before I saw him.

"Mrs. Priest," he called from a recess where he stood, over near a guard at a desk. "This is Mr. Trout."

Trout, a jovial-looking man, sat planted in his chair. A wide fellow, his chest strained against the buttons of his uniform. He had one of those Kaiser mustaches that Chaplin made popular. He didn't bother standing to greet me, merely pivoting a hand to its side, thumb up. I clasped his palm and shook.

"Al, the building manager here, hits the town on Saturday nights," Gould said. "He trusts Trout with all the security decisions."

"I don't know if 'trust' is the word," Trout said, snorting with a laugh. "I mean he says he doesn't trust me. But he does leave me in charge." He squirmed up from his chair.

With his belt cinched well below his swollen waist, his holster was barely within his reach. His stubby fingers twitched in the empty air like a gunslinger waiting for the moment to draw. Which he wasn't about to do; the action looked ridiculous.

"There's not much to my job," he continued. "Just say 'hello,' answer questions, and roust the occasional bum. The main qualification is insomnia and I'm good at that. Come along. To use the elevators at this hour on a Saturday you need a key."

Trout held out a key and followed it as though they were both drawn by a magnet.

"Mr. Trout has agreed to help us contact Abelardo," Gould told me.

"Help? Not so much. But I'll point you the way."

Trout fixed the key into a slot in a metal panel, turned it, and the elevator doors parted. "We don't need Lardo around, not often, just for cleaning and maintenance, but he's solid at his job. Keeps the clocks always running. We give him a cot up in the timepiece room and sometimes he stays for the night. Could be there now."

He planted his arms akimbo. "Take a ride up to the 26th floor. That'll bring you to the clock mechanism. If he's not there, you can post him a note. He'll call you back, we got a phone up there, and he'll help you out however you like. Like I said, he's a swell guy. Big as a bear, but peaceful."

Peaceful? He didn't sound like a killer. I began to doubt that this errand would get us any closer to the hunchback in the photo. Maybe for the better. I had built up Gould's expectations, so it might be best to disappoint him. Give him nothing, string him along while demonstrating how fruitless our outings can be and maybe he'd leave us alone.

A panel inside the elevator had two tall columns of red button knobs stamped with numbers. I worried about the future of elevator operators' jobs. Poor guys. I thought of that recent play about robots taking human jobs. It seemed like there was less and less employment for greeters and all those who bless your days with discrete bits of courtesy.

After the doors shut and we began to rise, Gould said, "One bonus about having you along is that the guard here treats me as harmless like I'm as sweet and tame as the girlie at my side." I scooched over to the distant wall shrinking away from him. "Far off from my side," he clarified.

As we ascended, I pictured the heights we were passing as they would appear outside the building, all the stacks of windows, the dizzying distance to the street below. I imagined a falling body and the splatter when its fall ended. I thought of the woman who tumbled past my office window the day I met Alan. Our first adventure together.

Our lives depend on the sturdiness of these elevator boxes and the strength of their cables. It seemed like a miracle to be suspended so high above the world, lifted by a string. It reminded me of those ballyhoo daredevils who walk on the wings of aeroplanes. I remembered Alan and I encountering the Skywalkers, the Mohawk Indians recruited to build the skyscrapers. Balancing on beams far above the earth, they seemed to walk on air.

"I'll keep quiet and let you sweet talk the guy," Gould said. "His body being warped and all, he'll probably go goo-goo for you like that monster in that Grimm's tale, Beauty and the Beastie."

A circle was cut through the cab's panel in the middle of the buttons. Numbers appeared in its window counting up the floors. 24 ... 25 ... 26. The elevator stopped and the doors automatically spread open, like welcoming arms.

When I was on the street below, the Metropolitan Tower seemed to rise into the sky like the forearm and fist of a giant. Here, on a lofty floor, the interior felt cramped. I thought of the inside of a church's steeple. The layout was crowded in the center by the bank of elevators and constricted by single offices at each of the corners. These carved the remaining floor space into the shape of a cross. A coldness seeped in from outside and I could hear wind sweeping the exterior walls.

A row of single bulbs marched along the ceiling to the area behind a clock. A leather-bound console, hip-high, looking like one of those cabinets that hide phonograph players, sat beneath one of the clocks. Planted in its center was a small timepiece. Cloth-bound wires snaked out from its base, running along the edge of the floor and turning the corner to connect to the other three massive clocks.

Four clocks in total, one facing each side of the building. They stood three floors in height. Here, on the 26th floor, I could only see their center slices from 3 to the left and 9 to the right. Their width took up all the wall space.

The backs of the clock faces were massive concrete disks. Spotlight canisters were set up behind the numbers to make them shine out to the world. A web of wires connected to other lights. The dial on the console read 6:15. Considering the span of the clocks, the minute hands had to be several times my height. I thought of the hour hand pointing toward the street and, imagining its plunge, I couldn't help but feel an attack of vertigo. Somewhere far above, a single bell rang the quarter-hour, its tone seeming to shudder and pass down the shaft of the floors as though the building were the chamber of a flute.

At the center of the dials were electric motors. I could hear their operation, a scratchy hum like a phonograph needle announcing the end of a record, like those old phonographs that used cactus spines.

"It's majestic," I said.

From behind the elevators, footfalls sounded on metal steps in a measured cadence, and someone spoke while descending the stairs. "It is most magnificent."

The speaker had the whiskey-smooth voice of an elocution instructor who advertises on the radio promising to transform his students into talkie stars. "The tip of the minute hand moves an inch every four seconds, more than a foot a minute. Slow but unrelenting. The teeth of gears rotate, chewing one another. Every present moment devouring the now and shitting out the past. Time has no mercy."

And time had no sense of polite language.

With the end of that speech, a hunchback appeared from behind the bank of elevators. He sported a black cape. Too perfect a match with the photos to be a coincidence, he must have been the hunchback at the murder scene. I flinched and then calmed myself: I wouldn't show fear.

And this man didn't evoke fear. His broad face wore the aspect of a tragedian, glowering. However, I got the impression that we, as intruders, were not the source of his distress but were, rather, its relief.

A muscular man, he towered over me, a full head taller.

It appeared that his hunchback cut short a true giant. He had a shock of raven hair drooping in front of his forehead. His eyes, dark pools, fixed on me, unblinking.

He patted the leather console with its small clock. "This is a chronometer," he said, "the device from which all time flows."

"Mr. Visconte ..." Gould began.

"Abelardo, please."

"I am Jessie Gould with the *Evening World*."

"And I am Lorraine Priest," I hurried to add.

"Lorraine," he said, focusing on me, "a musical name." He smiled and shut his eyes, taking a deep breath, as though inhaling a memory.

"You know how to run all this?" Gould asked, sweeping his hand.

"It knows how to run itself." The hunchback stepped up to a gear and trailed a finger around its rim. "In my reckless youth, I once put an Indian Head penny on a streetcar track. Those in my gang told me it would derail the trolley and I wanted to see. Ha! All I got back was a pinched penny with a smudged face. I saved it." He took the coin from his pocket and held it up for viewing, twisting his expression to match that of the chief. "That Indian is bent like me. If I put a penny in the gears of the clock, could I stop time?"

"We haven't come here to listen to your daydreams," Gould said, speaking through nearly closed lips, percolating with impatience.

"Fascinating, though they are," I added. This man was eccentric, but I could understand why the guard called him peaceful.

Gould nodded at me. He ceded to my approach, recognizing my honey was better at luring someone into talking than his vinegar. I went on. "My husband—not this man here—and I are investigating a murder at the site of the Chrysler Building. A hunchback was at the scene. One who wore a cape."

"Shakespeare called us bunch-backed," Abelardo said, ignoring my inquiry. "My friend Humpty taught me to love the great dramatists because they celebrate the deformed. Shakespeare and Hugo and Verdi."

The fragile partnership between me and Gould cracked as he chose to go on the attack again. "Would you like to tell us what you were doing at the crime scene, or should we talk to the police?"

"The police? No. No police, po-lease," the clock keeper said. "And I have nothing to say on that matter. Not to them. Not to you." With that, he walked away, rounding the elevator bank. I could hear his footfalls on metal stairs, clanging like bells, rising above us. Those footfalls suddenly stopped and the world hushed as though catching its breath. In the near silence, the clock gears and bearings ground out the time. Wind whispered against the tower's walls. We all listened as an elevator's cables hummed.

The elevator? I swiftly glanced back at the elevator we'd just vacated. A half-moon dial over its doors indicated its upward progress. Twenty. Twenty-four. Its arrow climbed to 26 and stopped. The doors parted revealing Sullivan and Bergen. Bergen's gun was drawn.

I backed away.

Gould stepped forward. "You're early. I was about to get a confession."

"A confession?" Sullivan said.

"The cripple. He climbed up the stairs. In back of the elevators."

Bergen hurried around the elevator bank. I heard his boots banging on steps as he ascended.

Sullivan glared at me. I glowered back as I took in that flat face and flat nose. His snarl. His fists bunching and opening.

"Lorraine," Gould said, sounding almost apologetic, "after you and me and Alan spoke, I went to the Tenth Precinct. They promised me the complete story if I led them to the hunchback. They've tagged him for the killer. So, hey, you and I will be catching the killer. Performing a good deed."

"You pathetic worm," I said. I really wished I could find a more graphic epithet, but loathing clogged my mind.

"Just doing my job," the worm said. "No hard feelings."

Footfalls clattered down the stairs and Bergen returned, breathless. "I can't find him, sir. Not hide nor hair."

"That's okay," Sullivan said. "We got the lady." Bergen marched my way, gun pointed, handcuffs dangling from his other hand.

"That wasn't part of our agreement," Gould said.

"Yeah?" Sullivan said. "I vote to break our agreement."

"But I'm a double agent. I should have two votes."

"You don't fucking know what that means," Sullivan said. He took a Peace dollar from his pocket and tossed it at Gould's feet. I suppose I should have been insulted, being sold for a dollar, but even Jesus went for a mere thirty coins. "Bergen," he went on, "take this gal to lock-up. Throw her in the tank with the razor dames. Make her ugly."

CHAPTER 33

Alan Priest

SEVEN P.M. My missing hand prickled. Maybe the weather. Or else … I got this sudden crazy notion that it was a ghost warning me of danger. Yeah? then why didn't it clue me in on the appearance of the Italian assassins or the visit from Sullivan? I decided my spectral hand was like my bullheaded instincts, its warnings were hit or miss.

The cab let me out at Lexington and 42nd. In recent days this area had become familiar stomping grounds. The site for the Chrysler Building sits diagonally across the street from the tower Chanin built. The Chanin Building is burly, gigantic: a Greek Titan. As a devotee of architecture, I regarded it as the most beautiful skyscraper ever constructed. It is a temple to dynamism trimmed in the styles of futurism and the modern French school, *les arts décoratifs.*

Its uppermost floors are surrounded by buttresses and

pillars. Its crown is highlighted by over two-hundred multi-colored spotlights.

Irwin Salmon Chanin was born back in the days when Salmon sounded like a good name for non-fishy beings. Perhaps his middle name inspired the bronze frieze that ran across the building's front brow. Titled "Evolution," it depicts the progression of life from primordial ooze through fish and on to geese (and yet no further, perhaps geese being the epitome of beasts). It reminded me of a poem by Langdon Smith, a wag who once worked for the *Evening World*. It goes in part:

Let us drink anew to the time when you
    Were a tadpole and I was a fish.

The lobby could humble Jove, Roman god of the sky. It is modernist and yet palatial, jazzy and regal. Overhead a series of slender chandeliers hang like luminous icicles. Bronze reliefs depict the theme "The City of Opportunity." Even the ironwork for the ventilation grills possesses an industrial grandeur.

The building is so massive that twenty elevators, each decorated differently, service its floors. A man stood in front of the bank. At first I thought that, at this hour, he might be an elevator operator. No, he wore a side holster. He was a guard.

Although muscular, he appeared far from formidable. He had an overly ripe face that said his sobriety began and ended with each shift. He leaned against a cane designed with a brace that strapped it to his forearm.

"Mr. Chanin is expecting me," I said.

"You are Mr. Priest?" he asked. I nodded. "The elevators are fully automatic. Press the button with the number of your destination. Floor 52."

"Thanks." I replied and stepped into an open elevator cab.

The elevator gave a sort of a grinding hum as it rose. I thought ahead about meeting Mr. Chanin. In my life, I've noticed little overlap between confidence and competence. That's a shame. Too many inept but self-assured people achieve success and lord their power over the rest of us with contempt.

Irwin Chanin was different. He belonged to a select class who were wealthy, capable, and honorable. Even though he could make more money creating cheap slums, he built good housing affordable to the poor. In his youth, being Jewish, he had to use a separate door to enter theaters. When he constructed his own theaters, he made it so all patrons had to use the same entrance.

I reached the 52nd floor, and the doors slid open. In contrast to the chandeliers in the lobby, spotlights, sunk into the ceiling, illuminated the passage forward. In front of the entrance to the executive suite, stood a heavenly gate. It was whimsical, strips of metal fanning out from the center of its base like peacock feathers. It was industrial, its rays chocked with loose gears and toothy arches. When I parted its doors, I expected a chorus of angels to start singing.

Hallelujah.

Irwin Salmon Chanin is an insubstantial man. Late thirties, short, balding. He wore round-lensed glasses with black wire frames, and a dark tuxedo over a spanking white shirt. He bristled with self-assurance, thrusting out a hand for shaking, bright-eyed as though excited to see me.

I extended my left hand, and we shook. His grip was firm, but not that sort of knuckle-crushing that comes with the insecure.

"Miss West …" I began and, because he chuckled just by my invoking her name, I halted for a moment. "Miss West told me you might be able to help me."

"I have only a vague understanding of how that could be." He rounded his desk and for a moment, I thought he was going to take a seat. Instead, he pressed a pair of flat palms against his desktop and leaned forward.

"Your missing hand? The war?"

I nodded.

"But your lungs are okay. You never experienced a gas attack?"

"No, but for the grace of God." I have often considered how my injuries could have been worse. I'm forced to. On too many corners, legless or blind veterans sell pencils or beg for dimes.

"Good. My first building as a contractor was to make a poison gas factory during the war. I was young and foolishly patriotic. I've never stopped reflecting over those whom I might have hurt or killed. How can I help you?"

"I'm investigating the case of the woman who was found murdered this past Thursday in the ruins where the Chrysler Building is to be built."

"I read of that."

"So much of your building overlooks the site. I was hoping that perhaps one of your late-night guards or other employee may have seen something to help me. About 3 a.m. on Thursday, or a little before. Perhaps one of them noticed a vehicle parked in front. And there was a hunch-backed man at the scene."

"A hunchback? How unusual."

"About 4 a.m. the police were on site."

"The local precinct?" Chanin asked.

"Number 10."

"A bad crew." He pursed his lips in thought and then spoke slowly as though choosing his next words carefully. "From my own lofty perspective, I have often gazed down upon the layers of rubble of that newly demolished site. They say their building will dwarf my own. That man, Chrysler, is singularly competitive. When I built this skyscraper, I purposefully chose not to make it the tallest, the most vain. As the Lord said to Samuel, 'Look not upon appearance or height … for it is not as man sees, the Lord sees into the heart.' I will send word to all my late-night attendants—there are not many—and ask whether they witnessed anything unusual or that otherwise might be perti-nent. Anything else?"

As a lover of buildings, I revered this man. Awestruck, I could think of nothing more to say other than, "Thank you."

The buttons in the elevator winked one-by-one as they counted down. I was surprised when the cab settled to a stop at floor 42. I supposed I shouldn't have been—someone must have called for it, interrupting my journey. The doors parted. No one was there.

Light from the elevator cut a swath of illumination into a dark expanse. I could make out the pillars of support beams, each a tree in a shadowy forest. A dim light leaked through distant windows in front of me and to either side. Peeking my head out I could see there were no internal walls. The Chanin Building wasn't set to officially open for another two months and while the exterior was complete, the 42nd story remained unfinished. I could even detect checkerboard spaces where the floor was missing altogether.

A man approached, a blocky figure like that of a fighter. The flashlight in his hand blinded me, his face unseeable and his body a paper silhouette. I made out the shape of a gun in his other hand. Snub-nosed with a fat-bellied cylinder.

"Step out of the elevator, Mr. Priest," he demanded. I recognized the voice: Legs Diamond. He nodded his firearm. "Don't you try and close them doors."

I hesitated. If he was inviting me to take a bullet, why oblige him and go into the big dark space where my body wouldn't be discovered until Monday? Maybe I *could* close the elevator before he could rush inside and join me. Even if I did take a slug, I'd be traveling down to the first floor where I'd get the guard to call an ambulance.

I stood motionless, collecting my thoughts. I came up with a different plan.

The only lighting, that flashlight. For me, the light blinded my eyes. For him, he could see a vulnerable target. Legs was cocky. He'd underestimate me. I stepped out onto the 42nd floor and let the elevator doors close behind. Without the light from the elevator, only the blinding beam from his flashlight remained.

"Follow me," he said. I suspected he meant to lead me to some corner or space to stash my body or maybe he planned to shove me out a window.

Back in my days as a magician, I learned a thing or two about misdirection, and I recognized that I could use the darkness to my advantage. I had a single glove in my coat pocket, left-handed. As he guided me on, I discreetly took it out and slid it over the stump of my right wrist. Legs knew of my disfigurement, but the moment was tense and dark. I could fool him.

"Here's about where," he said. "Have yourself a park."

"My hand!" I cried, lifting and shuddering my right arm as though I felt a sudden pain. I shook my glove free and it fell. As I intended, it appeared as though my entire hand had fallen off and Legs followed the glove to the floor with his flashlight beam.

Seizing the momentary distraction, I lunged at him, crashing chest-to-chest, thrusting my right arm against his forearm, turning his gun away so that the gunshot went off to the side. With the full force of my tackle, he toppled over backward, crashing against the floor, and I landed on top. With my left hand I liberated his flashlight, sending it skittering to the side. It struck a pillar and its bulb popped, sending our world into near complete darkness.

Still struggling, still pressed against his body, my hand came across a second gun, this one in a body holster. I snatched it and scrambled away, backing into the darkness.

He blasted a couple of shots in my direction, but not seeing me, missed.

The gunfire had illuminated me and his lying figure. I moved to the side in case he decided to fire at where he'd just seen me standing.

His labored breathing gurgled, telling me I must have busted one of his ribs. I steadied my own breaths. With my eyes closed, I focused on recalling the images that appeared in the brief moments of light. Construction beams rose, spaced out from each other, forming the corners of what would become walled-off offices. Empty areas without flooring, pits that descended to who-knew-how-far below.

I didn't get a glimpse of what sort of gun I held. Slender, it had a comfortable grip. Sleek line to its muzzle, no bulky cylinder. An automatic. Lightweight. I wondered whether it was even loaded. Still, shooting him was worth a try. I'd direct the first slug at the sound of his throaty breathing. It would provide a flash to see where he was. The second bullet would be on target.

I stepped out, intending to fire, but the trigger wouldn't move. Not even a click. I felt around with my thumb for the slide of a safety but didn't encounter one. *Stupid me.* I held the gun in my left hand, my only hand. Nearly all guns are built for right-handed shooters with the safety where the thumb would be.

I couldn't finger about for the safety latch without inverting the gun, so I did something that would seem strange to those with two hands. I pressed the pistol to my lips and probed its handle with my tongue, an organ as sensitive as fingertips. It tasted metallic, a bit leathery from its holster, a bit salty from the sweat of my hand. I came across the safety switch and scraped it back with my teeth.

Legs must have realized I could locate him from the noise of his labored breaths. That sound lowered to a sizzle as though he now breathed through clenched teeth. Along with a soft wheeze of outdoors wind, and an occasional peep of traffic horns from the canyon floor somewhere far below, nothing else was audible, not a whisper, no other notice of a world beyond the blanket of darkness.

We shared the same dilemma. Each of us had a gun. If we fired, our first shot would be blind. That little spit of gun flame would reveal our location. I had hoped it would be enough to illuminate our target for a solid second shot. But perhaps not. Not if he was hiding. I had to seek cover.

I slowly swept my right arm about probing for a support column, not wanting to strike it so hard as to make a sound. The tiny hiss of Legs' breath seemed to coalesce from the darkness itself and whisper directly into my ear.

I heard something like a coin striking the floor and rolling. *Ha!* The misdirection by throwing a pebble trick. Was I supposed to shoot that direction?

Stepping back, my wrist brushed against a column. I trailed my stump of my forearm along it. It was broad enough to provide cover. Once behind it, I could fire my gun from safety.

Without thinking, I carefully stepped around it, only to find the floor was missing, one foot dangling in the air. At first, I wobbled to the side, gasping. Then I found myself falling.

CHAPTER 34

Lorraine Priest

I'VE KNOWN men like Gould the whole of my life. They don't care so much about being heels, but they do care very much when an attractive woman recognizes them for what they are. He insisted on having the police allow him to ride with me to the precinct. As some sort of apology?

"Don't worry, Lorraine," he said. "I'll sort out this mess."

He failed to inspire my confidence.

Sullivan and Bergen marched us out of the Metropolitan Tower and with the help of two other officers herded us into the rear end of a paddy wagon where they chained us to the metal arm rests of a metal bench. The back doors shut with a *clank*.

We sat there surrounded by a disheveled crew of gaunt men, all of them dark-haired and olive-skinned. Some greeted me with wolf whistles under their breaths. I recognized Italian among their mumblings.

I had the distinct sensation we were all sardines crammed into a can. Any moment some Fe-Fi-Fo-Fum giant might use a slotted key to roll back the roof. I pressed my hand to the van's metal wall to feel some connection to the outside world. It felt cold.

The paddy wagon jerked to a start. The Tenth Precinct was in Midtown, Turtle Bay. I imagined that we would take the most direct route. I pictured heading up Lexington past the wreckage where the Chrysler Building was to be built. Past the Chanin Tower. I envied Alan and his boring meeting. I felt tense with fear. My fingernails clawed into my palms.

"Does anyone speak English?" I asked. A goodly pause and more mumbling before a polite voice answered.

"I do, ma'am." The man—no he was closer to a boy—trembled. He wore a thread-bare coat. He sat, chained to the bench opposite me, eyeing his comrades who in turn, glared back at him.

"*Cosa hai detto loro?*" an older man said, nearly spitting with anger.

"He asked me what I said," the boy told me. "He thinks anyone who speaks is a rat." The boy answered the man. "*Ho detto che è bellissima.*"

The man nodded. "Ah."

"I answered him saying that I told you, you are beautiful," the boy said.

Hmm. The older ones didn't mind if he flirted.

"The police, they are collecting us to send us back to the Old Country, not because we are Italians," the boy said, "but because we are the wrong Italians."

"The wrong Italians?" I asked. I added a blush to

continue the pretense that he had once more complimented me.

"We are loyal to the old men who brought us here. A new group is taking over. They are planning to kill the old leaders and the Jews."

Gould looked wide-eyed. This was deadly information.

"Who are they?" I asked the boy.

"My friends do not understand my English words, but they will understand names."

A purge in the ranks of the mobsters. I asked myself whether this was the information that Lyndon had. The knowledge that got him killed.

The paddy wagon pulled to a stop. I stood, tugging against my manacle. To continue the ruse that our conversation had been about flirting, I bent over and kissed the young boy on his forehead. The other Italians gave whoops of approval.

I sat back down to await the opening of the rear doors. I heard boots clambering. A horse clopping along the pavement. A distant door opening and banging. There were a dozen of us in this paddy wagon. The police would be arranging reinforcements before taking us into their building.

This waiting. I struggled to stay calm. Sullivan had given the order, "Make her ugly." Putting me in with some brutes called "the razor dames." I have always disliked my beauty. The way it turned men into idiots. Now it seemed to me that I would miss the luxury of disliking it. I was positively terrified that it was about to be taken away. I feared that even more than the expected pain of the being sliced.

"If there are murders being planned among the Italians,

we should tell the police," Gould told me. "Maybe they'll reward us for the info and let you off."

"You idiot," I said. "The police are part of the scheme. That's why they're rounding up the old guard."

Gould's expression fell flat. He looked like he'd just swallowed a rotten egg, whole.

The back doors parted. Sullivan and Bergen and two other officers stood ready with billy clubs.

"Unlock and take them to the cells, two by two," Sullivan told his men. "Take the lady last. If any of 'em should give you the fish-eye, break their dago noses."

The occupants understood the word "dago." They reacted with killer glares.

One of the police officers spoke in Italian, I assume he was repeating Sullivan's orders. Two Italians stood up, offering themselves to be the first to go.

"What have you good folks been chatting over?" Sullivan asked Gould and me, tendering a smile.

Even a half-wit like Gould knew enough to not answer that truthfully, offering only, "The young man said Lorraine is very pretty."

With the van doors open and the prisoners escorted out by pairs, the cold blew in. Wintry, real Robert Peary weather. I gazed out along the remainder of the block, willing it to be a direction I could run.

When I'd come here before with Alan at my side, I'd paid little attention to the place. Although less than a block off of the ritzy Lexington Avenue, the Tenth Precinct Station stood along a squalid stretch of road. Next door was a fire station. Firefighters, I told myself, they would surely come to my aid, right? Yeah, as though they'd go to war with the police for little old me. Beyond the fire station, a SOCONY garage and a pair of one-story shanty businesses that seemed ready to be squashed like bugs.

I leaned to the side and looked up. The police station house itself was six stories. Tall and narrow, an American flag projected from its third floor. Its building was plain in its features and soot covered. It could be mistaken for a rundown tenement.

Gould's turn came up and the sergeant did the honors of unlocking his manacles. "Sergeant Sullivan," he said. "I could serve you up some sweet ink in my paper."

Sullivan cracked a crooked smile. "Angling for some special treatment? Who needs that asshole Priest when I got me this beanpole to kick around? Bergen, let's find this man a place in the drunk pen. Let him stew in some vomit."

It was my turn. Bergen leaned in with the handcuff key. I tried to ooze some charm, hoping to stir in him some sympathy, but I couldn't fake it, the corners of my nostrils lifting in a sneer.

"Stick her with the lady goons," Sullivan said. "We'll rustle her up some fresh friends to show her a right old time."

CHAPTER 35

Alan Priest

I FELL THROUGH THE DARK, seemingly only for a moment, and slammed down sideways on my right side. The drop must have been only one story, ten feet, but it delivered enough force to smack the wind out of me and bruise me, shin to shoulder. Once, during the war, while marching alongside a road with my doughboy buddies, I was side-swiped by a careening ambulance. This felt the same, like someone had driven a thousand needles up and down half of my body.

Still complete darkness. My noggin hurt, I could feel a lump above my temple. My ears rang. While laying on my side, I worked my legs, bicycling them. I rolled my neck. I turned on my back and cracked open my jaw, screaming silently, taking a bite out of the dark. I felt my pistol laying beneath me, digging between my shoulder blades.

A match flame bloomed from the floor above. It didn't

illuminate much, just the disembodied head of Legs, looking down. That head shuddered, seeming to cackle. I'd bruised his ribs during our struggle, so that laughter must have hurt. *My* breathing certainly did. He let go of the match and it seemed to drift down as it came toward me. I rolled to the side as he fired his gun twice.

With the dying light of the match, I made out my surroundings. On this floor, there were walls. I was in a partitioned area set to be an office space. No furniture, not yet. No door to hide behind, to shut myself away when he came for me.

I saw a glimmer of light appear above, but not directly in my line of vision. Another match flame. I heard footsteps marching in a straight line overhead. *He would be heading for the elevators.*

No, he wouldn't wait for an elevator. He'd take the stairs. He'd come one floor down to hunt me. How would he find me? He'd lost his flashlight, but how many matches did he have? One thing for certain: this darkness made me blind.

I grabbed my pistol and scrambled to my feet. I felt unsteady, listing to my right, but my legs and ankles were still in working order, at least enough to plod. After groping my way through the doorless doorway, I paused for a moment, recalling which direction Legs's footfalls went.

I walked in that direction, toward the elevator bank, toward the stairway, arms out in front of me. When he did come for me, he would have to reveal himself with a lit match. I'd have a fighting chance to shoot first.

I thought of those Tom Mix cowboy movies, about how he cracked open the barrel of his six-shooter to count the remaining bullets. I tried to remember how many times I had already fired. The number didn't come to me. Having banged my head, counting seemed beyond my current capabilities.

As my eyes adjusted, the darkness was deep, but not so complete that I couldn't recognize a wall just in front of me. If I was right, it was the elevator bank. I pocketed my pistol and felt along the space waist high until I touched a recessed button. It was below another. I pressed it and it lit, illuminating a down arrow and my hand.

I heard the sound of feet, muffled as though behind a nearby door. That sort of clump that came with walking down stairs. *My hunter in the stairwell.* Several shuffled steps: he'd gotten to the between floors landing. And then they started again, descending.

I pressed my backside against the tiny light of the elevator button, covering it. I didn't want a peep of light to reveal me.

Not far away, I heard a door creak open. A match flame lit and a hand floated out of the doorway. Legs looking in before entering the floor. With his arm projected forward and his head still in the stairwell, he wouldn't be able to see me so close against the elevators.

Nevertheless, I had to scare him back. I seized my pistol from my pocket and fired it in his direction. The match and flame fell and the door shut. The spark of light slowly burnt out.

What would Legs do? Try to be silent? Risk sneaking out of the stairwell in darkness? Or would he burst in and rush across the floor, his gun blazing while presenting a fast-moving target?

It struck me that our odds were about equal. We were

both in close range. He was a gangster and had killed before. But I'd been a soldier. My training taught me to keep my cool. Wait for the enemy to make a mistake and provide me a target. Legs was a hothead.

I could hear the hum of the elevator below. Did that mean it was nearing? Or did its shaft conduct sounds from fathoms away? Could it be that the guard heard the gunshots and was coming to investigate? From forty stories below? And how would he know which floor?

I wished I could reach the indicator dial over the elevator to feel it and learn where it was. I considered that at this time of night, in this still half-finished building, it was unlikely I had summoned an elevator with a rider. No one else would be coming up. The elevator cab was on an express journey to rescue me.

I heard the nearby door creak again. Legs wouldn't know where I stood. All right, he had a general idea from the sound of my gunshot. I, on the other hand, knew where the stairway door was and where he would be in a moment.

He dove in, I heard him roll on the floor, making himself a small target. He fired my way, perhaps to illuminate me. I fired back, once. The second pull of my trigger clicked. Empty. He must have heard that sound. In the darkness, I heard him scramble to his feet. His footsteps calmly marched my way.

The elevator opened. Light. I threw myself inside before he had a chance to react. I slammed my right wrist against some floor buttons, any buttons and pressed myself to the side, out of the line of fire.

He ran in front of the elevator and fired twice more. As he was about to take better aim, I hurled my empty gun at him. He flinched, ducking it, allowing enough time for the doors to close.

I felt the elevator floor jerk beneath my feet as I began my descent. It took me a moment to realize that Legs could do nothing to stop my escape.

CHAPTER 36

Lorraine Priest

IN MY LIFE, I have visited several precinct houses. Some of those in Manhattan possess a classical architecture. In contrast, the Tenth Precinct station house looked like it belonged to a miserly landlord.

After freeing Gould from the back of the van, a cop cuffed Gould's wrists behind his back. His handler gave him a shove.

My officer unclipped me from the back of the van and secured the cuffs with my hands in front of me. A different rule for women? He pulled the chain hard, bruising me, tearing at my skin. I glared at him, wounded. He puckered his lips and popped a kiss in my direction.

At that moment I had an acute understanding why some people became criminals. I felt the urge to kill.

My jailer continued to tug me, dragging me along. A single step up brought us to the front door and inside the building. The first room we entered, something like a foyer, spanned the narrow-shouldered width of the building. My skin tingled. The space was overheated, even humid. Its walls sweated. The wallpaper was stained, yellow fingers trailing from the ceiling. Those blemishes were fringed with black mold. The room smelled of smut—the fungal kind.

An officer sat behind an elevated podium, more like a judge's bench. Behind him a hallway ended at a flight of stairs. "Booking?" he asked as Gould and I were guided in front of him.

"Straight away to the tanks," the officer to my side said. Gould was taken ahead of me. As he was marched up the stairs, the policeman piloting him banged him in the small of his back, trying to get him to stumble. Gould lunged forward but kept his balance. When it came my turn, I planted each foot solidly on the steps, in case my chaperone tried tripping me up.

For my trip to the Metropolitan Life Tower, I'd brought nothing more than a snap purse, figuring that, in the cold, I might need to drop a nickel to take the trolley over to the Chelsea. The police confiscated it before I got in the van and I realized, once again, I was broke. I needed to start hiding a bill in my shoes. *Ah!* A dime in my pocket. I squeezed it.

While standing at the top of the stairs, while Gould was herded off down a hall, a ham-fisted man patted me down, thumping my chest and butt. "Are you sure you ain't got yourself a weapon?" he asked.

"I'm sure."

"Would you like one? You're gonna needs it." He chuckled, and like the one before, he puckered his lips as though to kiss me. I wished I could smack him. All of them.

.   .   .

He led me to a hallway with two cells on either side, four in all. Not that they were all inhabited: in fact, the ladies—and there were a dozen of them—were all crammed into a single large cell at the end. The bars seemed thinner, flimsier than those I'd seen in the moving pictures. In Westerns and prison melodramas. I imagined a circus strongman could pry these apart.

"Stand aside girls," my chaperone said, raising his baton. The women shrank back. He unlocked the cell and pushed me in and then said, "Show me your bracelets."

I cupped my hands and offered up my wrists. He unlocked my manacles and drew them out through the bars. I turned around to face the women.

They were a mixed crowd. Some had skin-tight dresses and faces blushed and smeared with makeup, painted like tragic clowns: ladies of the evening. Some looked like street gang hangers-on, sneering tough and hands bunched in fists.

A moll stepped forward. "We got ourselves a society tramp," she said of me. "I bet her muff don't need perfume."

"I'll betcha it smells like strawberries," a lady of the night said.

I looked her straight in the eye and told her, "Thank you." I would not let them intimidate me.

She approached me. Standing nose to nose with me, she sniffed. I tried not to inhale, certain her breath smelled anything but fruit-like. She ended our encounter with a leer and backed away.

Among my fellow detainees, I was drawn to a lady separate from the others, one who shrank against the wall. She had that flapper look, as sexless as a twig. Beneath a sleeveless jacket, she wore a blouse that swallowed her thin body and a skirt that revealed her knobby knees.

Something in her coat pocket squirmed. She noticed that I noticed.

"I smuggled in a rat," she whispered to me. "I call him Milton. My dad's name. I can hold it out and keep the other ladies back. Good to launch at a face in case there's a rumble."

"I want to be on your side during a fight," I said.

"It's a deal," she answered, raising her hand for a shake. I was being flippant, but I suppose, standing all alone, she was eager for recruits. I winced, noticing several bite marks on her hand. She explained, "I rub Milton's gums with baking soda to make him look rabid."

I lifted my hand. "Lorraine," and we shook.

"Gabby. These gals here, they play tough, but they ain't the real McCoys. You got to watch out for the soldiers from the girl gangs. All muscle and mean."

As if summoned, the same guard who had led me to this cell, marched up to the door with two new ladies. They didn't wear handcuffs.

One had a hatchet face that seemed to have been recently taking whacks at a wood pile.

The other one had curly blonde hair that shot over the side of her head like a breaking wave. She parted her lips and teeth in a smile. She had a single-edged razor lying on her tongue.

They both wore gray pants and white pullover shirts, the sleeves cut off and ragged. No jackets.

The officer let them in and locked the door behind them. The other women drew back as though pressed by an invisible hand.

My nose drew back in a curl. They smelled of rotgut liquor, the kind that was equal parts alcohol and industrial solvent.

"Hey, chickadees, Lena and Boo have come to make merry," the hatchet-faced woman said. She was obviously in charge.

"Hey, Lena," a fellow inmate, braver than the rest, said and the hatchet-faced woman smiled. She wasn't hiding a razor in her mouth.

"Where we got a missy named Lorraine?" she asked.

"I am Lorraine," Gabby spoke up before I could. She was taking this partner thing seriously. I shot her a look of thanks.

Thanks quickly turned to dread as Lena plucked a razor from her waistband and fixed it between the knuckles of a fist. Her hand swayed like a cobra about to strike. Gabby sunk a hand in her pocket and drew out her rat, pinching it by its neck so it couldn't squirm and bite her. It did have foam on its mouth.

Boo circled behind Gabby, razor blade raised. I froze, transfixed by the sharp metal suddenly on display. Their weapons were small, but it didn't take a sword to cut a throat.

Just as Boo was about to strike, I cried, "I'm Lorraine."

Boo swerved and swung her razor, missing me as I flinched backward, banging up against the wall. I glanced wildly side to side. There was nowhere to escape the next swing of her blade.

Gabby hurled her rat and Lena swatted it midair. Milton landed with a roll among the feet of the cowering spectators and scurried to find shelter among them.

Were all of this precinct's police in on this? Maybe not. I might as well try to get help. As I opened my mouth to scream, several gunshots rang out from down the hall.

CHAPTER 37

Lorraine Priest

THE TUMULT outside my cell continued. More gun blasts and the husky screams of men. A thundering storm of feet, chaotic but moving in the same direction, rushed to some unseen location on the far side of the precinct house.

With all the sudden frenzy among the women in my cell, you would have thought the gunfire had been explosions, and British army cannons were pointing our way. With nowhere for protection, the horde of my fellow cellmates cried out and jostled one against the other, each vying to penetrate the center of the group. To be protected from bullets by using their fellow inmates as human shields. Gabby and I didn't dare move: Lena and Boo still pinned us to the wall.

With more gunfire, Lena and Boo refocused their attention. They pressed their faces against the bars as though to squeeze through and looked down the hall, desperate to see what was going on. "You got us in here," Lena called out, "what the hell you up to down there?"

Gabby dropped to her knees, crawled and jammed herself between the legs of the crowd of cowering women. That left me, alone and separate, my back pressed up against the wall, not wanting to move, not wanting to remind the razor blade women of my existence and hoping beyond hope that whatever madness was going on would get me out of this jam.

The gunfire abruptly ceased, but we could still hear the yells of men and the clang of metal on metal. A jailhouse riot?

Lena turned and sneered at me as though I was responsible. Gabby emerged from the forest of women's legs triumphant, Milton in her raised hand.

Now came the rumble of feet and the rush of what sounded like a mob, some clattering on stairs, all rushing down. A jailbreak. Then, to my astonishment, Abelardo Visconte marched down the corridor in front of the women's cells. With his hunchback and his massive presence, he looked like the bugbear from some folk tale. Lena and Boo shrank away from the bars. He had a thick-barreled key in hand, and I could only hope it fit our cell door.

"Miss Lorraine," he said in his deep timbre, "I have an ally in this station house. I had him sneak in a gun to the Italians in their cell, hoping to start a diversion. It worked." More shots. He glanced down the hall then jutted out his lower lip. "Perhaps too well." He inserted his key into the lock. "There are prisoners pouring out of the building. We have but a moment to join them."

The mere fact that Abelardo with his almighty presence had addressed me, provided me with a blessing of immunity. Boo and Lena parted to let me pass.

"I recommend that those of you with petty crimes stay behind," Abelardo said. "There may be repercussions for walking out this door."

I joined the hunchback in the hallway. Among the other women, only Gabby accompanied us. "We're a team," she told me, stuffing Milton back in her coat pocket.

"Come along, before Sullivan returns to the station. I have no doubt that he will restore the order and will be unrestrained in his retribution."

We rushed to the main room at the top of the second-floor stairs. Several police had batons and guns drawn. Everywhere pieces of furniture had been turned on their sides. A pair of Italians who had accompanied us in the paddy wagon crouched behind a thick oak table using it as a shield. One of them brandished a gun, keeping the police at bay.

Our brigade, two women and a man, barely drew attention. Abelardo led us down the stairs. No one seemed to inhabit the first floor. Perhaps the police were all one floor up, summoned to the battle. Perhaps those thundering feet had meant both a mass breakout and a herd of police who had gone chasing the fugitives.

Abelardo guided us to a motorcar, a Tin Lizzie. Ten years back, these Model Ts seemed like the only vehicle in existence. Already they looked like antiques. This one's motor had a fine rumble, and we pulled out along the squalid block of 51st Street, turning south at the corner onto Lexington to join a more civilized part of town. Immediately, I could see the crown of the Chanin Building with its multicolor light display in the distance.

"I can't go back to the Met Tower," Abelardo said. "They will hunt me down."

I thought of the Chelsea. A brooding hunchback? He would fit in with their Bohemian spirit. "You know the Chanin Building?" I said, instead. Perhaps Alan's meeting had run long and we could catch him there. "You can see it up ahead."

Abelardo nodded. He seemed so grim.

"Take us there."

That meant just continuing down Lexington.

"So, gal," Gabby said to me, "what did you do so criminal to get the coppers so hopping mad? I mean, what kind of fugitives are we?"

"Me?" I asked. "I …"

"I saw the police commit murder," Abelardo said, interrupting.

Gabby folded her arms and raised her shoulders as though only just now feeling the chill.

"Lyndon Warnecki?" I asked.

"Lynn Dawn," he said. "I had just come out of a drag bar. No, I am not among their fellowship, merely an admirer. I was there when she was arrested and knew quite well the Tenth Precinct and their petty games of shaking down drag players. I followed their wagon to the station where they set her free. She told me that she traded information for her liberation. I was set to take her to her place at the YMCA, but she had told me she had a meeting with a reporter."

"My husband."

As we waited at a light, Abelardo took a moment to eye me. I'd like to think he was assessing me with new respect, but I think he used the moment to connect the dots. "The one who wrote that piece in the *World?*"

I nodded.

"What Lynn Dawn told the police to gain her freedom must have been too damn toxic for them to leave her alone. They followed us. Lynn Dawn went into the wrecked building and after I saw the police pull up and follow her. I went inside to keep her safe. But in the dark and with all those corridors, when I came upon her, I was too late."

I said, "You were caught in a photo at the scene."

"I carried her body away and laid it out next to St. Agnes. She deserved a better resting place than a pile of rubble."

I took all this in, my stomach knotted. I glanced at Gabby. She seemed confused, not having had all the story. "A young man who shared the back of the paddy wagon with me," I said. "He told me the Tenth was rounding up the 'wrong' Italians. It's some mob maneuver against the older bosses now in charge."

"The Mafia," Abelardo said. "That's the Old World name for their crime organization. They often called themselves the 'Black Hand' here, although so did an assortment of rogue punks. I've seen the new generation. More coordinated. More domineering. Hungrier. More vicious."

I remembered that Gould the Ghoul was also with me in the back of the van. What had happened to him? Was he part of the jailbreak? Was he still in a pen in the Tenth Precinct?

I suppose I should rejoice at his comeuppance, but

Sergeant Sullivan can be particularly sadistic and, frankly, I don't get a kick out of vengeance. It doesn't change the past. Revenge is merely the loud echoes of cruelty in a world where brutality constantly shouts. Maybe I'm a pacifist.

Who knows? I imagined that Gould was trying to bargain his way out, promoting himself to triple agent.

Gabby spoke up, no doubt keen to fit her story in with ours to be equals. "I'm a nickel-a-dance girl," she said. "Ten cents if the customer wants a kiss, but never more than one. I got a copper who took me out to the alley. He wanted more. I scratched him. He cuffed me and left me on the alley floor for a time. That's where I found my friend Milton." She stroked the head of her pet. I felt a pang of pity for her meager life.

Abelardo pulled up in front of the Chanin Building.

CHAPTER 38

Alan Priest

When I was a slim thumb of a tyke, being hauled from town to town by a mother who toured with theatrical shows, I'd sneak out of our boarding room to present myself to the neighborhood as the new kid on the block. Lonely, desperate to find friends, I looked for someone to play with, for anyone who'd let me join them.

Being a new kid comes with a romance and a curse. I was considered exotic, having seen New York City and so many far-off places. I could tell the hicks tales of overhead trains and skyscrapers. I might as well have been describing knights on flying horses and castles in the sky. That was the romance. However, my appearance also acted as a threat to their already formed cliques. The young girls swooned over my cosmopolitan experiences and the boys responded with jealousy as though I was looking down on their bumpkin ways. Frankly, I was. Many of my ventures into the streets ended in fistfights.

When I returned to our rented room, my face smudged with dirt and my lips bloodied, my mother would inevitably say, "Look what the cat drug in." She never acted concerned, as though my injuries had come from a rough-and-tumble game of stickball.

Look what the cat drug in, I could hear her saying. I examined my face in the shiny brass plate of the elevator cab as I descended down the gullet of the Chanin Building headed to the lobby. My entire right side felt raw. I was a tenderized shank of beef ready for the backyard grill. My breaths came in shudders.

The floor indicator lights marched down. I felt seized by a sudden fear. What if Legs had caught another elevator and it was chasing this one? I pictured a broad elevator shaft with two cabs descending, one to the side of the other, both racing, the upper one gaining. I imagined the sound of that second elevator, whirring alongside mine. Our doors would open at the same time. A click as Legs pulled back the hammer on his gun.

Okay, I was just being paranoid. I shook off this image. It would take a while for Legs to summon another cab.

L. The lobby. The doors parted, revealing the cathedral-like first floor. The only person present was the same guard, leaning on the cane attached to his arm brace. The smile on his face collapsed as he stared with alarm at my disheveled figure.

I stepped out of my elevator and looked back at the overhead floor dial. Another cab was descending, only now passing the thirtieth floor. I thought of how long it would take. One minute?

Time enough to flee. Or. I asked the guard, "Do you know Legs Diamond?"

"I've read something of him."

"He attacked me. He's coming down in that elevator."

His eyes rose to read the dial above the elevator door. Twentieth floor and descending. His breath quickened.

"If you loan me your gun, I'll confront him," I said. "You can find a safe spot."

He drew his gun. "It's my job, sir."

The elevator counted down. Twelve … eleven … I asked myself, "What if it's not him? Someone else this dark hour?"

"Alan!" A voice behind me cried. I turned. Lorraine entered the lobby.

CHAPTER 39

Lorraine Priest

It seemed like ages ago since I'd stepped over the threshold of the Metropolitan Life Building. Even though that was a relatively new structure, being only twenty years old, it seemed old-fashioned compared to the Chanin Building skyscraper. This entryway concourse was marvelous, thrilling—I've never been to the great basilicas of Europe, but they must feel like this: like God was the architect.

My group, a towering hunchback, a nickel-a-dance girl and me, we must have seemed like a strange collection of humanity, and I thought that explained Alan's wild-eyed expression. No, something more was wrong. He looked like he'd slept a night in a trash can.

He shouted to me. His voice echoed across the vault of the room, "Legs Diamond is in the elevator. He'll be here in a moment. He just tried to kill me."

Gabby drew out her rat. Abelardo, more sensibly, pulled

out a pistol, the slender kind, one that until this moment he had hidden in his jacket pocket.

The only moving floor indicator was a semicircular dial. It crept down until it pointed all the way to the left. First floor. The lobby. Its doors parted.

Jack Diamond, gun in hand, stepped out, a smile on his face. He first pointed its barrel at Alan. When Alan did not reciprocate, he swung his pistol to target the guard. The guard, a cripple, leaned on the cane attached to his arm brace. It steadied his aim. "I recommend you holster your weapon," he said.

Legs didn't fire and instead focused on Abelardo and his pistol. He appeared to size up the situation: if he did shoot, he'd have to contend with return fire from two directions. Instead, he sensibly pocketed his gun. He strode by Alan and the guard as he whistled a tune. I recognized it as coming from *Die Dreigroschenoper,* a popular German musical, a song about a killer called Mack the Knife.

He tapped his fingers against his forehead as he passed me as a sort of salute, adding the two tones of a wolf-whistle to his melody. Gabby shook a hand in the air, waving to him. She pocketed Milton.

Distracted by Legs, I didn't notice Alan rushing my way until he was upon me, throwing his arms around me. I guessed I shouldn't have been so shocked by his kiss on my cheek. Even more shocking was how Abelardo pulled us apart. Alan shoved back.

"He's my husband," I said.

Gabby's eyes popped. "Oh!"

Alan looked over Abelardo, feet to haunches. "You're Abelardo. I remember you from Dreamland."

"And you are?" Abelardo asked in his resonant voice.

"I guess it's easy to forget a magician. Just a kid at the time."

"Albert … Alvin …"

"The Amazing Alan," my husband said, sketching a bow.

"Ah, yes, sleight of hand." Abelardo looked down at Alan's stump and shut his eyes, seeming to drink in the pain of the wound. "All of us are broken and endure."

"Tell me about it," Gabby said.

The building guard, leaning on his cane, tottered up next to us. I guess he felt he'd earned the right to know what was going on. Why not? "That Mr. Diamond. He's gone for good?" he asked.

"I suspect so," Alan said.

"We've found out what got Lyndon killed," I told Alan. "He learned about a plot by some of the Italian mobsters trying to take control. The police at the Tenth Precinct are in on it. They're rounding up the soldiers from the old gang before the new ones make their move."

Alan nodded in agreement. "It makes sense. Legs must be on the side of the insurgents. They are killing those who might know about the plot."

"But he only kidnapped me," I said. "He could easily have knocked me off."

"Yeah," Gabby added, as though she knew about my situation.

"They must have been trying to keep things on the hush," Alan said. "Maybe Legs figured that I'd spoken to Lyndon and planned to use you to keep me quiet. Or, maybe they were going to force you to call Rothstein and tell him everything was fine."

I imagined such a phone call. As though Legs could make me say what he wanted me to. I can be stupidly stubborn. Like Alan.

He said, "Still, they couldn't hold you for long. Which means the plans must be very advanced."

"The Italian in the police wagon said they were after Italians and Jews," I pointed out.

"Rothstein," Alan said.

"Rothstein," the guard echoed. "That man is a monster."

"There are much worse forces than Rothstein," Abelardo said. "He keeps the true darkness at bay." He spoke that with the deep voice of a prophet of doom.

"There's more to the story," Abelardo went on. "I was the reason Lynn Dawn went to meet you at the wreckage site. Ever since my job at Dreamland, I have loathed Mr. Reynolds. He was there when the park burnt to the ground. I believe he planned it, and then blamed it on careless workers. He even suggested that I had a part. I fit the public's imagination of a villain."

I squeezed Abelardo's hand.

He said, "I learned about his scheme to defraud Chrysler and told Lynn Dawn. He said he had a contact at the *World*."

"That was me," Alan said.

———

The four of us arrived at the Hotel Chelsea at 10 p.m., still early for a Saturday night. Alan considered Gabby and Abelardo to be in danger from those at the Tenth and promised to provide them a room for the night. I worried about his generosity and our finances. How long could jailbreakers—and that included me—afford to stay on the run in a city with Sullivan and his stooges?

Any concern that the Chelsea might turn Abelardo away disappeared when the desk clerk welcomed him by name. "Lardo! You've come to do some modeling?"

"Not for this visit. I'm here with a friend."

Abelardo, a model? Little did I suspect that he and I belonged to the same profession. Still, it made sense. He had a presence that would dominate a canvas. I imagined his brooding figure painted by a German expressionist or a hulking sculpture by Rodin.

"Are you still serving dinner?" Alan asked.

"You'll find comestibles on the buffet table."

Yummy. I could use a few choice comestibles.

Alan stretched side to side, perhaps squeezing out the pockets of pain from his bruising. "I'm calling up the *World*," he informed me, "to tell my bosses about Gould in case he's still locked up at the Tenth. I'm going to also ring up Rothstein to warn him, although I suspect he'll be hard to find at this hour of night."

Abelardo, Gabby, and I made our way to the dining room. A couple haunted a dark booth. A squinty-eyed scribbler bent over a corner table with a bundle of typewritten pages, marking them with a red pencil. A nodding drunk sat on a stool at the counter. He clutched an empty whiskey glass as though it anchored him from tipping over.

There on display atop a candlelit buffet table, a loaf of bread as large and as brown as a holiday turkey and blocks of sweating cheese. They seemed too good to be true: the mirage of food for my weary eyes.

A box radio sat on a side table in the corner of the room. It played, *"Can't Help Lovin' That Man."*

Abelardo said to Gabby, "As I recall, five cents a dance."

"And five cents for a kiss," she said.

He placed a dime on the table and scooted it her way. She stood and held out her hands. He took hold of one and wrapped an arm around her waist and leaned in. They stepped between the tables and swayed together. I would swear I heard Milton chirp with glee.

I sat down with my food, inhaled its aromas for a moment, then tucked a corner of the tablecloth into the vee of my blouse.

The drunk hailed me. "Hey, doll, you do any modeling?"

"Don't you call me, 'doll,'" Abelardo responded, intercepting the compliment. He winked my way and told the drunk, "My friend Gabby is a champion artist's model."

"Me?" she asked. Abelardo sealed her lips with a kiss. They lingered for more than a nickel's worth.

The music stopped and the radioman announced, "This is Gertrude Lawrence with *'Someone to Watch Over Me.'*"

I put a second dime on the table. "Have another whirl on me."

Alan returned and sat across from me, picked up my sandwich, and took a bite. "Chanin left me a message. His contacts informed him that Sullivan is KKK. That explains the sergeant's power. He has an invisible army of backers. The Klan often infiltrate positions of leadership and I'm guessing his allies extend to City Hall. I couldn't run down Rothstein. Perhaps he knows of the danger and is in hiding."

"And Gould?" I asked. After how he betrayed me, I suppose I should wish that he was rotting in jail.

"Gould made it out before reinforcements arrived, before Sullivan shut down the precinct station. He's at the *World*, bragging to his fellow reporters about his adventure and playing the hero."

God smiles on the fools of the *World*.

CHAPTER 40

Alan Priest

SUNDAY. God rested, but I suppose whipping together the Heavens and Earth in six days, he earned it. As for me, I headed to the *World:* my only creations are hacked-out stories.

Lorraine had long ago volunteered to serve as a greeter for a noontime rally for Roosevelt and Smith at Madison Square Garden. After that she was tasked with running down Rothstein. We agreed to meet up later at Lindy's Restaurant.

I reached the office to find Gould sitting on the edge of his desk in the middle of a cluster of reporters, spinning the yarns of his adventures. He glanced my way with daggers in his eyes. He knew I could destroy his entire tale. My fellow newsmen would take my word over his.

Leaving Gould to stew, I made myself comfortable in my chair. My tall, faithful Remington Electric awaited my brilliance. I fit a blank page into its carriage and rolled it into place. I released the carriage for a moment to align the page perfectly. One-inch margins.

I had thousands of words in me, perhaps tens of thousands. I opened my desk drawer and gathered a dozen more sheets to place on my desk. When that didn't seem enough, I added another dozen, squaring them.

I felt like a gunslinger, suiting up for a high noon duel. I looked around me. Just my stack of pages and my snake eyes were enough to gather the interest of my fellow reporters. They knew me and recognized when I was determined. They knew Gould and merely humored his fierce winds.

I began to type. My hand leapt from key to key, from side to side, flying about like popcorn on an uncovered pan. I sprinted at 48 words a minute, one-handed. The bell rang when I ended each line. Lyndon Warnecki, Lynn Dawn— Lorraine's discoveries. Mae West and the drag ladies. I completely forgot about the bruise that covered my entire right side.

I wrote about Sullivan and the Tenth Precinct, their association with the KKK, and how they rousted drag performers and how they chased down Lynn Dawn. Abelardo's statement on Lyndon's murder. How the police ran a secret operation rounding up the Italians in service of unknown mobsters. The recent murder of Salvatore D'Aquila and the hit on Joey Noes. The storm of mafia members being exiled by Benito Mussolini.

The Sunday editor, Yellen, recognized my seriousness. He split his time between his office and my desk, returning to scoop up new pages as they came off my typewriter. I paid no attention to his reactions as I pounded out line after line.

I wrote about Humpty Jackson and Abelardo Visconte. Gould's cowardice when he cooperated with those at the Tenth Precinct. The jailbreak. I wrote about Reynolds and his association with Legs Diamond and Reynolds' comments about using Diamond as muscle. I put together a first-person account of my showdown with Legs.

I tied it all together. The overthrow of the city's mob bosses was like the rise and fall of empires. I created a tableau as vast as the story of mankind. I wrote like a madman. After three hours, I totaled thirty double-spaced pages.

When I was done, I leaned back in my chair, and finally took a moment to acknowledge my surroundings. Yellen had returned my story and a half-dozen of my fellow reporters were poring over individual pages. It would take a labor of Hercules to restore the document to its proper order.

I noticed their faces. They seemed confused. Worried. They must have been reading them out of sequence. Where was Gould?

Yellen placed a hand on my shoulder. Never a good sign. "Can we talk in my office?"

Something was wrong. "Is it Lorraine?" I asked, following him. He closed the door.

"Have a seat." Another not-good sign.

"I'd prefer to stand."

He shuffled around and behind his desk. I didn't sit so he didn't sit. "I called up Mae West," he began. "She doesn't want to be associated with exposing her drag friends."

"Oh. We can change names. Anonymize it all."

"There are other problems."

My eyebrows rose. So did my Adam's Apple.

He dove right in. "We can't accuse a whole precinct of being KKK."

"Just the night shift," I corrected him. "Sergeant Sullivan. Irwin Chanin told me that."

"*The* Mister Chanin? Will he go on the record? Is his source air-tight?"

"I don't know." I considered the matter. He might not want to risk exposing his source. To risk personal retaliation. His building was in the Tenth Precinct. Being Jewish, he might be a particular target for the Klan. "Okay, it's an exaggeration to say the lot of them are KKK. Still Gould can verify parts of this." I regretted that the moment it came from my mouth.

"And what about your claim that 'unknown Italians' are taking over the New York underworld?"

I gritted a smile. Okay, that one was a bit vague.

"And you say Salvatore D'Aquila, a cheese importer, was actually the most powerful mob boss in New York?"

"Rothstein told me."

"And he'll go on record?"

Never. He would never squeal, not publicly, not even on his worst enemies. Yellen had to know about the gangster's code. "D'Aquila was *il capo di capo*," I said. "Chief of chiefs. For seventeen years he ruled the New York Mafia. He was assassinated in a gangland hit."

"Shot to death on the street, that much is for certain. We reported as much. Listen, Alan, you're an excellent reporter."

I was about to be patted on the head.

"Some of this is very usable. Your identification of Lyndon Warnecki." Lorraine's doing. "Your personal battle with Legs Diamond reads like thrilling fiction. And the fact that Lorraine's kidnapping took place in front of a variety of reliable witnesses, or, if not reliable, at least the Algonquin group has prominent people. That confirms your particular connection with him. We'll run that story tomorrow, front page along with the fact that the corpse in the ruin was Lyndon Warnecki, dressed as a female artist, but no more until you work further on … those other parts. Legs, unlike Reynolds, isn't going to sue us."

I took a moment to digest this.

"And, Alan …"

"Uh-huh?"

"About those other parts. The fall of the Roman Empire? The end of the Mayan civilization? A bit heavy-handed."

When I returned to my desk, I found my pages placed in a ragged stack, held in place by a gum eraser. Atop was a message. "Rothstein attends a poker game at the Park Central each Sunday night. Room 349. H.S."

Herbert Swope.

CHAPTER 41

Lorraine Priest

THE RALLY AT MADISON GARDEN, two days before the election, was filled with fellow fanatics, Democrats cheering on Smith and Roosevelt. I personally met up with Roosevelt's wife, Eleanor, a gracious but somewhat shy woman, and with their five children. A short distance away, Franklin himself struggled with his braces to rise to his feet, the force of his will overcoming his decrepit legs. When he flashed that famous smile? I think he was wincing.

From three o'clock on, I camped out at Lindy's restaurant. I was determined to see Rothstein. The restaurateurs told me that no one was seeing the big boss. They tried to give me the bum's rush, so I ordered iced tea after iced tea, insisting, loudly, that I was just an ordinary customer and had a right to be there. They even sent Icepick down to persuade me to go. They figured that we had some sort of connection. We did have. Some sort.

Icepick was such a massive, blocky man he could have

been fit with a motor and turned into a steam shovel. When he sat on the bench across from me, he made a loud thud and the wood creaked.

"Missy Marquette, the boss don't want to see anyone now, and he told me to twist your arm to get you to leave, only I don't want to twist your anything or hurt you. So go. Now."

While Icepick is not much of a conversationalist, the easiest way to distract him from a task was to engage him in a conversation. I asked him, "How did you get your start as an enforcer?"

"Huh?"

"An assassin?"

"I don't …"

"A killer."

"Oh!" That perked him up. "I had me a good friend, Cal, and we was on the street and not eating much, and he took care of me, and we made money killing pigeons, and then we just killed people."

Which explained everything and nothing. I asked myself how one set of murderers inspired so much disgust in me while Icepick always seemed so pitiful. Was I completely losing my moral compass? My head hurt. Too much iced tea. Thankfully, at that moment, Alan came through the door.

"I have an address for Rothstein," he said.

Thank God. I had to get out of there. And do what? Warn a mob boss to keep him safe?

. . .

"Why?" I asked Alan as we stepped out onto Broadway and turned the corner to connect to Seventh Avenue. "Why should we bother warning Rothstein?"

"Because murder is wrong?"

The fact that Alan phrased that as a question: it seemed as though he hadn't convinced even himself.

"Because in gangland wars innocents die," he added.

A little better. I leaned into my husband, against his left side, the one that was not so bruised and tender, and wrapped an arm around his shoulder. I squeezed and he rested his head on mine. Not the easiest for walking, but we managed.

The Park Central Hotel takes up half a city block. Two towers, one on either wing, are joined by a skirt of three floors and massive shoulders which span a recessed rear. It has a face of brown brick. I looked up, counting the floors.

Alan must have read my lips. "Twenty-five," he said.

I imagined it had a thousand rooms.

We were sensibly set to enter through the lobby, but when we came to the intersection of an alleyway, we saw Arnold Rothstein holding his gut and stumbling toward us. The alley was poorly lit save for a single door which spilled out a yellow light, framing a man in a chef's white coat. The chef said, "I called for an ambulance."

Rothstein's head was bowed. He looked up to Alan and me with a twisted smile on his face. "Lorraine, Alan. I hope you're having a better night than mine." Alan reached out to grasp an elbow, but Rothstein waved him off. He walked past us.

On the sidewalk, as he passed beneath the streetlamps, I could see the extent of his wound. Blood had soaked his shirt. It continued all the way down his left pant leg, and was dripping from his cuff onto his shoe. He staggered to a Yellow Cab. Before the cabbie reacted, Rothstein opened the passenger's side door.

"I was shot," he told the terrified driver. "It's not contagious." In Rothstein's line of work, it was.

"Who did this, Arnold?" Alan called after him.

"You don't know me by now?" he responded. "I'm no rat." He ducked inside the cab. "Stuyvesant Polyclinic," he announced, "I believe that's the closest."

He shut the door, and the cab sped off.

Alan grabbed my hand. "Come along." He drew me into the alley. "This is one of the biggest stories of the year."

We rushed to the door where the chef stood.

"I'm a reporter for the *World*. What's your name?"

"Bill Woods."

"Easy to spell. What did you see?" Alan asked while pulling me past the man. We entered into a long kitchen.

"He just came bursting through the door from the service hall," Woods said. "I asked him, 'What happened?'"

"And what did he say?"

"He said, 'I cut myself shaving.'"

Alan and I followed a trail of blood down an aisle between preparation counters. A boy with a mop was already swabbing the blood-stained floor. We stepped by him, continuing into an anonymous hallway. The blood trail stopped at a service elevator. Alan pressed the call button.

Having dragged me along, now that we paused, Alan

massaged my hand. I suspected it was to relieve his nervousness as much as mine.

"What if the shooter is still hanging around?" I asked.

"Shooting Rothstein? He's run for the hills." We could hear the hum of the approaching elevator. "We might have to stop to check every floor."

"His poker game was on the third," I said. "We can try there first. Why do you suppose he took the back way out?"

"Probably worried about a follow-up crew out front."

The elevator arrived. Alan stepped in front of me and yanked open the door. He does this to prove that his one hand doesn't limit him. We stepped inside and he shut the door behind us. I felt as though lately I've spent all-too-much time in these boxes.

Although summoning the elevator was automatic, the floor selection came via a lever. Alan pulled it up and we began our ascent. There was a puddle of blood on the elevator rug. We shuffled away from it, paying it respect.

"No bodyguard with him," Alan commented.

"Maybe we'll find one dead."

Third floor. Alan leveled the control, and we came to a stop. I opened the door. The trail of blood continued down the hall. As to which room, that was obvious from first glance. A sentinel stood outside a door. Short, thin, serious, he wore a loose-hanging suit, the sort that allows an easy draw from an inside holster. Could this have been the shooter? *No.* As Alan said, he had fled to the hills.

Walking down the hall, I counted room numbers up to his post, up to Room 349. To where the blood took a turn beneath the door sill.

"We've been invited," Alan told the guard. Such a bluff, so calm and matter-of-fact; he'd be a whiz at poker.

The guard patted down Alan and then me, not respecting my lady parts. He tapped the door twice with his knuckles, probably a signal that it was a friendly visit.

The door parted enough to allow me to see into the front room where four card players sat around a large table with wads of paper in the kitty. I've been a hanger-on at this type of high-stakes game. They played with IOUs, "markers."

"They say they were invited," the guard relayed to those at the table.

"You believed 'em and showed 'em our mugs?" one of the men said. Lean-faced, he sported a rich man's clothes: an immaculately tailored suit with a pink carnation over his vest pocket. The others seemed to have been there for days. They wore rumpled suits and dead-eyed stares, the kind I've seen in slot-coin junkies who haunt Liberty Bell machines. The small matter of a shooting wasn't about to stop their game.

As the guard was about to shut the door on us, Alan called out, "What happened to Rothstein?"

"He cut himself while shaving," the man with the carnation said.

CHAPTER 42

Alan Priest

I HAD the story of the year. Rothstein, the King of New York. Untouchable. He had a gut wound. He might survive for a time, but with that much blood lost and coming infections, his death was near-guaranteed. I used a hotel pay phone to call the *World* desk and caught Yellen, giving him the basic details. I asked him to send some reporters to Park Central for follow-up and to talk to the police. To send someone to Stuyvesant Polyclinic: I might be the only outsider who knew where he'd been taken.

"And don't include Gould," I said.

"Gould is slumped over his desk, dead drunk."

Lorraine and I took a taxi to the *World*. I urgently wanted my story on paper, fresh from my mind, a reparation that would make up for my overwrought reporting earlier in the day.

I stationed Lorraine at a second typewriter, asking her to compose her own account.

It took me an hour to pound out five pages. I was proud of my work. Clear-visioned, every moment had been seared into my mind. I didn't have to tell the whole of the story, the other reporters would fill in crucial details. The police statements. Whether or not Rothstein was still alive.

I was even prouder of Lorraine's writing. Understated, direct. *You are there.* Everyone who read it would shiver and say, "Wow."

Yellen, who had stayed on well past his work hours, read my pages and gave me a silent nod. He said, "With Rothstein's shooting, we're pushing the account of your gunfight with Mr. Diamond to page two."

I nodded, exhausted. I'd lived three lifetimes in the past few days.

Yellen said, "I received a call from William Reynolds. He already knew about Rothstein. He wants to meet with you and Lorraine for a truce."

"A truce?" I was skeptical.

Yellen stuck out his lower lip and shrugged. "He says he has a lot to offer."

"When?" Lorraine asked.

"Tonight."

"This late?" I asked. I glanced at Lorraine to share my puzzlement. "Why?"

"He said he wanted the cease-fire to start immediately. Before more stories came out."

"Where do we meet?"

"He said, 'At the gate to Dreamland.'" *Dreamland?* The beginning of all my nightmares. Burnt to the ground. Now a big, empty space.

"Sounds like a trap," Lorraine said.

When I last met with Reynolds, he'd dug himself a deep hole. Maybe if I gave him another chance, I'd have what I needed to sink him forever. "Tell him in two hours," I said. Time to change clothes. I promised myself again that I'd rustle up a gun.

"I'll call Santarelli and ask him to join us," Lorraine said. "To watch our backs."

When Lorraine and I returned to the Chelsea, Abelardo insisted on coming along. He offered to be our muscle. Running down a gun at this time on a Sunday night proved to be a fool's errand. Off to Dreamland. Judgment Day.

———

I'd visited the stretch of land that had been Dreamland exactly once after it had been leveled by its great fire, that being just after coming home from the war. At that time the empty lot had become a trampled-down meadow where children played baseball. To either side, independent amusement rides sparkled and roared.

When I'd gone to war, barely a man, I could inhale and exhale the world. I looked at the stars and believed my domain extended as far as my senses.

Before I'd ever reached the war front, while marching with my fellow soldiers along muddy roads, I saw men on pallets being taken the other way. Blistered and blinded, their heads wrapped in bandages, their breathing rattled and they coughed up blood. Mustard gas had stolen their eyes and lungs.

I learned how, as foot soldiers, we were there to be stepped on like bugs, as though we were no more than juice and shells. Like a woman carrying a stillborn infant, I returned from war with a dead child inside me. It felt as though the children playing in the trampled-down field of Dreamland were mocking me.

That was then. Meadows grow to cover the scars of battlefields. In New York, ultimately, meadows give way to tar. In the years since my last visit, Dreamland had been turned into a massive municipal parking lot, a testament to the recent dominance of the motor car.

Once upon a time, a giant angel loomed over the entrance to Dreamland. The path inside meant passing beneath her watchful eyes. Made of papier mâché, she ended her existence in flames.

To her side was Bostock's Arena. Its one-armed lion tamer was one of the most famous entertainers in the world. Beyond that, *The Story of Creation,* a living tableau with a naked Adam and Eve providing a stern and titillating Biblical lesson. Ahead, in the center of the dream, a spire to rival the Tower of Babel.

A metal, hip-high fence prevented automobiles from entering the parking lot anywhere but through paid access. A long, loose chain hung across the formal entrance. A measly attendant's booth was the tallest structure in the vast vacant space.

Midnight. Lorraine, Abelardo, and I stood on Surf Avenue by the entryway.

This being November and off-season, the major parks were closed. The lights of distant, independent rides winked. Their glow slathered the pavement. A stray wet dog loped by, leaving that familiar odor of damp fur in its wake.

Down the street, a truck approached, a great hulking dark wagon. Its only light: the glowing cigar tip of the driver. Only one possibility: Sergeant Sullivan. This meeting was to be a truce?

The paddy wagon pulled up in front of us. Only then did its headlights flare, temporarily blinding us. I supposed that Sullivan liked the dramatic effect.

I made out the doors to either side spreading like wings. The shapes of three men. Sullivan, the most massive of the group. I recognized Reynolds by his silhouette. Bent with age, he had the posture of a vulture. He proceeded ahead of the others. Then the third one came into view: Legs Diamond.

Sullivan drew his pistol. In my mind's eye, he always held a gun. Legs drew his.

Reynolds approached us. "Lorraine, Alan," he said, "and you are Abelardo."

The giant nodded.

"From the days of Dreamland," Reynolds went on. "Your frame is hard to forget. Let's take a walk."

With a wave of his arm, we were invited to go first, guns at our backs. He held out a flashlight, illuminating a spot of ground before us.

Lorraine, then Abelardo, and then I stepped over the chain.

My right half still felt the pain from my fall in the Chanin Building and I arched to the side as I walked. I should have been afraid. Very afraid. Still, I couldn't help but feel that this was a prelude to something more. Or else why wouldn't they have simply shot? The night was dark enough, the location, lonely. No witnesses.

Lorraine seemed calm. "We were supposed to discuss a truce," she said.

"Absolutely, a truce," Reynolds said. "But on my terms."

I heard the chain rattle behind me and the stumble of a foot as someone failed to step completely over it. "And these two goons are the enforcers of your terms?" I asked. "Mr. Diamond? Sergeant Sullivan?"

Legs and Sullivan remained quiet. Reynolds spoke, "I've given the chiefs at your news rag some precious information and they have promised to leave me alone. I will need that same promise from you."

"I intend to write that you are a member of the Ku Klux Klan," I said. It was a guess, but not much of a guess. His hatred of immigrants and so many other people. His work with Sullivan. "So, I suspect that, to get the *World* off your back, you named names of some of those in your secret society." Ralph Pulitzer, in particular, carried on a crusade against the Klan. He would let Reynolds off the hook for some choice intelligence.

"What the …?" Sullivan said. "You wouldn't—?"

"—Don't pay attention to his speculations," Reynolds said. "He's trying to turn us against one other."

He didn't deny the allegations. I heard Legs chuckling. I had the impression that there was more than one agenda taking place.

"With Rothstein falling, the entire face of the mob rackets will change," Reynolds said. "Including the protection of my properties."

And the mobsters' job of busting construction unions, I thought.

"We don't need to be enemies," Reynolds said.

We trekked along where there once had been a promenade called the West Walk, down past where they had the Infant Incubators and the Dog and Monkey Show.

Reynolds' flashlight beam swung side to side across the pavement. We came upon a roped off area and before us, a pit.

"A sinkhole," Reynolds explained. "After the fire, I filled in the crater that made up the subterranean chambers of Hell's Gate. The dirt settled and began to collapse."

"How deep is it?" I asked.

"I don't know. The original excavation was thirty feet." He aimed the flashlight beam into the pit. The bottom remained unseen.

"Forty feet," Abelardo said. He had worked down there.

Lorraine folded her arms across her body and squeezed herself. She was probably thinking what I was thinking. This was to be our grave. "And why are you showing us this?" she asked.

"To prove the sincerity of my accord," Reynolds said as though his meaning was obvious. "Legs?"

Legs stepped behind Sullivan and pointed his pistol at the man's back. "Drop your heater, bud," the mobster said.

Sullivan didn't move, holding on to his gun.

"You see," Reynolds said, "Legs and I are willing for bygones to be bygones. The sergeant here is not the kind to let go. A little human sacrifice will demonstrate our goodwill."

Sullivan twisted his head to the side, his neck bones

popping. "If you shoot me and I don't go and immediately drop, you will be dead in a minute. All of you."

"Shoot his spine," Reynolds said. "Make him crawl."

Legs shook his head. "That's chancy. Any slim move and I's bound to miss the mark."

Sullivan jolted to the side and Legs shot, striking Sullivan in his flank. The sergeant spun around and launched one of his massive fists at Legs's kisser and when Legs ducked, Sullivan directed his gun at the killer's chest.

Legs flew in and wrapped his arms around Sullivan, a boxer's clinch, only there was no referee to break them apart. Sullivan returned the favor by squeezing Legs who, being much smaller, struggled to stay on his feet. The sergeant's hand with his gun was behind Legs's back. He shifted his arm to aim his revolver at the back of his opponent's head.

Abelardo joined in, seizing Sullivan's hand, separating his fingers and wrenching the gun free. Sullivan lifted Legs from the ground and stepped toward the pit.

"Oh, don't do that." Santarelli's voice came from behind us. He stepped out of the dark and pressed his gun to the back of Sullivan's head.

"Gilberti," Lorraine said. "I was wondering when you would get here."

"I have been following your parade awaiting my moment to intervene."

"Is this it?" Sullivan asked. "A slug to the brain from a gutless dago?"

Abelardo struck out, grabbing Santarelli's gun hand, repeating the twisting motion he'd used on Sullivan.

Santarelli fired one shot into the air and then lost hold of his pistol. The police lieutenant nursed his wrist.

"This is my battle," Abelardo said. He squared off with Sullivan who was all too happy to let go of Legs and raise his fists. "For Lynn Dawn."

"Who?" Sullivan said, but didn't wait for an answer. He made the first punch, a right directed at the giant's chest. Merely a feint, it stopped short, but his left fist slammed against the giant's ribs, rocking Abelardo to the side. Abelardo swung back with lightning speed connecting below Sullivan's temple.

The sergeant stepped back, swiveled his jaw, and shook off the blow. He spit a gob of blood and grew a smile. He then undertook a strange ritual, lowering his fists to his waist and then pounding one on top of the other, switching back and forth as his fists ascended the empty air. Finally, with his fists cocked in front of his face, he dipped his head and leaned forward ready to strike. "You're big," he said. "But big doesn't kill."

That was not strictly true as Sullivan quickly found out. Abelardo rushed at him, taking a jab to the chin before he plowed against the sergeant. He drove Sullivan backward to the edge of the pit of Hell's Gate before letting go.

Sullivan teetered. Abelardo grabbed one of his shoulders, steadying him for the moment and, with his other hand, delivered a punch to the sergeant's face. Sullivan tried to wriggle free from the giant's grasp. He launched one strike after another against Abelardo's chest, but unbalanced, couldn't deliver the full force of his blows. Finally, he broke free from Abelardo's pinch-hold. When he did, he tipped over backward. From the length of the pause before the thud, I estimated his journey to have been thirty feet down.

Groans and rasping breaths rose up from the hellhole. Legs walked up to the edge of the pit and fired several shots down, each impact eliciting a grunt. Then only silence.

"There," Reynolds said, as though the outcome had been foreordained. "You have a sacrifice sealing our truce. I've given Mr. Pulitzer the names of ten prominent local Klan members, including an alderman who serves a Jewish district."

"Mr. Reynolds," Santarelli said, retrieving his gun, "you are under arrest for planning the murder of Sergeant Mitchell Sullivan."

"And will you arrest Abelardo for throwing him in the pit?" Reynolds said. "And Mr. Diamond for finishing him off?"

Santarelli and I exchanged looks. As a practical matter, we had to consider that Legs held a gun and was unlikely to surrender.

"Let's step away from this unfortunate ending," Reynolds said.

Unfortunate? It was the exact ending that he had planned.

Still, taking it all in, I had to agree with him. The loss of Sullivan was a boon to the world. The arrest of Abelardo would be a tragedy.

Santarelli raised both his hands as though in surrender, his gun pointed at the sky. Finger off the trigger, he lowered his weapon and holstered it.

"Let's go home," Lorraine said.

CHAPTER 43

Lorraine Priest

THREE MONTHS AGO, on Election Night, Tuesday, November 6, Herbert Hoover won the presidency over Al Smith, man of the people. The public didn't want a populist with a conscience. They wanted the wild prosperity of the twenties to go on and on. All of them were millionaires, at least in their dreams. At least according to the stocks they owned in Australia tin mines.

Arnold Rothstein dreams no more. On election night he won his half-million dollar bet on Hoover and lost his battle to stay alive. A gambler named McManus was charged with his murder. The motive, Rothstein had an unpaid gambling debt. From what I've read, the evidence seems flimsy and those from the poker game claimed they saw nothing. I doubt he'll be convicted.

Rothstein killed over an unpaid debt? That seemed too trivial. He had to be the victim of a war between the gods.

On the other hand, Alan says that, if it were a mob hit, there would have been several shots.

Roosevelt won the governor's race by the slimmest of margins. Strange how history can depend on a handful of votes. Maybe I helped sway a few of those.

The death of Sullivan went unsolved. *Good.* Otherwise, a certain secret society might be targeting all those involved, including Alan and me. Otherwise, Abelardo might be arrested and Santarelli would have gotten in trouble for keeping quiet.

The City of New York dealt with the rat's nest of the Tenth Precinct the way they do best. They renamed the station. Okay, they did promote Santarelli to Captain and put him in charge. I heard that Chanin pulled some strings to make that happen.

Gabby and Abelardo are still an item. When I asked them whether they were going to get married, Abelardo answered, "Marriage is a dying institution."

"In twenty years, no one will be married," Gabby added in agreement.

The Marx Brothers are splitting their time between Broadway and Queens, the latter being where they are filming a talkie. Margaret Dumont continues to work with them.

For her latest movie role, Gail Collinswood, my mother-in-law, played the part of a suffering scrub lady, fretting over her wayward daughter who succumbed to the glamour of Hollywood. The Academy of Motion Picture Arts (and Sciences!) has announced that they are starting an award for filmmakers and performers, and word is out that my mother-in-law's acting is prizeworthy. I've also heard they also plan to give an award to that dog, Rin-Tin-Tin.

Mae has yet to give in to the siren call of the talkies.

Chanin installed a 200-seat auditorium on the 50th floor of his building, the highest theater in the world, built for his employees to watch films and plays.

With no direct threat remaining, Alan and I moved back into our apartment. It felt good to be home and we re-christened our place with lovemaking, again and again.

———

A pair of manila envelopes arrived in the morning mail, both addressed to Alan. One read, Hoover, Washington, DC —that is, John Edgar, the head of the Bureau of Investigation, not the president to be. Alan had bundled up a collection of his research as to what comprised the mob network of New York, items which the *World* had deemed too speculative to print.

Alan tore the envelope open. It contained the same thick pile of papers that Alan had sent off. Scrawled on the front page in cramped letters: There is no such thing as organized crime. *-JEH*

Alan flipped through the pages to find further comments. None.

The second envelope had its return address stamped in the upper left corner:

Black Mask Magazine
25 West 45th Street, New York

Alan had spoken of this publication with reverence. They were the home for two-fisted action stories. He especially sang the praises of Dashiell Hammet and his detective, The Continental Op.

The thickness of the envelope said that his story had been returned. Alan broke open the seal with care.

Paper-clipped to his story was a handwritten note. It read, "Excellent effort. Too overwrought. Sorry to decline. Please send more. *Cap Shaw.*"

Alan looked as happy as I imagined he would for an acceptance. "A personal note from Shaw?" he said. "That's like Hemingway giving his blessing."

As I mentioned, Alan had spoken of this publication with reverence. I listened. I had yet to tell him I'd sent to Black Mask my account of Rothstein's murder. Shaw wrote me an acceptance. I had been waiting to tell Alan in the hopes he'd receive news that we were both to be published.

I wasn't about to turn down Shaw, not to salve Alan's ego. That's not my personality. But how was I going to break the news?

I started with a kiss.

AUTHOR'S NOTE

Many of the characters and events in this story are fictional and any resemblance between them and reality is coincidental. Alan, Lorraine, Gilberti Santarelli, Gail Collinswood, Jessie Gould, Abelardo Visconte, Gabby, Icepick, Sergeant Sullivan and Bergen are wholly creations.

Other characters were real and populated New York in the 1920s.

The Algonquin Circle was a famed group of writers and actors who met regularly for extended booze-filled lunches at the Algonquin Hotel on 44th Street. In this novel, thumbnail portraits were presented of Robert Benchley, Robert Sherwood, Alexander Woollcott, George S. Kaufmann, Edna Farber, and Dorothy Parker.

Perhaps Dorothy Parker, beautiful and serpent-tongued, best exemplified the group. Among her memorable sayings, "I'd rather have a bottle in front of me than a frontal lobotomy." In regard to men seducing women, she proclaimed, "Candy is dandy, but liquor is quicker." When she was late writing her newspaper column because of her honeymoon, she sent a note to her editor, "Too fucking busy and vice-versa."

Mae West was a Broadway and Hollywood star, play- and screenwriter, and provocateur. She developed for herself a unique personality for her time: a commanding presence with a sizzling sexuality. For her, men were … accessories.

After spending years working the vaudeville circuit, during the mid- to late-twenties she made a name for herself with her a series of scandalous plays that featured a broad-minded take on sexuality: *Sex* (1926), *The Drag: A Homosexual Comedy* (1927), *The Pleasure Man* (1928), and *Diamond Lil* (1928).

When *Drag* was set to debut on Broadway, the powers that be decided that they had had too much of her provocations and her play *Sex* was raided by the police. A new law was passed: theaters that ran such filth could be shut down for a year.

In her eighties, sixty-seven years after her Broadway debut, she starred once again as a sex siren, this time in the film *Sextette* (1978).

During her career, she coined many famous double-entendres that are still spoken today, such as "Is that a gun in your pocket or are you just happy to see me?" and "It's not the men in my life, it's the life in my men."

By coincidence in the melting cauldron that was Manhattan, during the time of this story, Mae West lived in the same building as did Legs Diamond.

Her sister, Beverly, and her lawyer, manager, chauffeur and lover, James Timony, are much as depicted in this novel.

The Marx Brothers were to comedy what The Beatles

were to music: immensely popular and wildly creative. For a brief time five of the brothers performed together: Groucho (Julius), Chico (Leonard), Harpo (Adolph), Zeppo (Herbert), and Gummo (Milton). Gummo dropped out before the group made it big on Broadway. The four Marx Brothers first scored a hit with *I'll Say She Is,* (1924), then with *Cocoanuts* (1926), followed by *Animal Crackers* (1928). With the advent of talking pictures, they took their act to the movie screen.

Harpo, who is featured in this story, never spoke in his film and stage productions. By all accounts, he was the gentlest in spirit of the Marx Brothers, the others being abrasive, compulsive gamblers, and womanizers.

As Groucho Marx described her, Margaret Dumont was "practically the fifth Marx Brother." Beginning in 1925, she starred with the Marx Brothers in two Broadway plays continuing on with seven motion pictures, working with them until she was in her late fifties.

Thomas "Humpty" Jackson and his wife Bella were much the same as described in this novel. Humpty, a hunchback, ran a Gas House gang at the turn of the century. His center of operations was the 11th Street Cemetery where he ruled from a roost atop a gravestone. During a stint in jail, he learned to love classic literature. He quit the gangster business and opened a pet store on the southern end of Harlem where his woman helped keep him straight.

For most of the 1920s in New York, Arnold Rothstein served as the king of the underworld. The ultimate fixer, he owned politicians, police, and judges. An inveterate gambler, he was said to have rigged the 1919 World Series.

On Sunday, November 4, 1928, he was called to the

Park Central Hotel where his regular poker circle met. What happened there remains unclear: beyond the fact that he was found at the service entrance, shot. Rothstein survived for two days, dying on election night; his half-million dollar bet on Hoover's win went uncollected. A gambler, George McManus, was charged with the crime, but the evidence proved flimsy. Shortly after his death, Arnold Rothstein's personal papers, filled with information on bribes and blackmail, disappeared.

His widow, Carolyn Green Rothstein, wrote a book about her husband and his murder called *"Now I'll Tell."* It was made into a film starring Spencer Tracy as Arnold.

Arnold Rothstein's death helped pave the way for a restructuring of New York's organized crime scene. The Mafia would be headed by the Five Families, bringing about the extinction of the old guard, derisively referred to as the "Mustache Petes."

Jack "Legs" Diamond, born in Philadelphia, was for a time a loyal lieutenant to Arnold Rothstein. Handsome and vicious, he epitomized the character of a suave killer. After surviving several assassination attempts, he quit New York City to move his gangsterism to Albany. He was shot to death on December 18, 1931, probably by rival mob members. His murder went unsolved.

Irwin Salmon Chanin built the Chanin Building, a marvel of art deco, topping off the building in October of 1928, and officially opening it in January of 1929. In the timeline of this novel, the interiors of several stories were still incomplete.

A humanitarian, Chanin had a philosophy of building for the people. His Green Acres housing project in Valley

Stream, New York, included open spaces for families to recreate and enjoy nature.

William P. Reynolds is more of an enigma than the other real characters in this novel. His life story is available only in glimmers of achievements, indictments, and disasters. He was the architect of Dreamland, a deliriously surreal amusement park. He was the builder of the opulent Long Beach Hotel which also spectacularly burnt down. He helped build the city of Long Beach, New York and tried to keep out minorities and Catholics. He regularly ripped off his investors. He became mayor of Long Beach until he was found guilty of embezzling funds. That his racism extended to being a member of the Klan is speculation on my part.

Throughout the 1920s, Herbert Bayard Swope and the heirs of Joseph Pulitzer ran the *New York World*. It was a remarkable paper for its time: populist, crusading, and sophisticated. It had a reputation as the premium of newspapers and a destination for the best of writers. Although Ralph Pulitzer was the responsible son and the driving force of the paper, Joseph Pulitzer, Sr., deeded most of his fortune and control of his estate to his incautious son, Herbert. In 1931, Herbert helped sell off the *New York World*, ending a great enterprise, with 3,000 losing their jobs.

On the one hand, the Pulitzers did award an unusual number of Pulitzer Prizes to their *New York World* employees. On the other hand, their paper did demonstrate the highest standard of journalism. Herbert Swope was the recipient of the first Pulitzer Prize for journalism. After Ralph Pulitzer's death in 1939, his wife, Margaret Leech, went on to have a successful career as an author, twice winning the Pulitzer Prize in History.

Historic buildings are as important to this story as are the historic characters. Four buildings are prominently featured: the Chanin Building, the Hotel Chelsea, the World Building, and the Metropolitan Life Tower. The soon-to-be Chrysler Building also serves as a backdrop.

Beginning in the late 19th century, Reverend Charles H. Parkhurst acted as a religious firebrand fighting political corruption and crime in New York. In 1906, his church was torn down to make way for the Metropolitan Life Tower.

In exchange for the land, the infamous architect, Stanford White, designed a new church for Parkhurst just one door down. Parkhurst lived to see that church also demolished. It was demolished in 1919 to make way for Metropolitan Life's expansion into their north building.

The Metropolitan Life Tower was briefly the tallest building in the world. Its clock faces are larger than those of Big Ben. Among massive, hour-ringing bells, its are still the world's highest.

The Hotel Chelsea has a remarkable history as an artist's colony, being the temporary home to many of the greatest painters, sculptors, authors, songwriters, and musicians now for a century-and-a-half, from Mark Twain to getting a call-out in Taylor Swift's *Tortured Poets* album. The poet Dylan Thomas died in the hotel, drinking himself to death.

From 1890 to 1895, the World Building, the home of the *New York World*, stood as the tallest building in New York and as the tallest office structure in the world. It was destroyed in 1955 to make way for new ramps accessing the Brooklyn Bridge.

Catty-cornered across from the Chrysler Building, the

Chanin Tower was the first to represent a move by the architects of skyscrapers from downtown to midtown Manhattan. It was for a time, the fourth tallest building in the world and it was the first major U.S. structure to fully embrace the French Art Deco and Italian modernist movements.

The spire of the Chrysler Building is an iconic symbol of New York City. The excavation of its foundation came in November, 1928. The building was topped out within a year, and took its place in the march of the world's tallest buildings, reigning until it was surpassed in 1931 by the Empire State. Among the Chrysler Building's decorations, gargoyles are mixed with eagles, along with representations of radiator ornaments, and automobile hub caps. Like forty other Manhattan buildings, it has its own zip code.

Along with the shooting of Arnold Rothstein, the Park Central Hotel was the scene of a second historic mob land murder. In October 1957, Albert Anastasia, chief assassin and head of Murder, Incorporated, was taking a shave in the hotel barbershop when two masked assassins maneuvered to his either side. They shot him five times. His bodyguard sat in the next chair. Taking no action, he went unscathed. The murderers were never found but behind the scenes, Crazy Joe Gallo took credit. Coincidentally, and having nothing to do with the mob, earlier that same year, Ingrid Bergman won the Academy Award for playing a very different Anastasia.

Which leaves the tale of Dreamland. Built in 1905, it was one of the three great parks that comprised Coney Island, the other two being Luna and Steeplechase. William Reynolds set out to make something bigger, brighter, and more audacious than his competitors. It was equal parts insane and marvelous.

The park never made a profit, with Reynolds stiffing his investors. Its end was a bit too symbolic: a fire rising up from the depths of Hell's Gate amusement ride. It was never rebuilt.

Fires haunted Coney Island. Steeplechase had a major fire in 1907. Luna Park was closed after a major fire in 1944.

ACKNOWLEDGMENTS

I would like to thank those who reviewed early drafts of this novel and provided feedback. This includes local authors Bob Ritchie and Diana Renta. Members of my Mystery Writers of America, Florida Chapter manuscript group also helped. They are the authors Diana Stuckart, Bruce Kubec, Holly Thompson, and Kathleen Baldwin.

Thanks to the good people at Oliver-Heber Books, including the Crosbys: Tanya Anne Crosby and Alaina Crosby, along with Kate Ward, Hilary Brown, Sally O'Keef, Evelyn Adams, and Eli Brewer.

Thanks for insights into the game of roque from David Haggstrom. Also, a shout out to all those in Angelica, New York who help keep alive the traditions of the game.

ALSO BY MARTIN HILL ORTIZ

The Skyline Murder Mystery Series

Floor 24

The Missing Floor

Never Kill A Friend

A Predatory Game

Dead Man's Trail

A Predatory Mind

ABOUT THE AUTHOR

Martin Hill Ortiz is a professor of pharmacology at Ponce Health Sciences University in Ponce, Puerto Rico. He received his undergraduate degrees at New Mexico State and his doctorate at George Washington University. He is the author of three novels. Many of his short stories, including those that introduced Alan Priest, have appeared in Mystery Magazine.

He has one son who lives in Panama.

Previous books by Martin Hill Ortiz

A Predatory Mind
A Predator's Game
Never Kill A Friend (as Martin Hill)
Dead Man's Trail (a novella)
The short story compendiums, The Best Short Stories

Volumes I through III: Chosen in 1914 by the most prominent authors of the day.

More about Dr. Hill Ortiz can be found at mdhillortiz.com